THE LOCUST ROOM

John Burnside has published two previous novels, *The Dumb House* and *The Mercy Boys* – which was joint winner of the 1999 Encore Award – a book of stories, *Burning Elvis*, and seven books of poetry. His most recent collection, *The Asylum Dance*, won the 2000 Whitbread Poetry Award and was shortlisted for the Forward and the T. S. Eliot Prize. He lives in Fife with his wife and son.

THE
LOCUST ROOM

JOHN BURNSIDE

Jonathan Cape
London

Published by Jonathan Cape 2001

2 4 6 8 10 9 7 5 3 1

Copyright © John Burnside 2001

John Burnside has asserted his right under the Copyright, Designs and Patents Act 1988 to be identified as the author of this work

First published in Great Britain in 2001 by
Jonathan Cape
Random House, 20 Vauxhall Bridge Road,
London SW1V 2SA

Random House Australia (Pty) Limited
20 Alfred Street, Milsons Point, Sydney,
New South Wales 2061, Australia

Random House New Zealand Limited
18 Poland Road, Glenfield,
Auckland 10, New Zealand

Random House South Africa (Pty) Limited
Endulini, 5A Jubilee Road, Parktown 2193, South Africa

The Random House Group Limited Reg. No. 954009
www.randomhouse.co.uk

A CIP catalogue record for this book
is available from the British Library

ISBN 0-224-05292-6

Papers used by Random House are natural, recyclable products made from wood grown in sustainable forests; the manufacturing processes conform to the environmental regulations of the country of origin

Printed and bound in Great Britain by
Biddles Ltd, Guildford and King's Lynn

for Lucas

As for future unions, too soon to think about it.
Let there be clean and pure division first, perfected
singleness. That is the only way to final, living
unison: through sheer, finished singleness.

D. H. Lawrence

Prune

when the knife is sharp,
taking care that the scar be neat.
To share the surgeon's belief in healing,
you must trust what has been taken from you
is a blessing.

Allison Funk

Being a gentleman is the number one priority,
the chief question integral to our national life.

Edward Fox

CAMBRIDGE, 1975

He was sitting in a chair, opposite the bed. The girl he had chosen was still asleep, totally unaware of his presence in her neat bedsit room. By the light from the window, he could tell that she was dreaming; he had seen enough sleeping women to recognise the look of the dreamer on her face, and the faint blue tremors of attention that flickered beneath her eyelids. He had been in her room for some time, excited by the thought of what was to come, but comfortable and easy in himself, in no way anxious or troubled, in no way afraid. He had come in through the window and closed it carefully behind him. He was good at this; it was what he knew best, this ability to *be*, to move silently around a house or a room, to go where he chose and leave no mark. It was a source of continuing pleasure that he possessed this particular ability to slip in through the smallest gap and, once inside, to become transparent, a negligible presence, so absorbed in the act of watching, in paying attention and being aware of every flicker and murmur of the house, that he himself became almost invisible. It was a skill he had been born with. When he was approaching a new place, he always knew the best way in, as if he belonged to that borderline of cool air at the window, to the half-life of greenery and rain in the almost imperceptible gap between the frame and the sash. He belonged – he had belonged all his life – to the places that other people treated as dead space, to attics and stairwells and narrow rooms at the back of the house, to old larders and closets with their tiny windows or rusting iron grilles that the occupants had long since forgotten. No matter how secure they thought it was, every building, every home, had a gap where he could slip in and wait, for hours if need be, as still and silent as a hunting cat. On trains, he would sit by a door and press the palm of his hand to the space where the cold entered; out walking, or cycling back across the fen, he was happiest when a sudden gust of wind found him, brushing his face, or filling his eyes with momentary tears. It felt more real, more like life, to be in this world of borderlines and spaces, and he couldn't help thinking that it was nothing more than an accident that he had been born into the cluttered world of others. Long ago, he had realised that he should have been an animal – a polecat or a wolverine. In school, the one phrase in the Bible that had made sense to him was where it said that the spirit moved on the waters, like a breath of wind. It had pleased him, even then, to think that the spirit, which was something better than God, should be such an inhuman presence.

Afterwards, when he was remembering, he would some-times wonder if this was the moment he enjoyed the most – not just for the anticipation, when it seemed that anything was possible, but also for the quiet of it, for how the tension he carried through the working day would settle and dissolve, till he felt so light and easy that he almost believed he could have flown out of the window and away over the sleeping town, over the roofs and chimneys and the lit shop fronts. At times like these, anything was possible. He would allow himself this moment to stop and look around, to take in the details of how each girl lived, with her books and her clothes around her, her

2

posters on the wall above the bed, her photographs and knick-knacks on the table. He could have stayed there all night, he could have emptied the drawers and the handbags and taken anything he wanted, and they would never know who had been there. He was so good at this now, so skilled at his trade. He could cross a cluttered room in the dark and make no sound. There were times when he was sure he could stop breathing if he had to.

And this was it. This was the key to everything a man did, the secret at the heart of it all. Silence. Stealth. That quality hunting animals possess, of moving silently in the night, aware of everything – aware, even before it happened, of the sudden rush of wings, or the quick magnetic glide of skin and bone through water or undergrowth. It had always been like this; even before, when he'd only gone to steal, he had lingered over his work, stopping to touch their things, to handle their hairbrushes and discarded underwear, their books, their bottles of perfume, their love letters. He had earned the right to everything he found in those rooms, and it had been the most logical thing in the world to move on from their jewellery and skirts and make-up to the bodies themselves, each one different, yet all of them his by right Naturally, they were afraid – and he came to see, as he learned to enjoy it more, to relax into it, that he even had a right to their fear. There had been a night, less than a year before, when it had come to him that the fear only arose because they could never see the whole picture; they could never see this act from his point of view. It was impossible for them to understand the change in him. Occasionally, he lamented the fact that he would never be able to explain himself. He felt an odd regret, close to grief, when he realised that nobody would ever understand, not the journalists and policemen who wrote and spoke about him in the newspapers, or the people he overheard on his rounds, discussing his work with a quiet, shocked pleasure, taking their angel's share of his power, imagining, dreaming, pretending they despised what secretly enthralled them. What they didn't understand, as they said all the usual things, running through what was expected of them with an absurd, apparently practised ease, was that he wasn't a man any more: he was something else. As he rose from his chair and stole silently across the room towards the sleeping girl, he was a character they would have recognised on film, or in a book, but would never acknowledge in real life: a vivid creature, part man, part animal, but also something more, something indescribable. For hours at first, and then for whole nights at a time, he was a fragment of hideous beauty and power; an elemental presence; a natural force. For a long time now, he had understood that he was immune to their world — that, unless he allowed himself to be caught, they would never find him out.

ACTS OF CONTRITION

At around five or five thirty, Paul would stop at the bakery and buy hot rolls or a loaf of warm bread that he would slip inside his jacket to keep it warm on the walk or the cycle ride home. It was a routine into which he had gradually fallen, one of those everyday rituals that meant something, for no particular reason, and for a good half-hour before he stopped making photographs he would look forward to walking into the warmth of the shop and allowing the smell of it to connect him, at some level, with a whole other world that was only half-imagined. Though he didn't know quite what it was, there was something remembered there too, some link or kinship in the spirit with heat and mugged windows and strip lights. He had felt it working nights at the Post Office over Christmas vacations, when he should have gone home, but didn't leave until Boxing Day, when the worst of his mother's traditional Scottish Christmas was over, and it was there in his memories of childhood, in the grey, early morning cool of his paper round, or the long drives with his father, out on the weekend, when they escaped from the suspended animation of the house, on their contrived fishing trips. This daily ritual had something to do with the gap between the warmth of the bakery and the cold blue of the sky, with the slow shift from dark to light and with the sense of distance that came in the early morning, when most of the city was still asleep. At the baker's shop, you could walk right in to where the bread was made, the loaves coming out of the ovens on those wide metal trays, and set to cool on the side, the new bread and confectionery racked up along the walls, a richness that left him feeling quietly happy when he left and stepped back out into the waiting cold.

He rarely slept, but it didn't bother him now as it had done, when he thought everyone had the same needs, the same basic requirements for rest and food and contact. People found it difficult to believe that he could survive on so little, but even as a child he had been an insomniac and, though it had troubled his mother, sleeplessness had been more of a pleasure to him than a burden. At night, while his parents slept – he imagined them settled deep in their separate beds, warm and thoughtless as wintered cattle, his father snoring quietly in his closed room, his mother mute and still, just visible through a door which always stood slightly ajar – at night, while they slept, he would get up and walk the house, going from room to room, listening to the silence around them, surrounded by the stillness of the gardens and the lit streets, and the exit road that reached away through the woods and the fields to the mystery of the distance. He was never tired after these sleepless nights; in the morning, after he had gone back to bed and slept maybe two or three hours, if that, he would rise as easily as anyone, and do whatever was required of him, getting ready, eating breakfast, putting his things together for school. Sometimes those sleepless nights turned into private feasts, when he raided the fridge for milk and cheese, or took down the tin of home-made cake from the tall cupboard, and cut himself a slice; sometimes he would sit by a window and flick through one of his father's books. It had never bothered him, sleeping so little – though it worried his parents, especially his mother, who seemed to blame him for his condition. Once or twice, she had risen in the night and found him sitting by a window, eating cake, or reading, and she had wanted to know what was wrong. He knew there was a simple explanation, he felt sure there was something he could say that would get her to leave him alone, but he could never work out what it was.

'I can't sleep,' he would say, hoping that this was enough and knowing that it was not.

His mother would stand watching him a moment, in her slippers and dressing gown, with that sceptical, careworn look on her face. She would wait a long time – maybe a minute or more – before she spoke, always quiet, but always with a note of suppressed annoyance, always on the verge of an accusation.

'You can't sit up all night, you know. You have to sleep.'

'I'm all right,' he would answer, trying to keep his voice flat and calm, though he knew it was useless. 'Honest I am.'

If it had been his father, he would have been allowed to stay where he was. His dad might be strict, and he always spoke his mind when it mattered, but there was no point – as he frequently said, when called upon to intervene in these subdued confrontations between his wife and son – there was no point whatsoever in trying to force the issue. It had been stalemate: Paul never could explain what it was that made him want not to miss a moment of the night, while his mother could never overcome the basic fact of nature that, no matter what she did, she could not force her son to sleep like a normal human being.

Then, some time during his teens, he had discovered photography. To begin with, he had used an old Voigtlander he'd found in a junk shop; he had heard somewhere that the Emperor of Japan refused to have his portrait taken with any other camera than a Voigtlander, because the lenses were so good. He liked the Germanic authenticity of the name as much as anything, and the weight of it in his hand; at the time, it had been the best he could afford with the money he had saved from his paper round and various odd jobs. Later, however, he had started with the Minolta. It wasn't that he had needed, or even wanted a modern camera – he would have had something older, something with glass plates and a long exposure time – but his father, who always encouraged any interest Paul might develop for craftsmanlike or skilled tasks, had bought him the X300 and a good-quality camera bag one afternoon on the way home from work. From then on – especially after he had gone away to college – Paul had taken the business of photography seriously, not as a hobby, but as a lifelong discipline. From the first, he had seen no point at all in taking the usual pictures, whether that meant the kind of snapshots his mother expected, or the craftsmanlike, camera-club work that was exhibited from time to time in the town hall or the library. What he wanted, though he had still not come anywhere close to achieving it, was a photography of the night, of the gaps between the hidden and the revealed, that would more closely resemble natural history than anything that might be called 'art'.

So it was that, halfway through his first year of college, this early morning excursion had become an important, even vital, ritual. Occasionally, he would stay out all night, but his customary routine was to take his camera bag and a notebook and go out into the streets for a couple of hours in the early morning, before it got light. Sometimes he took the bicycle; more often, he walked. It was essential to this nightly routine that he keep moving – though not too quickly – in order to cultivate that sense of things one has when on the move. It was the single most important thing he had learned about looking: just as most people are more conscious of being seen than of seeing, so there are those who only see fully when in motion, picking out essential details with a sidelong look, or learning how to be attuned to those shifts in colour and form that only occur at the edge of vision. Sometimes he would stay out for hours, cycling from one place to another in search of the perfect contrast, the perfect expression of the night's logic. What he wanted was a photograph, not of the darkness itself – which he knew was impossible – but of the colours that darkness revealed: the gardenia of a lit street sign; the egg-yolk gold of a Belisha beacon; the shell-pink of street lamps, still burning in the milk-and-ash grey of the dawn. And though he had always loved darkness, though it was true that, even without his camera, he would probably have gone out into the night at some point, just for the smell and the taste of it, there was no doubt that the act of photography itself, the process of choosing and focusing and singling out colour and detail and form, added something he could only think of as metaphysical. Ever since he was a child, on long drives with his father, going out to make a special delivery, or on the way to their fishing spot, early on Saturday mornings when it was still half dark, he had guessed that there was something there, some state, resembling absence, that might be achieved in the half-light, achieved or chanced upon, perhaps, by simply staring out and catching a glimpse, here and there, of lit windows through the woods, or passing through those small towns on the road home, after a day's fishing or walking, narrow villages with the one shop still open, the houses hooded and still, a few children here and there, standing under street lamps, or walking back with milk and bread and bottles of cherry cola. Now, when he took night pictures, he felt he was setting in motion a process

9

that might end with that absence, a form of invisibility that would consist of nothing but attention, nothing but being itself.

When it was too bright to continue, when the sky cleared and there was a softness in the air, he would put the camera away, carefully packing the body and the lenses into their separate compartments, and he would start for home, stopping at the bakery on the way. It was the best part of his day; he was happiest in those first couple of hours, from the last of the darkness to the first of the light: in the faint, ice-blue intimation of a spring dawn, or the lime-coloured wash of a summer's morning over fields and meadows, a light with no trace of white in it, no glare, no ordinary brightness.

Though he had cleaned it himself only a couple of days before, the kitchen had managed to transform itself, as if by magic, into the usual mess. The sink was stacked high with plates and coffee cups, some of which stood proud of the rancid grey pool of dishwater, recongealed grease, bacon rinds and bloated scraps of pitta bread that had gathered there over several days of deliberate neglect. The draining board, the floor, even the low window behind the sink, were splashed with tomato sauce, gravy and egg-fried rice; every available surface was littered with beer cans, half-eaten chop suey in foil containers, blotted newspapers, spills of sweet-and-sour sauce, dirty glasses and cups, grease-crusted plates and various other, less explicable traces of the decayed and the inedible. In the middle of the table, a pair of rugby boots had been deposited, their cleats packed with mud and grass, as if to perform the office of some bizarre ornament, between a near-empty vodka bottle and a jar of pickled onions from which the lid had obviously been missing for some time. On the chair, set at some distance from the table, yet implicated nevertheless in the general chaos, a pair of maroon socks, scabbed and clouded with pewter-coloured mud, lay neatly folded beside a box of Tide. Blotting from his mind the image of Clive, his sixteen-stone, rugby-player housemate, standing over the sink, carefully hand-washing and rinsing his kit, Paul dashed to the cupboard, removed a jar of strawberry jam and the sliver of Lurpak butter which sat, still unmolested, on his personal shelf, and retired to his own room, where he kept a clean knife, a spoon and a glass for just such occasions. He hated eating in a dirty kitchen. He couldn't understand how Clive could let things degenerate to this level. Because keeping things in order seemed so natural, so very straightforward a thing to him, he usually suspected that this mess was deliberate.

He took his time over breakfast: a glass of milk, some fresh bread and butter, a spoonful of jam, a banana – the simplicity, the ritual of it, had become one of his deepest pleasures. Yet the thought of the chaos downstairs nagged at him and soon he was back in the kitchen, cleaning up. In spite of the elaborate mess that Clive had contrived, it took less than an hour to restore some semblance of order to the place. It was something he had learned in his first year: if you shared a house with other men, you had to decide on your policy right away, then stick to it. You could take on the unacknowledged, even despised role of housekeeper, or you could let things continue to slide and fester, till the house was, in Paul's terms at least, close to uninhabitable. It had surprised him how people like Clive, or his previous housemates, Tom and Adam, could live in such porcine squalor, and for a while he had tried to call their bluff, to see if one of them would snap, and do something – anything – to help. They never did. They lived by the simple rule that there was always someone else who would clean things up, as there presumably had been at home, before they came to college. Not that Clive ever actually intended to leave this midden for someone else to deal with: the presence, here and there amongst the debris, of washing-up liquid containers, rancid dishcloths and a single, sad-looking Brillo pad, floating in a battered and blackened saucepan, testified to his pathetic goodwill. Besides which, the mere presence of someone of Clive's bulk, in a space so small as their shared kitchen, struck Paul as absurd, even ugly. Whenever Clive was indoors, Paul preferred for him to remain at rest, preferably seated, with something to occupy his hands.

On this occasion, however, Clive was not the sole begetter of the chaos with which Paul had to contend. At some point, presumably when the house was otherwise empty, the new tenant, Steve, had descended from his room, made soup from a packet, and left what he had been unable to eat in an uncovered plastic bowl, in the middle shelf of the otherwise empty fridge. There was no doubting that this blood-red liquid with spaghetti rings and rehydrated onion floating on its surface belonged to Steve; Clive would never have eaten anything from a packet. He was strictly a tins-and-takeaway man: if you had to add water, or break eggs, he was sunk. Steve's empty Knorr wrapper still lay, like a vital clue, on the floor under the kitchen table – and it was enough, as insignificant as it was in the overall scheme of things, to get Paul wondering about the new man. Steve had moved in just six weeks before and, after the first couple of days, he had kept himself apart, preferring to stay locked up in his room, and only emerging to leave the rent, in a plain brown envelope, on the kitchen table, where Paul would find it. Pretty soon, Paul never knew when Steve was in the house: the little man would sit upstairs for hours, even days at a time, or he would come and go, silent and invisible, sneaking in and out of the house while Paul and Clive were out, or otherwise occupied. The only conclusive evidence of his presence would be the rent, the occasional bowl of unfinished food in the fridge and, every now and then, a vast mess of sweet papers, abnormal quantities of Quality Street wrappers, empty Black Magic and Jaffa Cake boxes, crammed into the swing-bin till it was full to overflowing.

After a month of this, Clive had had enough. One morning, when Paul returned from one of his night photography sessions, he was confronted in the kitchen by the big rugby player, who was very obviously hung over and dissatisfied in the general way that Paul had come to think of as Clive's trademark. It was something he had noticed about the men he knew, not just from college, but pretty well everywhere he went: there was a disgruntled quality, an air of dissatisfaction about nothing in particular, which they seemed to think went along with being male. The few men he knew who seemed more or less accepting of their lot – his father, his friend Richard – were the exceptions rather than the rule. Not that they were happy so much as curious and alert, as if the question, for them, wasn't so much whether or not they were content with their lives, as whether or not the world was still interesting enough.

'What do we know about Steve anyway?' Clive had demanded. 'I mean – what does he do?'

'I don't know,' Paul replied, trying to make light of the whole thing. 'I got the impression he was a student.'

'He doesn't look like a student,' Clive said.

Though he was tempted to enquire what a student looked like, Paul could see the point. Steve was an odd-looking little

13

guy: yellow-skinned, prematurely balding, thin as a rake, he looked more like an undertaker's assistant, or a gravedigger. At times, in fact, Paul was tempted to think of him as a phantom, a revenant from the graveyard at the end of the street, come to haunt them. Still, it was none of his business, or Clive's, what the guy did, as long as he paid his rent – which he did, religiously, every Friday. This was more than could be said for Clive, as it happened, who had been late more than once with his share of the money.

'I don't see why you let him have the room,' Clive continued. 'The truth is, he gives me the creeps.'

Now it was Paul's turn to be annoyed. 'I let him have it,' he said, trying to hide his irritation, 'because nobody else wanted it. And because we needed the money. Unless, of course, you want to split the rent two ways instead of three.'

Clive was standing at the sink, concocting one of his exotic hangover cures, a process which involved honey, milk and some kind of dried herb.

'The lad doesn't seem very bright,' he said. 'I'm sure there's a brain installed as standard, but whether it's switched on is another question. Besides which, there's a smell.' He flashed Paul a quick, interrogatory look. 'There's a definite, ratty kind of smell, coming from his room.'

Paul shook his head. He'd noticed a thin odour on the landing outside the new man's room, reminiscent of animal pens, or damp straw, but it was nothing compared to some of the aromas Clive had created in the upstairs toilet, on his more colourful Sunday mornings. Or the warm, slightly fenny scent of the pick-me-up that Clive had just set down on the table, in a chipped beer mug, with SKOL stencilled on the side.

'Maybe he's got a pet,' Paul ventured.

'What kind of a pet?'

'I don't know. Just a pet. A hamster or something. A lab rat. A spring-tailed Siberian gerbil.'

Paul ventured a quick glance at Clive's face, which wore an expression of distaste, though whether this had to do with Steve's unofficial roommate or the glass of curdled milk and fenugreek, or whatever it was, that he had just downed in one, it was impossible to say.

'That has to be unhygienic,' the big man said, setting the empty glass down on the table and wiping his mouth.

Paul held his tongue.

'I'm surprised at you,' Clive continued. 'I thought you hated germs.'

Paul sighed. 'I don't know if Steve has a pet,' he said. 'And I don't much care. It's not our business really, is it?'

Clive had given up then and gone off to the gym, or the pool, muttering something about rodent infestation and bubonic plague. Yet Paul had to admit that, on some level, the other man had been right: Steve really *was* odd, and if Paul had had any choice in the matter, he would have given the room to someone else, if only to keep Clive happy. He had known, as soon as Steve had turned up, that the big man wouldn't like him. Not that this made Steve so extraordinary. No one could have denied that Clive was generous in the range of his dislikes: he didn't want women staying in the house, because you couldn't relax when they were around, you always had to be on your best behaviour, you couldn't swear, or fart when you wanted, you had to keep the toilet clean; he preferred it if they didn't have music students, or anybody musical, in fact, because he'd had a bad time with some clarinettist in his first year; before Steve, a thin, angelic-looking, somewhat vague art student, in a tie-dye shirt and white drainpipe jeans, with straggly dyed-blond hair and painted fingernails, had turned

15

up, having seen Paul's ad in a shop window, calling himself Marc-with-a-c and enquiring if the room was still for rent. By this time, Paul had been desperate – they had gone three weeks without a third person to share, and Mrs Yazstremski had said that, if they didn't get somebody within the month, Paul would have to make up the rent out of his own pocket. It was hard to find anyone who wanted to share the house, especially mid-term, and Paul would certainly have let the room to Marc, if he could have done. But Clive had been at home, and had proceeded to behave as badly as only Clive could – it was his chosen field, after rugby and drinking; as he himself would often admit, with a cheery smile, he could have represented England at Olympic level in obnoxiousness. Marc's response had been exemplary: though he had obviously decided, within the first five minutes, not to take the room, he had persisted in showing a keen interest in the let for as long as he thought he could get away with it. His parting remark to Paul, with Clive safely out of earshot, had said it all.

'I'm sorry,' he had murmured, with a wave of his alarmingly white, purple-tipped hand, 'but I was hoping for something a little less bucolic.'

Marc had been lucky. Steve had come along on a wet Wednesday evening, when Clive had been at the gym, doing circuits with the rugby team, and he had taken the room immediately, saying it suited him down to the ground. Yet, looking back, Paul realised that he hadn't gleaned much information from Steve's conversation and, in idle moments, he had stopped to wonder, much as Clive was wondering, exactly what he knew about his new housemate. Obviously, Steve was a student: he had to be, since he kept such irregular hours. True, he always had the money to pay his rent, and never used any of Paul's stuff from the cupboards, or the fridge, but that didn't mean he couldn't be a student, any more than the fact that Steve – as he had told Paul when he came to see about the room – did not drink. It seemed that the guy's only problem was that he was painfully shy. He may have been afraid of Clive, and perhaps with good reason, which partly explained why he kept to himself so much. In fact, the shyness, the fondness for sweets, the way he talked put Paul in mind of a displaced schoolboy; in spite of his sallow skin and balding pate, it was hard not to think of Steve as an overgrown child. It was obvious to Paul, though he would never have admitted it to Clive, that Steve had a pet of some kind locked in his upstairs room, probably a hamster, or a guinea pig. His only other interests, as far as Paul knew, related in some way to nostalgia: he had a collection of old records from the Forties and Fifties, mostly children's songs like 'Tubby the Tuba', and 'Sparky's Magic Piano', and he could occasionally be found in the front room, watching children's television. It was the only time he ever used the front room – though whether this was because he only liked children's programmes, or because it was the time when Clive was least likely to be around, Paul couldn't be certain. Steve avoided Clive like the plague, and would probably have preferred to be left to his own devices generally, but he seemed less intimidated by Paul, and would even occasionally stop to exchange awkward niceties over a cup of tea, or the handing over of rent. Only a few days before, Steve had engaged him in something close to real conversation, in this very kitchen, as Paul sat reading the *Evening News*. The headline had been that The Rapist had been sighted, on three separate occasions, the day before; Steve had been on the point of leaving when the story caught his eye.

'Has he done it again?' he had suddenly asked.

17

'No,' Paul had replied. 'It says here he was foiled trying to break into the New Hall hostel on Madingley Road.'

Steve had lingered a moment then, as if there was something he wanted to say, but for which he couldn't find the words.

'Do you ever wonder about it?' he asked, finally.

'About what?'

'You know. The rapist.' Steve looked awkward, yet it was obvious he wanted to carry on; Paul got the impression, just for a moment, that he didn't really know what to make of the situation, that he wanted to hear how someone else felt about it. 'What he does. To those girls.'

'No.' Paul had lied, without knowing, until he said the words, that he *was* lying, that he would have lied, no matter who had asked him this question. It was an enquiry he had never made of himself; yet now, when Steve put it to him, he realised he wondered about it all the time.

'I try not to think about it,' he continued, carefully, though he could tell Steve didn't believe him. 'It doesn't do any good.'

Steve had studied him a moment. Paul felt uncomfortable.

'I can't help it,' he had said. 'I wonder about it all the time.'

He rose slowly, and started for the door, then turned and studied Paul for a moment, as if he were trying to decide whether he could be trusted. Paul had the familiar impression – an impression he had often had from other men, at just such moments – that this was the first time Steve had taken any real notice of him. Men did that all the time, though he knew very few women who were so casual, or so ready to take others for granted. For most of the men Paul knew at college, other people were like furniture, objects which existed, and took up space, and occasionally got in the way, or proved surprisingly useful.

'I've been stopped eight times so far,' he said, 'by the police, I mean. Apparently, I fit the description.'

He waited a moment, just long enough to give Paul time to speak, but Paul couldn't think of anything to say, and Steve had left then, looking sad and – this seemed odd to Paul, but he couldn't think of a better word for it – strangely triumphant. It was as if Steve had been included in something – some ritual or sacrament – from which normal men like Paul or Clive, ordinary men who did not fit the description, had been excluded, and this had bestowed upon him a special, indefinable status that only a martyr, or an innocent, might share or understand.

Paul was almost finished in the kitchen when Clive appeared. As always, even when he had a hangover, he looked fresh and rosy-cheeked, like a freshly scrubbed pig farmer, or a schoolboy just out of the shower after a hard afternoon's rugby. Nothing ever showed on the surface. It was all buried, deep under the healthy, flushed skin. When he finally noticed the state of the kitchen, he grinned and shook his head softly, but he didn't say anything.

'A good night?' Paul enquired.

'Mm.' Clive filled the kettle, scooped two heaped spoonfuls of instant coffee into a mug, spilling a few grains on the freshly wiped draining board, and sat down. Even from where he was sitting, Paul was able to observe the spilt coffee grains gradually dissolve and spread over the stainless-steel surface, like the aftermath of some failed experiment in chromatography.

'Where did you go?'

'The usual.' Clive seemed to be searching for something.

He often became disoriented in very neat surroundings. A minute or more passed before he found what he was looking for and the look of vague dismay passed from his face. The kettle began to sing gently, as he spread the *Evening News* upside down on the table so Paul could see.

'Bastard's been at it again,' Clive said.

'Oh.'

Paul studied the front page. Headed by an appeal to landlords – 'Police believe the rapist lives alone in a bedsitter or flat', it said, without a trace of irony – the story was the familiar one, with an ugly twist.

NEW LEAD IN RAPIST HUNT

The Cambridge rapist may have patrolled the Chesterton area in make-up, a wig and dark glasses yesterday before pouncing at a house in Church Street where he raped and stabbed his seventh victim in his most macabre attack to date.

Soon after the weirdly dressed man was seen round about 12.10 to 12.25 p.m., a 21-year-old secretary was raped in the house and stabbed – and this time the attacker had the word 'Rapist' printed in white capital letters on the forehead of his black leather hood.

The dramatic development of the man in make-up was revealed last night after police officers had questioned dozens of people in the area of Pye Terrace, Church Street, Chesterton, where the rapist struck.

'UNNATURAL'

He was seen riding an old black bicycle which witnesses said rattled. And he was seen to cycle past the house on the terrace twice – once up the road and then down again. He may have been to other streets nearby.

He was described, police said, as young, probably in his twenties, wearing a tan-coloured anorak or wind-cheater. He was thought to be wearing a fair or light brown wig, dark glasses with steel rims and had what witnesses called 'an unnaturally tanned complexion'.

'When they catch that fucker,' Clive said, 'the police are going to give him a good kicking.'

'Probably.'

'*If* they ever catch him,' Clive continued, staring sadly at the paper. 'I mean, how hard can it be?'

'Well, they know it's a man in his twenties who lives in a bedsit,' Paul said. 'They're bound to get him soon.'

'Sometimes I wonder,' Clive answered, oblivious to the ironic note.

They'd had this conversation several times. It was probably the most boring of a number of boring conversations they were capable of having. Sport. College. Women. Pubs. The rapist.

Paul had been treated on various occasions to theories ranging from the vaguely credible to the ridiculous. The rapist was known to the police, but he was an important or influential person, and they were afraid to arrest him. The rapist was a policeman. Once, coming home more drunk than usual from the Sports and Social Club, Clive had explained how, taking certain pieces of evidence into account, the rapist could have been a woman. No theory was too preposterous for the guys on the rugby team, who took the existence of the rapist as a personal affront. Clive, in particular, seemed to be almost obsessed by the rapist, and possible explanations for his

21

freakish behaviour. Now, drawing together personal animus and his usual wayward logic, he had a new idea to try out.

'Listen, have you seen Steve recently?'

'Yes,' Paul answered. 'I saw him two days ago.'

'Really? What time?'

Paul shook his head. He could see what was coming. He hoped, for Steve's sake, Clive hadn't run through this particular line of reasoning with his team-mates.

'About eight,' he answered, with all too obvious patience.

'Was he going out?'

'No,' Paul said. 'I was. Why do you ask?'

Clive glanced at the paper. 'Listen,' he said, 'I'm not saying it means anything. Probably it doesn't. But I'm pretty sure Steve was out on Wednesday. Which was when this would have happened, right? And he didn't come back till next morning.'

'So?'

'Well,' Clive said, his face a mask of assumed innocence, 'you never know. He pretty well fits the description. And this thing here – about his complexion. Unnaturally tanned, it says. Which could be Steve—'

'So now you think he's the rapist?' Paul said. 'Which means it isn't a woman. Or maybe Steve is a woman in disguise?'

Clive shook his head and took a long sip of his coffee. His mouth looked wet and dark.

'I'm not saying that,' he said. 'It's just that we don't really know anything about him.'

Paul waited. He was beginning to tire of this. He wished Clive would just say what he had to say and be on his way. Not that the idea that Steve might be the rapist hadn't occurred to him in his more idle moments. But then, it was a suspicion he had entertained about any number of men he knew at some time or another. According to Penny, or at least, according to her friend Marjorie, all men were rapists anyway. Or potential rapists. He remembered the time he had repeated this notion to his housemate, and the look on his face. The idea that, even in theory, Clive could be considered a rapist was the worst, the most unjust suggestion he could imagine, worse than murder, even worse than being queer. And he had been right, of course – though for all the wrong reasons.

'I'm not saying he *is* the rapist, but he could be,' Clive continued, staring into his coffee cup like some fortune-teller. 'I mean – anybody could.'

'You could,' Paul said. 'So could I. So could Steve. It's not very conclusive. Besides, Steve lived in Huntingdon before he came here.'

Clive looked up. 'How do you know that?'

'Because he told me,' Paul replied, matter-of-fact, with only the smallest trace of meaningful finality in his voice.

'Oh, I see. He *told* you.'

Paul said nothing. Sarcasm was always a good sign. It gave Clive the opportunity to make an exit while he thought he was still winning. A moment later, the other man stood, carried his mug to the sink, rinsed it carefully, and set it down on the draining board.

'I'm sorry about the mess,' he said. 'I meant to clean it up.'

Paul nodded. 'It's all right,' he said, making every effort to remove any trace of irony from his voice. 'It was no trouble.'

'That's all right then.' Clive grinned. 'You seeing Penny today?'

'I don't know.'

'Now that's what I call the female of the species.' Clive

shook his head. 'A cold-hearted bastard like you *does not* deserve *her.*'

Paul decided to ignore this clumsy attempt at affection. 'Bye, Clive,' he said, as the other man lurched towards the door. There was always the possibility of real destruction if Clive was distracted while moving around indoors. Once, Paul had distracted his housemate while he was fetching something down from a high cupboard, and Clive had pulled the whole thing off the wall, spilling jam jars and coffee powder and cornflakes all over the floor. As colourful as that had been, it wasn't an experience Paul was prepared to repeat.

When Clive had gone – the front door slamming behind him with a force that Paul felt he could never have managed, even with an effort – Paul stopped and listened. The house was still. There was never any sure way of knowing when Steve was at home, which bothered Paul more than it ought to have done. He liked to be alone in the house after his nights out. It was good to lie down, pleasantly tired, in an empty house, and know he would sleep sooner or later, drifting in and out of a dream state that was so close to the surface he would remember everything he saw and felt there – even to the point of believing, when he woke, that something really had happened. There was an abandonment – of the world, of himself, of existence – in this daily ritual; he was in no doubt that these hours he spent alone in his room, half asleep and, at the same time, keenly awake to all the underlying thoughts and processes that the noise and blur of the day usually concealed, were the truth of his days. He was capable, at such times, of a kind of absence, a self-abandonment that led to visions, streams of words, images, ideas that almost translated themselves into something meaningful, something he could see, or name. Yet these private hours were less satisfying when he thought someone else might be in the house. Climbing the stairs, he stopped on the landing and listened. Steve's room was the smallest and darkest, towards the back of the house, overlooking the graveyard; it was totally silent, totally still. Paul walked to the door and knocked – he wondered if Steve could ever hear the conversations he had with Clive, sitting up here, directly above the kitchen – but there was no answer and, reassured that he was alone in the house, Paul crossed the landing to his own room and lay down.

He slept for a short time – he couldn't be sure how long – then drifted slowly back to the light. He had been dreaming, but he couldn't remember details; all he knew was that, when he came to, he was thinking of a photograph. It wasn't a picture that existed, even in his mind, but it was real, as an idea, as an impossibility, nevertheless. It was the picture he had been trying to take for almost three years, ever since he had first begun to realise that the Sixties were over, and the world he had expected to inhabit did not exist. Because something that had happened in the late Sixties, and persisted into the early Seventies – as far as 1972, say – was finished now. All through his teens he had been impatient to grow up, to be away from home and part of that life. He had been waiting years for an impossible freedom, preparing himself for his arrival in a world that had melted away on his fingertips and lips, like new snow. It had become history: you could read the documents, you could see the films, and you could remember it from a great distance, not the way it had really happened, but the way it had *transpired* on television and in the newspapers. Some of the people who had lived through that time had been so self-conscious as to have been destined for history from the first; even as they posed for themselves, they

25

had seen their lives as recordable events, and they had died into the visuals and sound effects – but there had been others who were intent on loss, intent on becoming, and they had been too real to be included in the narrative. Paul had wanted to be a part of that experiment; he had anticipated alchemy, transformation, an absolute integrity, a variation on the idea of disappearance. He had wanted, not to *make*, but to *be*. He had hoped for a kind of work – a discipline, a craft – that was continuous with his life – not something practised, not something separate, but a magical pursuit that was integral to his very being. Now, he had settled for what he could only describe as 'thinking of a photograph'. An image. He wanted it to exist outside time, outside narrative; he wanted it to be cryptic; he wanted it to be clear.

For a long time, he had imagined that chance would play some part in its composition. He would take his camera out on cycle rides or drives, and point it randomly at the world but, though the results were sometimes interesting, they lacked the particular quality he wanted. After a while, he had begun taking night pictures, still using chance, looking for a compromise, something not quite abstract, but a pure image, in black and white, of light mingling with darkness, not entirely abstract but not figurative either, something which, in the spirit at least, recalled Cézanne's painting of Jacob and the angel: light mingling with darkness then coming clear, at that implausible moment before the divine animus seizes you in its arms and the struggle begins. As he had expected, it hadn't worked – and failure to find the compromise pushed him back towards the impossible with a sense of privilege and an absurd gratitude. The idea that he was on a hopeless quest meant he had nothing to lose; he could take all the time in the world, and it didn't matter whether he arrived at anything. He had always known – he had almost trusted in the notion – that what he was looking for might not exist, and even if it did, it might be wholly meaningless to other people. He couldn't visualise it, but he knew it had an abstract quality, an essential detachment from human concerns. He wanted something akin to that moment at the end of *Zabriskie Point*, where Daria Halprin sees the house in the desert exploding. The critics, his friends, so many people he knew had failed to appreciate that moment, because the beauty of it was too remote, too detached from what people thought of as narrative. Yet, for Paul, it had signalled the beginning of a long process that was still continuing, of moving out and away, towards the unknowable, towards the impossible which was, in every meaningful sense, the fundamental ground of whatever he could think of as reality. When he was alone, he caught glimpses of that reality; when he was with other people, it vanished. Together, people constructed a narrative that did not include the fundamental, but made of the world what was needed for social life to continue. Paul wanted to go beyond that.

Photography had something to do with this desire. For a long time, he had been cautious about looking at other pictures. There was something seductive about them, an almost unbearable allure in the photographs he saw in magazines, for example, or at exhibitions, a gloss that they gave to the surface of things, a glamour that absolved the object of its being, to make it a thing more looked upon than seen. Slowly, however, sitting in the large-format and reference sections of the public library at home, or here in Cambridge, he had stumbled upon the masters of the craft – Kertész, Avedon, Strand, Cartier-Bresson and, finally, like finding the key to something that had been locked all his life, a slender book of twenty pictures made by Raymond Moore for a small Welsh Arts Council exhibition in 1968. The pictures were exactly as he had imagined photography might be, at its best – images of frosted planks, rock pools, seaweed, a street in Alderney, they possessed, or were possessed of, that quality of estrangement that seemed to allow the things seen to move away from the viewer's gaze, to set each thing, each pebble and plank and scab of weed, in its own inviolable space, not as a mere object, but as something respected, something loved and so left to be itself, beyond possession, beyond comprehension. It was precisely the opposite, this work, from what was said of photography in the sociological theories of critics – that it was a form of theft, that it violated its subject, that it was an act of appropriation. Even the one image of a person – a woman named Miss Hooper – set her apart, and not only did not intrude but made the occasion of the photograph an act of courtesy, of withdrawal, that surprised Paul. When he read the introductory statement to this thin volume – a modest catalogue of a mere twenty images – he understood why he had been unable, till now, to formulate his ideas.

Statement

Photography is a means of sifting or abstracting visual phenomena – it can be solely concerned with conveying factual information about objects in a particular position in time and space – or it can convey an awareness or revelation of the marvellous.

For me – the no man's land between the real and fantasy – the mystery in the commonplace – the uncommonness of the commonplace.

An understanding of the limitations of the photographic encounter or event. Awareness involves these limitations.

The encounter

The subject is limited. This defines its personality or existence. It is a particular thing or combination of things.

The photographer is likewise a limited entity.

The positive phenomenon of the encounter occurs when the photographer's being is triggered into activity by the subject – the subject depends for its photo existence on the photographer. No other can reveal it – an awareness is involved both of the subject and the self – one almost becomes the other.

It was still theory – it was still a paraphrase – but this statement opened his eyes to something. If Moore was right, you had to go beyond the social, you had to refuse the given role, in order to perform a kind of alchemy that would be at once a disappearance and a way of remaining utterly still. As a photographer – as an amateur, in every sense of the word – Paul had fallen in love with the idea of an impossibility, half-knowing all along that the beauty of the impossible would cast its shadow over everything else, every possible fact, showing it up as the temporal, contingent thing it really was.

He had been dozing for a while, drifting in and out of a half-sleeping state, when he heard voices in the hall and sat up with a start. A moment later, Penny appeared at the door.

'Hiya,' she said, a little too brightly. He had been seeing Penny for almost a year, and she still seemed wary around him. Or not so much wary as awkward, in the way people are when something is unresolved between them. Penny was tall, with thick, honey-coloured hair that fell in waves over her shoulders; she considered this her best feature – she had even said as much, on more than one occasion – but what had first attracted Paul to her was the roundedness of her body, the way her breasts looked in the cashmere sweater she sometimes wore to lectures, and the astonishing, smooth curves of her legs. When she was present, he was possessed – there was no other way to describe it – quietly but completely possessed by a hopeless desire that, no matter how urgent it felt, never quite found its appropriate form. Yet, though they had been seeing one another for months, they had never slept together. This was at least part of the reason why Penny usually didn't come to the house – they would meet at Belinda's, or The Copper Kettle, or in the college canteen, their meetings formalised in a way that kept just the right distance between them, a distance whose function Paul was never sure he understood. In all the time he had known her, Penny had only been to the house on a handful of occasions, and she had only set foot in this room twice.

'Were you asleep?' Her voice was musical, always light and slightly mocking, as if she knew something he didn't, and was waiting for him to figure it out.

'Dozing,' he said. 'Who were you talking to?'

'Your flatmate,' she said. 'Steve, is it?'

'Oh.' So Steve had been in the house all along. Paul wondered that he hadn't heard him.

Deciding that she wasn't going to be invited, Penny took it upon herself to slip in and set herself down on the one chair, by the table, at the far end of the room, near the wardrobe with its full-length mirror. Sitting like that, opposite the window, she was lit like the figure in an old painting, and Paul was struck once again by her straight, Florentine face, and her dark, slightly heavy-lidded eyes. This Italian look was the first thing he had noticed about her. When they had first met, Paul had decided this look made her seem mysterious, more beautiful for being slightly remote.

It had taken him only a month to realise that nothing could be further from the truth. Penny was anything but a mystery; her motives, her desires, her opinions, her personal history, her moral code – all were fixed, open, utterly unequivocal. Everything about her was knowable. Everything she owned – clothes, jewellery, records, books – all of it had a known history, either as a simple narrative she had told him, in the full confidence that it would not only be interesting, but even significant to him, or as something that could be surmised from simple clues. Her boots, for example, the ones she was wearing now, had been bought on a birthday shopping trip with her mother – black leather, with heels and almost square toes – a little *different*, her mother had said, in that first shop, but Penny hadn't been sure, and they had gone on, trying on all kinds of footwear – white brogues, fur-lined ankle-boots, the knee-high fashion boots in bright blue or pearl-grey that Penny favoured. Finally, they had gone back to the first place and bought those very first boots she had tried on. Penny's mother had pointed out, again, that, although they were plain, they were a bit different, a bit more stylish. You could wear those boots for years, and they wouldn't go out of style. They were, quite simply, classic. Penny and her mother were great friends, more like sisters than mother and daughter, and Penny had to say she would always talk to her mother, if she had a problem, before she talked to her friends from back home. Not that she didn't have good friends, back home. Most of the girls she knew she had known since middle school, friends who would always be there, girls she could trust. She didn't know anyone like that in Cambridge; though she had friends, she didn't necessarily feel she could talk to them. She felt lonely, sometimes, when she thought about it — with the rapist going about, and nobody knowing who he was, or what he might do next, it was hard having nobody to talk to. When she talked like this, Paul knew — without having to be told — that there was no irony intended.

For a while after they had first met, they had skirted around the idea that they were a couple — what Penny, and probably her mother, would have called an 'item'. They did not touch; they did not arrange to meet at set times, or in specific places, they simply drifted together at lunch times, or after lectures; they were not going out; their lives were separate. The first time they had been alone together for any length of time, on the closest they had yet come to a proper date, they had gone to the Botanic Gardens. It had been Penny's idea; Paul had hardly ever seen the place in the daytime. He liked to climb the fence at night and be alone there, looking at the plants in the dark. Sometimes he stumbled across a couple having sex amongst the low shrubs, or a band of dope-smokers, but most of the time he was alone, and he would stop from time to time to feel himself being happy, to be aware of it, trying to fix it and understand what it was like. He was always happiest in the dark, and by himself; though he enjoyed swimming at the Mill Road pool in the early mornings, two or three times a week, it was never as good as the rare summer nights when he'd cycle over to Newnham, lock the bike on Grantchester Road, and climb the fence into King's Swimming Club.

On that first date, they had walked by the long chronological beds that showed the plants in the order they were introduced into England, first by the Romans, then from various parts of the Continent and, later, from Asia and America, the various semi-exotic flowers and fruits, irises and tomatoes and lilies, and spiny shrubs with strange half-flowers, weeds he would have thought were native, if he had thought about it at all, plants he had seen in his father's garden without really noticing them. Here in the gardens, isolated in little individual plots, attached to their names, classified and fixed, they were all so intensely physical and lit, so utterly distinct. There were times when Paul was amazed by the sheer mass of information in the world – subtleties and strands of difference, generic and specific terms, systems of division and classification, the infinite complexities of identification and taxonomy – and it occurred to him that, if he wanted anything from a photograph, it was to suggest something else, some unity, some underlying oneness.

It was a warm, bright afternoon. At the far end of the gardens, by the administrator's house, they found an apple tree that, according to the plaque at the base of the trunk, had been grown there from a cutting taken from the very tree Isaac Newton had been sitting under when he discovered the principles of gravity.

'I thought that thing about the apple was a myth,' Penny said.

Paul didn't answer. He was reading the plaque that told about Newton. He remembered something his father had said about Newton, about how he was the most remote man in history, because nobody had ever understood him. Paul hadn't understood the remark, and his father had never bothered to explain it.

'In the nineteenth century,' Penny said, 'when they were uncovering the Egyptian tombs, they found thousands of mummies – not just people, but animals too. Cats, mostly, because they were sacred to some goddess, I suppose. Or maybe the people just wanted to take their pets with them to the afterlife. There were thousands, literally, all pretty much the same and of no particular archaeological interest.'

She glanced at him to see if he was listening. It bothered him, even then, that small gesture, this personal indifference in his heart that she had already guessed at – yet, at the same time, he felt that she was to blame for this seed of indifference, if anyone could be blamed. It had been his error, perhaps, to mistake her sexual coldness for a magical remoteness on their first meeting, but over the weeks they had known one another, as she patiently fended off his attempts at physical intimacy, he had come to feel that she was the one at fault, that she had been guilty of a deliberate deception.

'Anyway, the archaeologists didn't have any use for them, but they didn't want to just throw the mummies away. So they bundled them up, put them on a ship and sent them home to be used as fertiliser in English gardens. Very rich source of minerals and trace elements, apparently, your average mummified moggie.'

She paused, waiting for something.

'And?' Paul had no idea what the point of this story was.

Penny had shaken her head and walked off in the direction of the small artificial lake, where Paul had once seen a grass snake, coiled on a slab of limestone, warming itself in the early morning sunshine. It had been an inauspicious start to an affair that had quickly grown tight and habitual without ever becoming close. Paul had always blamed Penny's sexual problems for this – she said she wanted to wait, not necessarily until she got married, but at least until she knew for sure that it was right, before making that commitment. This coyness struck him as curiously old-fashioned, even a little touching; at the same time, it seemed frivolous on her part, a kind of pretence in which she expected him to collaborate, as if it were the most natural thing in the world. And, as far as Paul was concerned, it *was* frivolous: that Penny said she wanted to sleep with him and, at the same time, wouldn't risk it until she felt certain of something – he was never quite sure of what – meant that she wasn't taking their relationship seriously. A few weeks after that walk in the Botanics, Paul met a lithe, sarcastic, utterly compelling woman named Nancy, who worked as a nurse at Addenbrookes. He'd had no intention of being unfaithful to Penny, but he'd drifted back to Nancy's rooms, from passivity and boredom more than anything, and he had stayed several hours, before walking home in the rain – guilty, angry, disappointed in himself and, at the same time, painfully aware of the fact that he wanted to see this woman again. He could have ended it there, that night, but he didn't and, when he took time to think it through, he told himself that it wasn't his fault. It wasn't even his choice. That he occasionally slept with Nancy was wholly justified, under the circumstances.

Nevertheless, he felt guilty. On the one hand he continued to see Penny, without knowing why. He suspected he simply didn't have the courage to break it off; yet, in spite of everything, he knew he liked her. Had they been lovers, he could have imagined a kind of happiness with her, or at least something easier and more pleasing than the troubled affair with Nancy, whom he only saw once a week, on nights designated by her, for drunken, slightly perverse bouts of brittle sex touched with bitterness and mockery.

It was the more or less chaste nature of their relationship that left Paul feeling awkward and unhappy when they were here together, in his room. It struck him as odd, on the few occasions that they had been alone together, that he always wanted to get out, to be amongst other people; he and Nancy had never gone out together, they always stayed in her room, drinking Cinzano or vodka, or having sex in the narrow white bed that smelled vaguely of the hospital where she worked. When he was with Penny, it struck him as odd, and slightly perverse, that he was always the one who suggested they go out, to Belinda's, or the Sports and Social, or wherever, but he couldn't help himself. He even thought it was unfair of Penny to come to the house at all.

'Do you want to go to Belinda's?' he asked, after a moment.

'If you like.' Penny would appear amused and oddly detached at such moments. 'I've got an essay to do later, so I can't be too long.' It was another of her apparently deliberate strategies: she would come to see him, or arrange to meet, then announce that she had work to do, the moment she arrived, like a claustrophobe who needs to leave a door open, whenever she comes indoors.

'Okay,' he said. 'I can't be long either. I have some film I want to develop.'

It always stunned him, leaving the house and walking to the end of Mill Road, past the college and the swimming pool, and out to Parker's Piece – it always stunned him, the way his head filled with light and space, when they came into the open and made their way slowly across the Piece. He had often taken pictures here, especially at night: it was something of a cliché, the wide empty park, with its long narrow walks crossing at the centre under a high, ornate lamp, but he kept trying, vainly, to make it new, to find some way of revealing the magical quality of the space and the light, without

36

allowing it to become merely romantic. It always defeated him – like photographing a Christmas tree, or a sunset – yet he felt an attachment to the place, a fondness for the patterns people made, crossing from the centre to the eastern side of town, and for those who loitered in groups, drinking or playing ball games, the winos and foreign students, the girls from Parkside in their perfect, clean sports clothes. Today, in the surprising warmth of the May sunshine, the regulars were in evidence: three drunks on their bench at the far end of the Piece, within easy walking distance of the wine shop; a band of Italian kids in Snoopy sweatshirts and pale blue jeans; couples on the grass, twined around one another like mating snakes and – right at the centre of the Piece, standing stock-still under the tall, elaborate street lamp – the creature Paul and his friend Richard had fondly christened Aqualung, though his real name was Nick something – a sad, confused man of around thirty, with long, grimy, black and grey-streaked hair, who went about the town in a matted RAF greatcoat and battered baseball boots, no matter what the weather. As always, Aqualung greeted Paul, lurching out of his trance and nodding wildly.

'Hey, man,' he said. 'How's it going?'

Paul never knew if the man remembered him from the last time they had talked; it was Aqualung's custom to greet almost anyone who didn't look positively hostile. It had got him into trouble a few times, when he'd picked on the wrong passer-by.

'Hey,' Paul said, repeating the formula response. 'How are you doing?'

'Not so bad, man.' Aqualung nodded sagely. He always appeared to believe he was in possession of some grave secret. 'Not so bad.'

37

'That's good,' Paul replied, slowing a little but not actually stopping. 'Take care, then.'

For a moment, Aqualung regarded him with dark, sad eyes, as if there was something that remained to be said, some transaction that ought to have taken place between them, then he jerked back into his semi-trance, and Paul walked on, with a relieved Penny, who always seemed anxious on these awkward occasions – so anxious, in fact, that she waited till they were well out of earshot before she spoke.

'Who in heaven's name is that?'

'Just a bloke,' Paul answered, feeling unhappy and vaguely guilty. He didn't know why, but it always happened, when he met Aqualung, or one of the other ghostlike men who wandered the streets, that he felt sorry afterwards, preoccupied and troubled, as if he had failed, at some basic, undemanding human level. Though he saw the man several times a week, he always felt that Aqualung was waiting for something, that he had looked for some trace of fellowship or compassion that Paul had failed to provide.

'How do you know him?' Penny continued, intrigued.

'I don't know him,' Paul said. 'I don't know him at all. He's just some bloke who hangs around the Piece.' This answer troubled him, but it was the only answer he could give. As absurd as it would have seemed to Penny, he felt angry that the world let things happen to people like Aqualung, and nobody – Paul included – bothered to find out what was going on, or to help. As much as he knew it wasn't his responsibility, he felt accused by Aqualung's parting look, though he was sure no accusation was intended. It was a look he knew from elsewhere – he had seen it in his mother's eyes, and in the eyes of others he had known – a look of irrational yet deeply felt disappointment: in him, and in the world to which that look condemned him, a world that usually seemed, when he was alone, or distracted, the world of others.

True to her word, Penny left him two hours later. Paul was annoyed and relieved in more or less equal measure. For some time now, his frustration had been slowly mutating into a quiet indifference. He was annoyed that she took it for granted that they had a tacit agreement about sex, and about the time they spent together, but he was happy to have the whole evening ahead of him. On the way home, he decided to phone his parents from the phones near the Piece, a chore he performed every week, just to show he had not forgotten them, and from which he derived no pleasure. Though he missed his father and would have enjoyed talking to him unimpeded, it was always his mother who picked up, and even on the rare occasions when she fetched his dad in from the garden or from his workshop, she would loiter in the background, listening and chipping in comments and reminders. It made for an awkward and stilted conversation and Paul was always happy to finish the call and get away. Still, once it was over, he could at least rest easy in his mind, knowing he had done his duty for another week; so, stopping off at one of his two or three usual call boxes, he fished out as much change as he had in his pockets and dialled the number.

As he had expected, his mother answered the phone.

'Hello?' She always seemed surprised when the phone rang.

'Hello,' he said. 'It's Paul.'

'Oh.' She seemed flustered. 'Okay. Tell me the number, and I'll call you back.'

Paul told her the number twice, then hung up and waited. It was a minute, at least, before the phone rang.

'Hello?'

'I'm here.'

'Uh–huh.' There was a longish silence, just long enough for him to sense her casting around for something to say.

'So, how are you both?' he said. He wondered why it was always this awkward.

'*I'm* fine,' she said. 'Your father's not been so well.'

'Oh?' He couldn't tell if he had detected a note of real concern in her voice; she always sounded so weary and put upon. 'What is it?'

'He says it's just this flu that's been going round. But I'm not sure. Still, you know your dad.'

'Yes,' Paul said. 'Has he been to the doctor?'

'Of course not. You know what he's like.'

'I'm sure he's fine.' Paul couldn't help thinking that his mother's concern was as much of a burden as the illness itself. She had a way of making every little problem seem an inevitable and wholly justified affliction.

'Anyway, he's here,' his mother said, abruptly. 'I'll put him on.'

His father came on and promptly denied that there was anything wrong. He had a bug, nothing to worry about. Before Paul could press him, he turned the conversation around so they were talking about him, about college, his photographs, stuff his parents had been reading in the papers about the rapist. There was no further mention of his father's health. Paul could have predicted as much. It was just his mother making a fuss, as usual, he concluded, when he put down the receiver, left the telephone box and started for home. It was evening, all of a sudden, the light over the Piece a soft, greyish green, and Paul walked back slowly. After these calls, he realised how much he missed his father, and was always surprised again at how strong the feeling was, considering how rarely he thought about it. His mother had long since ceased to trouble him: he had made a more or less conscious decision, at around fifteen, to treat her as politely and kindly as he could, but he would never engage with her, he would never be available to her – to feel guilty, to participate in the tight, care-filled household that she had created over the years. And once he was away from home – at college, or working over the holidays – he rarely thought about her. There was no reason for this animus – for animus it was, a feeling much stronger than antipathy, or even dislike; there was no sin, no crime; his mother had never deliberately harmed him. What he had decided upon, years ago, was an almost theoretical distance between himself and this woman he barely knew; a stranger locked in her own remote world, who was, he suspected, both offended and bewildered on principle by the choices he had made: to go to college as far away from home as he could arrange; to find work in Cambridge, rather than going back to Fife over the Christmas and Easter breaks; to tell her almost nothing about his life or his studies, only ever responding to her questions in the vaguest, most general terms.

His father was different. A quiet, distant man, he possessed a depth of intelligence, an informed curiosity about the world and a sense of the continuous nature of the real, that seemed to come from nowhere. He had left school at fifteen, and pursued a series of manual jobs, finally ending up at Mackay's, where he worked in the customer supply and transportation department. The job itself hadn't been a hardship, Paul suspected, but his dad's real interests lay elsewhere. It seemed a long time ago, almost impossibly remote when Paul thought about it, but as a boy his father had been something of a local phenomenon: inventive and able, good with his hands, he had

41

built model aeroplanes for a while, which he gave away or sold to other children in the village, before moving on to kites, which were, paradoxically, simpler and at the same time more difficult to make. Some of the neighbours still remembered his dad's kites: they had always been brightly coloured and ornate, sailing out above the sea, or over the fields that ran down to the cliffs nearby, floating on the blue air like huge, formal birds, scarlet and green, or crimson and yellow, miraculously beautiful, almost alive, in the first years after the war. His dad still had one of those kites – though it was faded and torn now, with part of its streaming, phoenix-like tail missing – on the wall of the room where he slept, the one splash of colour in that otherwise austere space. In spite of its condition, this kite was evidently his prize possession.

There were people who said Paul's father could have been somebody, if he'd had the chance – or maybe if he had been interested. He'd never had the benefit, or the burden, of what was commonly referred to as a formal education; other than the journeys he had made for work, especially in the early days, when he had visited ports all over Britain, he had hardly travelled. As a family they had been to Spain twice, because Paul's mother had decided she wanted to go; it hadn't been his dad's idea – which struck him as odd, considering how interested he was in other places, with all the atlases and maps and history books from the library piled up in his room, and especially considering his interest in Italy and all things Italian. For a long time, Paul couldn't understand why his father had not only never visited Rome, or Florence, or Venice, but had never even expressed an interest in going. Eventually, though, he realised that his father's interest was in something mythical; he had no desire to see the place, or meet the people. It was an idea he was after. His father's Italy was a place in the mind; it could just as easily have been France, or Greece, or Tibet; what mattered was that it was unlike the place where he was obliged to live, that it was as unlike Scotland as it was possible to be. For his father, Italy could be reduced to a pile of books, a few records, and a shoe box full of postcards.

Still, his father's Italy had touched Scotland, too – literally. A few miles from home, on the back road to Cupar, was the place where the legendary balloonist, Vincenzo Lunardi, had landed after completing the first recorded hot-air balloon flight in Scotland. It was no more than an ordinary field, which belonged to a local farmer, but that didn't matter to his dad. If anything, the very anonymity of the place appealed to him. Here, he was free to imagine what he liked: the weather that day, the wind over the firth, the astonishment of the locals when the huge silk balloon came down amongst the sugar beets, or clover, or whatever they were growing there at the time. There was nothing to say where the balloon had landed – Paul had no idea how his father had worked out that it was this particular spot – and there were no books about Lunardi's Scottish flight, but his father had known all about it, from the distance the Italian had travelled, to the weather on the day, to what colour the balloon had been. It struck Paul that the great aviator had not travelled very far: he had ascended from Edinburgh and crossed the Firth of Forth, before putting down here, just a few miles inland. Perhaps he had intended to go further. He pictured the man as small and fine-boned, like the only real Italian he had ever seen, to his knowledge, a fragile, birdlike waiter from a café in Portobello. Lunardi had probably been thin, with a shock of dark, wavy hair; perhaps he had been a little nervous as he began his descent; or he might have been happy to have made it over the cold grey water, casually taking his place in history, with a wave for the bemused locals, and a Neapolitan song running through his head, as the balloon floated gently to earth. It was odd. In school, Paul had always thought of the people who made history as different from others, but when he was out there, in that ordinary beet field, with his father, he had begun to realise that history was made in just such ordinary places, by people who were not so very different from himself, and everything he had learned, every battle and king and Act of Parliament, had come to seem irrelevant now, compared to what that little man might have felt on landing. And this was all Paul wanted to know. If Lunardi was a person, like Paul, or his father, what had he felt up there, close to the sky? Maybe the idea of history hadn't even occurred to him, maybe he had never even thought about it. Maybe what he valued was the things he had seen and done up there, the experiences, the details, the passing moments. All the things he couldn't have described when he came down to earth. It would have been just the same for the astronauts, when they flew in space, or when they walked on the moon. Sure, they could make speeches, or bring back rocks and pictures, but there was something else; there was the fabric of things, there was the moment by moment experience. History recorded the facts, but the facts weren't what happened. What Lunardi thought and felt, the taste he had in his mouth, the colour of the fields, the shapes he had seen on the water – these were the things that history ignored. These were the things that had really happened.

This was his father's world: an imagined place, a refuge he had acquired by a process of negotiation, trading the world that others inhabited – a world, for some reason, where he could not feel at home – for a provisional, invented freedom. Ever since Paul had been a small child, his father had been there, moving about the house or the garden, a presence in the same space as Paul and his mother yet, at the same time, slightly apart from it all – a person, it seemed, who had chosen to live at one remove from the society around him, courteous to a fault, even kind in his way, but no more engaged with the everyday business of those others than an animal might be. It was his father who had taught Paul to drive, starting him early, out at the old aerodrome on Sunday mornings; it was his father who gave him the books he had collected over the years – books he had not understood to begin with, books of poetry, art books, science texts, not the usual things you gave to children, not the openly educational works they had in the school library, or the adventure stories his aunt sometimes gave him, but the kind of books adults read if they were interested in a subject. For several years, Paul had flicked through those books, staring at the pictures of leaf-sections and turbines, repeating the lines of poems he did not understand, but whose music he could feel somewhere deep in his body, a rhythm that haunted him through school lief-times and the long sleepless nights. Another child might have given up on those books, but Paul didn't: though nobody in his house ever spoke of love, the fond obligation to persevere, the sense he had that his father was entrusting these complex texts to him alone, the fact that no judgement was ever implied, no expectations voiced, no hopes invested in him, was as close as he had ever come to manifest affection.

At the same time, once Paul had become involved in some way in his father's world – when he had started fishing with him, or when his driving lessons had started taking them out on to the road – he was never in any doubt that the standards his father demanded of him would be as high as those he imposed upon himself. It was his peculiar ability to make this

45

feel like a privilege, a special kind of gift. More often than not, Paul found it encouraging, even flattering, to have someone expect so much of him – and in this his father's attitude stood in direct contrast to his mother's. He always expected the best, yet he never saw anything as final. Nothing was irremediable. When they had first started going out on driving lessons, he had taken Paul to the aerodrome and let him build up his confidence, but he hadn't taken him out on the road for a long time. Finally, Paul had become impatient.

'When can we go for a proper drive?' he demanded one Saturday afternoon.

'When you're ready,' his father had answered.

'I'm ready now.'

'You think so?'

Paul stopped the car. 'You don't think I am?'

His dad looked at him, a faint smile playing about his lips.

'You have just enough basic skill,' he said. 'Do you think that's enough?'

'What else is there?'

'Courtesy,' his father replied, not missing a beat. 'Courtesy is everything. Without courtesy, you're an accident waiting to happen, no matter how skilled you are.'

Five minutes later, they were on their way home, with Paul at the wheel; three months later, he passed his driving test, on the first attempt; but it was a year before he understood what his father had meant.

Clive was waiting for him in the front room, with a bottle of brandy and a couple of four packs of lager. He seemed worked up about something, and at first Paul thought he'd discovered some new secret about Steve; he was almost relieved when the big man started in again about the rapist.

'I've been thinking,' he said, 'and I'm really getting somewhere. Look.'

He waved his hand vaguely in the direction of the corner table. For the first time, Paul saw that there was a large map of the city, pinned to a board and set out in the corner, with bright blue and red pins, like the kind you see in war films, inserted at various points, mostly around the edge of the city centre, in the areas where student flats were the most prevalent.

'A red pin is for a rape,' Clive said. 'A blue one means he's been sighted, or he tried something, but was disturbed and had to get out quick.'

Paul nodded. 'So I see,' he said. He watched Clive as he explained the logic of the thing, his face flushed with the drink, his breathing a little heavier than usual, almost laboured even. It always amazed Paul that this man, who seemed so clumsy and awkward most of the time, was the same graceful athlete he had seen at the one or two rugby games he'd watched. Meeting Clive off the field, Paul would have thought of him as some kind of bruiser, one of the heavies in a scrum or a ruck, so it had come as a real surprise to see him run with the ball, dodging tackles, alert and alive to everything that happened around him, finding his team-mates with perfectly timed, accurate passes. Of course, he'd been happy to mix it up a bit, too, but Paul had come away with that vivid image in his mind of a running man, full of grace and physical intelligence, forgetting himself in the flow of the game.

'So you have to admit there's a pattern,' Clive concluded. 'All we have to do is study the pattern, and we can predict where he might turn up next.'

Paul shook his head. 'I don't know if it's going to be that easy,' he said, hoping Clive wouldn't notice he was being

47

humoured. 'And even if it was, I'm not sure the police would listen—'

'But we're not going to show it to the police,' Clive interrupted, his voice rising. 'I've got a few of the lads together. We're going to form a night patrol, based on this map, and put ourselves where we can do the most good. We can't wait for the police to catch this bastard.'

'So what are you going to do?'

'We're going to catch him, and we're going to give him a taste of his own medicine.'

'How do you mean?' Paul kept his voice level, seeming only just interested. He had begun to suspect that this could go either way: sound dubious, and he risked hurting the big man's feelings; take it too seriously, and he might find himself being invited to join the vigilantes.

'I mean we're going to do to him what he did to those girls,' Clive said through his teeth. He was starting to get worked up now, which was an unhealthy sign, especially when he'd been drinking. 'He didn't just rape that last girl. He used the knife on her – the poor bitch.'

Paul nodded. He'd heard rumours, including a rather graphic hint from Nancy, that the rapes had become steadily more sadistic.

'Christ!' Clive erupted. 'It must be terrible, being a woman. I think I'd rather die, myself.'

'Oh, I don't know,' Paul said, taken aback somewhat by the non sequitur. 'I know quite a few women who would disagree with you. It's just hard to imagine—'

'No.' Clive put on his unequivocal face. 'I can't imagine it. Thank God. It makes me sick just to think about it.'

He poured himself another brandy and sat down to think it over. 'You want some?' he asked, almost wistful now.

48

Paul shook his head. He wanted to get out, to get away. At times like this, Clive frightened him. There was an edge, a not-quite-contained rage to the man that reminded Paul of a large dog, an Alsatian, say, or a Doberman. It was a rage he had no use for, a festering thing that probably couldn't be transformed into anything else; there were times when Paul felt it in himself and it bothered him. Feigning tiredness, he headed for the door and, when Clive didn't say anything more, he slipped out, leaving the big man to his fantasies of expiation and revenge.

Saturday was his night for seeing Nancy. All week, he would try to keep her out of his mind, but when the day came – a different day each week, depending on her schedule at the hospital – he could hardly stop thinking about what would happen when he saw her again. It wasn't that he particularly liked her; far from it. He didn't even find her that attractive. She was too thin, with a hard, slightly mocking face, small breasts, jagged, mousey-coloured hair. Certainly – and this thought passed through his mind often – she was no match for Penny in looks. The sex, however, was both unsettling and compelling. There was no fondness in it, no affection. Nancy always set strict limits on how much time they spent together: she never allowed him to stay overnight; they hardly ever talked. When he left her, in the small hours, she didn't even bother to say goodbye. In so many ways, it was a cheap, mean-spirited relationship, yet it had been going on for a couple of months now: one night a week, he would go round, and they would drink and fuck, then Nancy would send him away. It was entirely physical; it was just sex. Most of the time, he felt he wasn't even being unfaithful to Penny. It was convenient, and it was exciting, but he had no feelings for

49

Nancy other than a slight mistrust. On the other hand, he knew Penny wouldn't understand that, if she were to find out. He wasn't sure he understood it himself. The worst thing was when he was with Penny in the afternoon, having tea in The Copper Kettle or Belinda's, knowing he would be seeing Nancy later. The two women were so different, and played such different roles in his life that there were times when they seemed to cancel each other out, so much so that it often crossed his mind that he would be better off alone.

Nancy had already started on the Bianco when he arrived. It was her favourite drink: Cinzano with nothing added, sweet and sticky, like sweets in a glass. As usual, she was preoccupied with something that had happened at work: it was a basic element of the ritual that he had to hear all about the day's worst events, in full and occasionally gory detail.

'What's up?' Paul asked her.

Nancy gave a sharp little nod and lit a cigarette. It was the signal that she was about to launch into one of her Casualty Department stories – a road traffic accident, a multiple amputee, a baby with a spike in its head. He was never wholly sure if she was telling the truth when she related what had happened to her on the last shift; her stories had the ring of crafted invention about them, like tiny novels, the characters too real, too well-drawn. Not for the first time he realised that this was her favourite part of the evening, better than sex, though it had something to do with it, a lead-in, a kind of foreplay even. Every time they had gone to bed together – even on the first night – she had told some such story. Surgery; burnt flesh; death. Then sex.

'I was on duty when they brought that girl in,' she said.

'What girl?'

Nancy flashed him a look, but didn't say anything.

'Oh,' Paul said, as the penny dropped. She was talking about the girl in the paper, the student who had been raped and stabbed. He could never keep track of her shift rota.

'That bloke really enjoys what he does,' Nancy continued, quietly. 'Do you want to know what he did to her?'

'Not particularly.' He remembered what Steve had said, and he felt troubled again by the unavoidable knowledge that, in spite of his protestations to the contrary, he was curious about the girl who had been brought in. It was important that he did not allow Nancy to see this.

'No?'

'No.'

Nancy laughed and filled her glass. She had obviously had a few during the afternoon. 'I couldn't tell you anyway,' she said. 'It's confidential.'

'Good.' He already knew he wouldn't be getting off that easily.

'She's in deep shock,' Nancy continued. 'It will take her years to get over it.'

Paul nodded. 'It's terrible,' he said, lamely.

They finished the Cinzano and had opened a bottle of vodka before they got as far as the bed. It was an unspoken rule that Nancy had to be drunk before he even touched her. This way, it seemed incidental. No matter how drunk she got, no matter what she was wearing when Paul arrived, no matter what they did, Nancy created a special illusion, a trick by which she seemed never to be wholly naked. She was always somehow veiled. This first fuck was always hard and urgent; often, when it was over, Paul would feel vaguely uneasy about how quick and thoughtless it had been. For as long as this phase lasted, they were no longer persons. It wasn't a question of love, or even lust: it didn't matter that Nancy could have

51

been anyone, because he knew that he, in turn, was nobody to her. Not at that moment. All that mattered was the smell – the scent, the traces – of their bodies, the heat that formed, then evaporated, on the surface of the skin, in the hair, on the lips.

Gradually, however, things changed. They would lie for hours in Nancy's bed, drinking vodka, coming together from time to time, then slipping apart gratefully, shedding like spent skins the bodies they had contrived for one another. Whenever they stopped, Paul would find himself unable to look at her, postponing the moment that had to come, when the fluidity that had existed for a moment between them – or not so much between as around, encompassing them, cancelling them out – would disappear, and she would become set, fixed, self-possessed. For as long as he could, he would avoid looking at her directly, lingering instead on the scent of her, a vapour she had become on his hands and his skin. It surprised him, every time, that they could have become so much one person, so outside themselves and their bounds, and then could so quickly revert to who they had been, as if nothing had happened. For some time, as if to make up for this obvious distance between them, Nancy – for whom nothing Paul did, outside this room, held a shred of interest – would probe and pry, asking him questions about his sexual history, what fantasies he had, what he wanted to do to her, what he wanted to do to other women. She often asked about Penny and, though Paul had never actually admitted the truth of that situation, Nancy had quickly guessed what was going on. She made no secret of her contempt for the other woman, whom she had never seen and, to divert her attention from his current girlfriend, Paul talked about other women he had known, or wanted to know.

Once he had made the mistake of telling her about

Caroline. It had seemed innocent enough to begin with: over a bottle of wine, Nancy had asked him about the first girl he had ever liked, the first crush, the first time he had been in love, and he had remembered Caroline Henderson, who lived three doors away from him back home. They had talked about her for a while – what she looked like, what happened to her – then, as far as Paul was concerned, they had let it slip. It was only later, when they were in bed, that she raised it again – and this time there was a fresh note in her voice, partly curiosity, but also something else, something darker.

'So,' she had said, in the seemingly matter-of-fact tone that Paul had come to mistrust most, 'what is she like?'

He hadn't registered at first. 'What is who like?'

'Caroline,' she said. It was like her to have remembered the name. Everything was stored away; everything had its possible use.

'Well,' he said, carefully, 'I haven't seen her in years—'

'No.' She lifted her hand, as if to wipe something away. 'Not that Caroline. I mean – the one you still think about.'

'I don't understand.'

'Well. You don't think about the real Caroline, do you?' she said. 'The one who's grown up and become a shop assistant, or whatever. You think about the girl in your mind. The one you used to know, when she was still in school.'

'I suppose so.' Paul lay back and closed his eyes. 'Some-times.'

'So what is she like?' Nancy was gazing at him with that fixed, curious look of hers. 'The girl in your mind.'

'She's—' Paul thought a moment. He could see Caroline Henderson in his mind's eye, exactly as she was when she was thirteen, and he had been two years older, slightly embarrassed

53

that, whenever he met this girl on the street, he didn't know how to act or what to say. 'She's just as she was then.'

'Which is?'

'A girl. Blonde hair. Blue eyes. Just a girl.'

'Oh come on,' Nancy said. 'You can do better than that.' She laid her hand on his stomach. 'What's her body like?'

'Slim,' he said. Nancy's hand slipped down to rest lightly on his thigh. 'Thin, I suppose.'

'What is she wearing?'

'The usual. A skirt. A blouse.'

'Her school uniform?'

'Yes.'

'What colour?'

'Navy. Navy and white tie. White blouse. Navy skirt.'

'Uh–hm. Knee socks?'

'No.'

'No?' She sounded surprised, even disappointed.

'It's summer,' Paul said, aware that he was making an effort to reassure her. He had a fair idea as to where this was going.

'So?' She slipped her hand down along his thigh and began to stroke him.

'So she's not wearing anything on her legs. They're . . . bare.'

'Oh. So – where is she?'

'Walking to school.'

'It's morning, then.'

'Yes.'

'So.' Nancy closed her hand around him. 'It's morning. She comes out of her house and you see her. She's a bit sleepy still; if you were close enough you could smell it, a little sleep-warmth clinging to her skin. She's just brushed her teeth. When you kiss her, she'll taste of mint.'

54

Paul smiled and shook his head.

'Don't you want to kiss her?'

'Of course I do.'

'What else?'

'I don't know. I don't think about it—'

'Yes, you do. Or if you don't, you ought to.'

'Why?'

'Why?' Nancy laughed. 'You don't think about it? You don't wonder what it would be like to fuck her?'

She waited a moment for him to answer, but he couldn't speak now.

'It's summer,' she said, 'but it's still morning. When you touch her legs, her skin is cool. She's wearing her uniform, but she isn't wearing socks. Maybe she's wearing stockings?'

Paul shook his head.

'No,' Nancy said. 'She's too young for stockings. That would be sixth form, and it has to be younger.'

'Why?'

'You know why.'

'How young?'

'I don't know,' she said. 'You have to choose. But sixth form is too safe. We'll have to find a girl from middle school. Or a third year, say.'

Paul knew what she was doing, but he couldn't resist it. He lay still and listened, while Nancy's hand worked beneath the covers.

'She's just woken up, and put on her uniform. She's just brushed her teeth. A bit sleepy. She's wearing a white blouse and tie. A little short pleated skirt.'

'What colour is her hair?'

Nancy laughed. 'Blonde, of course.'

'Blonde like you?'

55

'Of course,' she said. 'You haven't got much of an imagination, have you?'

It had been going this way for some time. Early on, not long after they had first met, Nancy had uncovered something, some memory, some minor detail, that had led her to this, but there was nothing playful in the game, there was no lightness, no sense of fantasy in these stories she invented. Nancy would feed him a line, she would isolate a remark, or a single word, and he would feel himself being drawn, only half against his will, into a mock admission of guilt. Then, afterwards, when the game was done, she would give him a knowing look, as if he had just confirmed something that she had always suspected, not just in him, but in all men. He had already begun to recognise the nature of this theatre she made of their encounters, but he couldn't stop himself, he was always drawn in, partly because he desired her more when she played this game and partly, at some other level he had never before encountered, he wanted to admit to the fantasy, he wanted to play the parts she assigned him. Everything, he told himself – remembering something Man Ray had said – everything is permitted to the imagination. The trouble was, Nancy was a literalist, and for her, this shadow–life was real. What Man Ray had wanted to say – that a game is a game, both as real and as necessary as anything else, but never the whole, never the exclusive truth – was lost on her. As a child, Paul had often wondered what it would be like if his mother were dead, but that didn't mean he actually wanted her to die. Everybody knew that those thoughts were part of the complex world of the imagination, where contradictory wishes and fears could easily coexist, it had nothing to do with the facts. Yet Nancy seemed unable to understand this. In her own mind, she had caught Paul out – though what she made of her own part in these games he could never tell. Even as he played along, he was struck by the way she always chose for herself the role of the innocent, or the victim; on the one occasion when Paul had refused to be carried along by the game, she had wanted him to play the part of the rapist, mask and all, and he'd been so frightened by the thought of that, and by his own arousal, that he'd walked out, sick to the stomach, with her laughter ringing in his ears, triumphant and bitter and utterly merciless.

Nancy never let him stay overnight. Sometimes they got drunk and fell asleep for a while, but she always woke him before dawn and asked him to leave. She had told him, the first night they had gone back to her rooms, that she expected him to leave before morning, so she could wake up alone. It had seemed odd to him, at first; after a while, though, he didn't mind at all. To be honest, he was glad to get away from her. Though he would look forward for days to seeing her, though the excitement would mount, sometimes to an almost unbearable level, as he cycled over to her building on the evenings she allowed him to visit her, he always felt odd after it was finished: odd, and a little demeaned, even tainted. The other odd thing was that, no matter what time of the night or morning it was when he left, he was always ravenously hungry – though even if Nancy had offered him something, he wouldn't have been able to eat it. Besides, he enjoyed the cycle ride or the walk home in the cool of the early morning. He would slip out of bed and dress; no matter how quick he was, she would always be asleep again before he actually got out the door. He often wondered what he was doing with Nancy; he had soon become aware of the fact that he didn't like her, and he was pretty sure she didn't much like him. The sex was something impersonal, something almost abstract, and that troubled him – yet it was also part of the pleasure. He could never have imagined sex like that with Penny. As he walked home, he would be aware of his body, aware of the smell of sex on his skin, that sticky heat of coupling that was more than either of them, and had nothing to do with who they were, or what they felt for one another. No matter how little they had in common, these nights with Nancy had taught him something about lust – not lust the deadly sin, but lust as it really was, not pleasure, not a chosen thing, but an involuntary, fundamental, life-affirming, yet wholly neutral force. It wasn't good or bad; it had nothing to do with love; there was nothing clean or contained or polite about it, nothing defined. It had to do with life in its own right, like when you sift through a handful of silt and find all the creatures it contains, appetites and senses and fleshliness, brimming with the same urgency as yourself. It was a blind, neutral kinship with everything; it was total abandonment. He had been waiting for it to happen all his life, and now that it had, it dismayed him.

Later, far into the night, he rose quietly and dressed. To his surprise, Nancy was still asleep, though light was just beginning to bleed through, over the roofs on Trumpington Road. She had to have drunk more than usual before he arrived, to sleep on like this, and he was troubled by the thought that, over the last few weeks, she had been slipping into something that seemed more like depression than the usual self-sustaining bitterness. For a moment, he even considered staying, in case that was what she really wanted. Maybe she needed someone to be there, and just couldn't admit it; maybe she wanted something else from him that she didn't know how to ask for. But the moment passed. Nancy stirred slightly in her sleep, and Paul quickly pulled on his shoes and let himself out.

Outside, the streets were quiet and still. A white cat darted across Lensfield Road as he passed the Catholic church and turned into Gonville Place, but there were no people, not even cars. It was still early, early on a Sunday morning; and he didn't see another person till he reached Parker's Piece. There, under the high ornate lamps where the paths crossed, stood Aqualung, still as a rock, staring up into the pinkish lights, as if he had not moved a muscle for the last two days. For a moment, Paul considered crossing the Piece, to see if he was okay, then thought better of it. He didn't know what Aqualung was on; it wasn't really his business. Maybe the guy was happy in his own way. Maybe he was better off like that than he might have been otherwise.

Some time mid-morning he woke with a start. When he hadn't slept properly for days like this, the dreams that came were vivid, but what was happening now wasn't really a dream; it was more of a memory.

He was walking in the woods around the Den, as he had done so often, but this time – and this was the only dreamlike element in the whole cycle of events – he was looking for the boy he had seen there so often, the boy who might have been his own age but looked older, a thin raggedy kid in a tatty pullover and greying jeans. As a child, Paul had imagined him living out there in the woods, alone and self-sufficient, with only a dog for company and protection, sleeping in the narrow shelter of the rocks, hunkering in under a tree to get away from the rain, as much animal as boy, alone and totally self-sufficient. Part of him knew it wasn't so: the boy came to school sometimes and Paul knew he had parents because he had seen them once, at Mass, with the boy in tow, standing next to his mother, silent and withdrawn from everything that was going on around him. Nobody could have lived in the woods. Yet Paul could imagine this boy out there, for days or weeks at a time, crouching amongst the undergrowth, looking for traces of spoor or abandoned kills, with a knowledge of the outdoor world that no other boy had, because he himself belonged there. He had nothing to do with school, or Christmas, or homework, and he obviously scorned other children. Nothing impressed him and there was nothing he trusted.

All his life, Paul had lived a street away from the shore and he had spent most of his time on the beach. He felt safe there, in that world of light and weather, and boats in the harbour, crowding against the walls, red and blue and yellow hulls with friendly names – *Shirley, Margaret-Ann, Morning Star.* Paul would spend whole days just hanging around on the front, watching the men unload nets or lobster creels; in winter, he would go out to the end of the East Pier, and stand as close as he dared to where the big waves crashed into the harbour wall – but he never felt that the water was dangerous. Inland, though, crossing the wide fields, or entering the darkness of the woods around the Den, it was different. It was only a three-mile walk – five miles on his bike if he followed the road – but inland was a whole other territory. Once, a farmer had appeared suddenly, with two large dogs and a gun: Paul had been convinced that the man was about to shoot him, because he was trespassing on his fields and, in spite of the fact that his father had told him never to run from a dog, he had turned and fled in panic. The inlanders he had seen – not just farm people, but everyone he saw from the road when he cycled by – all seemed strange to him: dark, lonely men, in scabbed, heavy clothes and big, ugly boots; shadowy, unhappy women, standing around in yards full of straw and run-down tractors. They looked so grimy and weighed-down, as if gravity here was twice as strong as it was on the coast.

Yet he couldn't resist the pull of the interior. He had always thought of it that way, ever since Mrs Greer had talked about the dark interior of Africa, and he had assumed that every country had two geographies: a clear, weather-beaten coast-line, where things were constantly changing, the endless motion of the sea eroding and cleansing whatever it touched, the wind honing everything down to the bone or the bare wood, and that dark, still interior, where things lay still and rotted, like the fallen trees in the Den woods, that lay for years turning black in the rain and finally flaking into great rancid pieces, or the huge tips of slurry and straw in the farmer's yards, that appeared never to diminish. If anyone had asked him which he preferred, he would have chosen the coast, without even thinking about it, but on Sundays, after lunch, when he had time to himself, he almost always rode his bike out to the Den woods. The Den proper was an old Pictish site – or so his father had told him, though there was nothing to mark the place as historically important – and consisted of a series of odd-shaped rocks with what seemed to be narrow steps cut into the stone and a few bleared carvings on the walls of the narrow passage that ran between the two largest outcrops. If you looked closely, you could see a vague dog-like animal on one rock, and a circle just above the flight of steps that led up to the highest stone. Nobody knew what the purpose of the site had been, but there was something compelling about the place. Paul could easily imagine it as a place of sacrifice or pagan ritual, and – though he would have been hard pressed to say if it was a sense of sin that drew him

in, or the possibility of something quite other, some sacramen-
tal moment, some dark and holy vision – he gravitated
towards that central spot, which was always damp and moss-
green, even in high summer. When you were in the Den, you
were completely surrounded by the only real woods for miles;
elsewhere the trees were scattered and sparse, usually no more
than hedge height, and twisted every which way by the wind,
but the Den was tucked into a long, barely perceptible fold in
the land and, for a long strip about a mile in length, the woods
grew thick and dark and lush. Out there, you could find the
ashes of a stranger's fire, still warm sometimes, amongst the
autumn leaves, or sodden with two days' rain; out there, you
might find a strange bone hidden amongst the bedsprings in a
midden; somewhere across a summer's afternoon – somewhere close by, but not so close that you could trace it to its
source – you might hear the small cry of a wounded animal
that could just as easily have been a child; at such times, you
would stop dead in your tracks, all of a sudden, and you would
be aware that you were being watched, though no one else
was visible.

When you were within their bounds, the woods seemed to
go on forever. Paul was aware of the points at which they
stopped: the old kilns, on one side, which had belonged to the
estate, back in the old days, but were ramshackle and empty
now, and the border where the wood met farmland on the
other, towards the north. This was no man's land: a battery of
fences and hedges and yards that marked where people were,
the domain of men with guns and dogs who seemed to spend
their entire time posting signals – poisoned rats, crows hanging
from wire or baling twine in a hedge or a fence – that he
knew were intended for him. If you walked north, you came
to a marshland: a vast expanse of black, acid water and reeds,

succeeded on the far side by a stretch of scrubby grassland and low birches; the only colour here, besides a range of dull greens, was the yellow of the odd clump of wild irises in early summer, and another, more buttery yellow in autumn, when the birches shed their leaves. It was here that Paul imagined the boy lived, when he stayed away from school.

Once, when he was quite small, he had gone out there with two slightly older boys from the village. They hadn't wanted to take him at first, but he had followed along behind till they relented and let him walk with them, wading through the dark mud towards a wide bed of reeds and scrubby willows. It was late in the spring; one of the boys had said they would find coots' and moorhens' nest out in the middle, and Paul had wanted to see what the eggs looked like. The oldest boy, John Greig, had said they would take a couple of eggs, but no more; the rule was, you left the rest to hatch, so there would be more birds next year. Paul had watched him blowing the eggs, making tiny holes at either end of the shell, and blowing out the yellow mess inside, and it hadn't bothered him. He didn't want any eggs for himself, though. He just wanted to see the nests. All the way out, he had been listening to John, and trying not to think about the other boy, Mickey, who was generally considered a bad sort. The rumour was that when Mickey found a nest he would take all the eggs – five, six, or even seven at a time, however many there were, he always left the nest empty. Even when he climbed into a tree after wood pigeons and suchlike, he didn't stop till he had taken everything, bringing the eggs down in his mouth, if he had to use both hands to climb. Paul had tried that once, just to see what it was like, and the warm egg had broken in his mouth as he was climbing down, filling his throat with a thick, sticky sweetness. He felt sick after that, and he had suddenly

63

understood that, in taking the eggs, he was doing wrong. It was as if the chick had broken and dissolved between his teeth, and what he had swallowed was its blood, or the soft makings of feathers and wingbones.

By the time they had reached the centre of the marsh, it was getting dark. Paul was already thinking of going back, before they found the nests; then, quietly, like a hunter, John Greig had told them to stop.

'Look,' he said, 'there's two nests just above.'

He pointed across the reed bed to where, first one, then, a few yards off, another dark, untidy nest lay cradled amongst the reeds, all twiggy and jagged, like the crown of thorns they put on Jesus' head for Good Friday. John stopped and took stock: the ground was wet and heavy between the nests and the relatively solid ground where they were standing, and it had taken them a few minutes to cross the gap. Finally they stood over the first nest. There were eight eggs.

'Moorhen,' John said.

He bent down, picked a single egg from the clutch and held it up so Paul could see.

'Can I hold it?'

'Be careful.'

Paul had taken the egg and nestled it in his palm: it was warm, smooth, unbelievably large; holding it, he felt there was something alive inside, something on the point of being, a whole chick, maybe, and he didn't want them to take it. He wanted to put it back and go, but there was no chance of that: Mickey was already kneeling beside the nest, with a handkerchief spread out amongst the reeds, ready to contain his find. Suddenly, a voice sang out from across the reed bed.

'Hey. You.'

Paul looked up. The others had jumped to attention. Across

the reeds, about fifteen yards away, the boy from the woods was watching them; he had what looked like a sheath knife in one hand, and a long, pointed stick in the other.

'Get away from there,' he shouted, his voice darkening with menace.

It was a rash act: one boy against three – or two, at least, for Paul would no more have dreamed of fighting him than he would of flying home across the woods – but Paul was surprised to see John and Mickey step away from the nests, and back towards the dry land of the further side. The boy was probably about the same age as Paul – which made John at least two years bigger – but that didn't count for anything now. Out here, in the growing twilight, on his territory, Paul realised that the others were as scared as he was.

'Look,' Mickey said, almost under his breath. 'He's got a knife.'

For a long moment, Paul could not believe that the others believed this boy would use the weapon – not for the sake of a bird's nest; then, with growing horror, he understood that the boy would not only use the knife, but would also be quite prepared to kill any one of them before he let them get away with a single egg. He didn't understand why, but he understood – because the others had understood, and their fear was obvious, even to him. The boy hadn't moved since they had become aware of him; Paul knew he was giving them a chance to run, to get away unharmed. For the first time in his life, Paul realised that a boy could be as serious as a man, and it was frightening.

'Come on,' John said, starting back towards the far side of the marsh.

'He won't use it,' Mickey said.

'Want a bet?' John looked more worried. 'That's Patrick Connor. He's Michael Connor's son.'

Mickey didn't say anything, but Paul noticed that he looked suddenly more concerned, and moved a little closer to John. Patrick hadn't moved a muscle. He stood his ground, the knife held casually in his left hand, his eyes fixed on John. Paul didn't know who he was, but he couldn't help being impressed by the effect he had on the older boys, who had forgotten the nests and were moving away slowly, heading back towards the woods. Paul couldn't take his eyes off Patrick Connor. All the time, he was waiting for him to turn away, knowing he had won, but he stayed where he was, watching, on guard, till they were away from the nests and back on the far side of the marsh where it was suddenly obvious they belonged.

As he grew older, Paul understood a little more about Patrick's circumstances with each passing year. Patrick's parents were travelling people, which meant that their children would disappear from school late in the spring and only reappear in the middle of autumn term, when school had been going for three or four weeks. For this reason, they were always behind. The teachers made no secret of their dislike of the parents, but they were kind to the children, perhaps because, as Paul had once heard his mother say to another woman after Mass, they had no prospects. That phrase had always stuck in his head. He wondered, from time to time, what it was to have no prospects, just as he wondered about his brother, who had died a week after he was born, before he could even leave the hospital. There were even times when his brother – who, coincidentally, was to have been baptised Patrick – and the boy in the woods became one person: in his nightmares, say, or in the long, slow daydreams he had in school, during Scripture classes. His brother had no prospects either, but he still had a soul. Even if he had died at birth, even if he had died in the womb, he would have had a soul.

Paul had been five when it happened. There had been an atmosphere of muted excitement in the house for weeks before his father took him out in the car for a drive and told him that they both had to be very good to his mother, and help her all they could, because she was going to have a baby. Paul had been noticing changes in how his mother looked; he had even asked her, only the week before, why she was getting so fat, and his parents had laughed. Now he was about to have a little brother or sister.

The weeks passed and, without particular warning, he came home from school one day to find a neighbour in the house, and his mother and father gone. The neighbour, Mrs MacMillan, had explained that they were at the hospital, and that everything would be fine. She fixed his tea and, when it came time, sent him to bed. Much later, well after midnight, he heard his father come in. There were voices below, talking quietly; then the front door closed again. Paul got up and looked out just in time to see Mrs MacMillan heading back to her own house, two doors up. It was a bright, moonlit night; he could hear the sea down below on the front, a long, low murmur, turning in the shingle. His father came upstairs, slowly, trying to be quiet, heading for his own room in the dark; when he saw Paul, he stopped on the landing, but he didn't switch on the light.

'What are you doing up?' he said. He sounded tired and defeated.

'I can't sleep,' Paul answered.

'Try,' his dad said.

'Where's Mum?'

'She had to stay at the hospital for a while. She'll be back soon.'

'Where's the baby?'

His father made a sound then, a short, muffled moan, and his body sagged, as if someone had winded him; but he immediately pulled himself up.

'He's gone,' he said. 'Go back to bed.'

'Where's he gone?'

His father looked at him in the dark. Paul thought maybe he had been crying.

'Go back to bed,' he said. 'We'll talk about it in the morning.'

But they didn't talk about it in the morning. By the time Paul got up his father was gone and Mrs MacMillan was in the kitchen, making breakfast. Later that day, when he came home from work, his father sat down with him and tried to explain what had happened, but what he said didn't make much sense: his baby brother, it seemed, had gone to heaven, the way old people did when they died, which struck Paul as odd, but he didn't ask any more questions. Mrs MacMillan tried to explain it to him too, a few days later, while his father was at the hospital, getting Paul's mum ready to come home, but she didn't say anything new. His brother had gone to heaven. He was with the angels.

Paul felt cheated. It was as if they had made a promise to him that they couldn't keep, like the time when his mother had said maybe he could have a bike for Christmas, and he had got some books and a toy panda instead. Later, though, he decided it was his brother who had decided not to come and stay with them, because he wanted to stay outside, and there were times when Paul thought of him walking away to where

68

the angels were, crossing the piece of waste ground beyond the yards, and disappearing into the woods. He knew he was supposed to forget about Patrick – when he asked questions about the baby, his mother didn't answer, the way she did when he asked questions about catechism, or the things the priest said in church – but he never did. Even when he got older, and realised that it hadn't been his parents' fault, he kept thinking about the boy who should have been there when he went swimming off the pier, the brother who should have walked to school with him, and maybe slept in the same room, just feet away, another set of dreams laid down beside his own. He felt a trick had been played on him. The boy with his own personality who would have made a snowman with him in the back garden, or borrowed his things, the one person who could match him, his other self, the brother he had never met, was missing. He had never forgotten that.

Before he arrived in Cambridge, it had never occurred to him that he might have friends, as such. There had been a couple of boys at school that he'd spent time with, mucking around with George Murray down at the harbour, or playing records round at Gary Wilson's when his parents were out, but he had never thought of them as in any way significant, or even particularly interesting, in all the years he had known them. It was a mystery, a kind of girls' thing, when Penny spoke about her friends back home: how Mary from next door knew her mind almost as well as she did; how she wrote letters back to old schoolmates every couple of weeks; how it made her day when a letter arrived from Alice, or Sandra, or one of the others, with news about weddings, or broken-off engagements, or new jobs. Paul had left home without even saying a proper goodbye to his former schoolmates; if he hadn't known about Penny's arrangements, it would never have occurred to him to write them letters, or wonder what they were doing. At the same time, the men he knew at college – classmates, fellow tenants at the house, casual acquaintances – seemed almost unreal; occasionally mildly interesting, or provocative, or annoying, they moved through his world and made no lasting impression, like zoo animals, or the people in movies. The one exception – the one man he thought of as a friend – was Richard. Yet he didn't even see Richard that often. Most of the time, he was alone. This hadn't seemed unnatural; he hadn't even noticed it until Penny pointed it out.

'Why is it men never have any friends?' she had asked one afternoon, out of the blue.

They had been having tea in The Copper Kettle. Penny had been describing her friend Miriam, who was about to get married, back home.

'How do you mean?'

'You know,' she said. 'Men friends. Not guys from the pub, or the rugby team. People you talk to. People you feel comfortable with.'

'I feel comfortable on my own,' Paul said. The idea of Penny's friends – people who knew your every thought, girls from back home who thought of themselves in little, chuckling, like-minded bands – had already struck him, more than once, as deeply claustrophobic. 'Anyway, I have friends. It's just that they don't live in my pocket.'

Penny laughed. 'All right,' she said. 'Tell me about your friends.'

'Well,' Paul said. 'There's Richard.'

'Oh yes. Richard.' She gave him a meaningful look. 'Good old Richard.'

'What's that supposed to mean?'

Penny shook her head. 'The only man I know who is more remote than you is Richard,' she said. 'The only reason you two are friends is that neither of you asks anything of the other. It only works if you never need anything.'

'So what's so wonderful about need?' Paul was irritated. There was something insulting about this glib analysis, something demeaning about the basic assumptions that it was built upon. What was wrong with self-sufficiency? Why did everyone think in terms of the relationships between people?

The reason he liked Richard so much, the reason he trusted him, was that there was a distance between them, a respect, a feeling of space, that he could always count upon. With Richard, there was no sense of being invaded, the way there sometimes was with Penny. Richard was a man who knew his own mind: he had travelled around in the East, and in Australia, where his mother had family; he had once stayed in a Buddhist monastery, but he never spoke about any particular beliefs, he didn't belong to a religion or group. In the monastery, one of the monks, a middle-aged man who never stopped smiling, had shown him his prize possession – a brand-new, possibly unused SLR camera – then had sworn him to secrecy. Material possessions were not encouraged in the monastery, and it had struck Richard as both amusing and poignant that this pleasant, proud man was ready to break the rules of an institution it had taken Richard some time to gain access to, for the sake of something so banal. A few days later, Richard had left the monastery and travelled home, ending up in Cambridge, where he worked at the Plant Breeding Institute. He'd done his degree in botany, and had come to the conclusion that he found plants more interesting than people.

'Only a handful of people matter,' he would say, half in

71

earnest, but also partly as a provocation to people like Penny. 'Some people feel guilty accepting this, but it's true. If we're honest, we have to admit that it's things that matter to us. The work we do. The places we live in. An old shirt. A glass bowl. A favourite pen.'

Paul couldn't have agreed more. The interesting thing about Richard wasn't what he felt but what he thought. Like Paul, Richard liked people who were interested in the world around them.

Richard had been the first person he had met in Cambridge that he liked, and was still his only real friend. Everyone else he had met seemed vaguely unconvincing: strangely polite and, at the same time, lacking in courtesy; unthinking, for the most part; opinionated, yet lacking in passion; self-regarding, naïve and uncritical, the men, in particular, seemed convinced that the world only existed to accommodate their own narrow interests and desires. He liked the city – he liked the open spaces, especially Midsummer Common, and Grantchester Meadows – but the Tech, with its prefabs and Nissen huts, was ugly and cramped and colourless, and the course he was taking, which had promised so much, was a huge disappointment. After a month, in spite of the fact that he had chosen Cambridge for its remoteness from his mother's house, he was already thinking about going home and trying something else. Having arrived full of ideas and angry passion, he had soon come to dislike everything about the place. After school, it should have come as no surprise that the whole academic exercise struck him as boring and overly self-conscious: students who rehearsed what they needed to say to strike the right balance between originality and the approved thinking, lecturers who lacked passion for their subject, the careful, stepwise exegesis which was the only accepted way of conducting any enquiry – all of it bored and irritated him. As far as the other students were concerned, he was unpopular from the first. An obvious outsider, he was often aware that he was rubbing people up the wrong way, but he couldn't help himself. He had chosen his course – a joint honours in English and European studies – because it covered so much for which he felt a consuming passion, a hunger, almost, that drove him to impatient and often aggressively outspoken lengths; it had not occurred to him, through most of the first year, that other students – not to mention the odd tutor – found his enthusiasm abrasive and threatening. Many of his fellow students were people for whom Cambridge had been a first choice, because of what it was, and what it represented; when they had failed to achieve the grades that would get them to the university, they had, like Paul, opted for the Tech, which was, if anything, one step lower than a polytechnic on the scale of things, in order to live what they must have seen as the Cambridge life. Englit was seen as an easy and mildly interesting degree; European studies seemed suitably vague and undemanding. The course covered some philosophy – a fact which most students regretted – but it also dipped into sociology, psychology and, best of all, was heavily literature-based. You could get through Dante without being blown away by the poetry, or the thinking, and you could still come out with a decent 2:1. Someone from his tutorial group in the first-year Italian option had expressed the view, more or less in those very words, a few weeks into the second term.

Penny said he had a chip on his shoulder. The truth was, like her, most of his fellow students were perfectly pleasant middle-class people with a mild interest in the arts. Many were 'mature students' who had come to college from jobs in the city, or cheery suburbs in Kent, or Surrey. They were far too well-mannered for Schopenhauer or D. H. Lawrence, but – as far as Paul could tell – they didn't see that. Everything was the same for them – Jane Austen, Nietzsche, Lawrence, Dante – it was all literature, to be studied and thought about and solved, like a crossword puzzle or a problem in trigonometry. They had every right to read and think and live exactly as they pleased – Paul knew this. At the same time, he wondered that they never saw the irony of their situation. With scarcely a second thought, he put his own unpopularity down to the fact that – in all he said and did, in his passion, in his gauche enthusiasm for ideas – he was a constant reminder, when no reminder was wanted, of that very irony.

The presence of The University only made things worse. He was painfully aware of having come to Cambridge from what most people considered the back of beyond, and he was already expecting to feel out of place when he got there – out of his depth, lacking in sophistication, awkward and inferior. At the same time he was excited about what he might learn from the well-educated and worldly people he would encounter. While he'd nurtured the chip on his shoulder, he had also dreamed of the democracy of learning, the shared passion of intelligence. So it came as a surprise that, while he did feel like an outsider, like a peasant almost, with his obvious passions and his sense of urgency, he nevertheless found that the sharp minds he had expected were far duller than he had expected. The only difference between most of the people he met and the people he had left behind was social: these people were roundly educated, they possessed a certain uncanny poise, they had somehow inherited a comfortable self-confidence that was easy to recognise, allowing them to see one another as kindred types, like Masons, or rugby players, but they were not the gifted souls he had hoped – and perhaps feared – to find. There were beautiful, remote girls with perfect voices, and robust boys with the easy confidence he had expected, but there was no wit, no obvious ability; most of all, there was no passion for art or thought, or for anything else that Paul could see. From a desire to be impressed and a fear of being intimidated, he had passed quickly to a vague, ingrained remoteness, the charmed detachment a visitor to a foreign country might feel when he doesn't know the language but isn't particularly interested in what is being said. From the first day, he was an outsider: these people who slipped into an easy familiarity with one another, immediately saw him as one who need not, even should not, be recognised. He was never quite sure why it should matter so much, or whether it was his own manner that contributed as much to this exclusion as their lightly held snobbery; perhaps it was his surprise and disappointment in them that had been obvious from the beginning – a disappointment that was sincerely held, but was also tinged with what he felt was a justifiable resentment. If these people were so ordinary, so merely adequate, why did they enjoy such privileges and, worse, why did they not see themselves as privileged? It took him the first year and a half to understand that, for them, there was nothing special about the life they lived, that it was all just business as usual. Whereas, even as an outsider, he had always enjoyed the city – the buildings, the concerts, the libraries, the Fitzwilliam and Kettle's Yard – like a tourist, or a boy up from the country. By the end of his second year he had realised that the people he was meeting really did belong to a different world, but it wasn't a particularly interesting one. It was simply a world of expectations and assumptions, a world much simpler and more navigable than his own, where success in some form was to be taken for granted. These were people

75

who knew they belonged – that was obvious; but, for the life of him, he had no idea what it was they belonged to.

One consequence of his growing alienation was that, when he met new people, he would lie about himself. It embarrassed him sometimes, afterwards, but it worked as a strategy: the stupid, pointless questions people felt obliged to ask were easily and more divertingly deflected with a lie than with the truth. Sometimes he delighted in an exceptionally tall story, something so incredible that he was surprised when what he said was taken at face value. More often than not, though, whenever he was talking to someone new, he found himself falling into simple, not particularly interesting untruths – stories that he told, not for profit, or to impress, but to keep something of himself back, to avoid squandering himself in small talk and chit-chat. He would lie about what he did, about where he was from, about what interested him, in an almost mechanical way. He would meet someone at a party, or in the pub, and he would tell them he was a dustman, or a night watchman; when people wanted to know where he was from, he would make up perfectly banal stories, pure lies that he knew, even as he told them, were transparently false and easily disprovable. It didn't matter to him that people knew he was lying. All that mattered was to seal himself off. He seemed incapable of simply keeping quiet, or of deflecting the questions people asked. He was awkward and unhappy in company, and often drank too much. The strange thing was, the lies he told were never very interesting or exotic. He was always something unglamorous; his family were always ordinary people; his personal history was never romantic, or adventurous, or tragic.

Then, just as suddenly, he stopped with all that. He lost interest in other people altogether and began to feel almost invisible in public places. He began to enjoy his own company. At around the same time, he took up meditation. There was a group of men who met, in a dim, narrow upper room above a shop in the Kite, to sit for two hours every Wednesday evening, and when he found out about it, he was intrigued and wanted to know more. Perhaps it was this – the meditation, the little rituals the men had, with sticks and bells and incense burners – that made him see how invisible he could be; though he only attended a dozen sessions, he felt that this meditation class had revealed something to him about being with people, about the difference between being with others and being amongst them. It was something he had read about in philosophy books: you could exist among other people and go untouched, unseen, like an alien, like a stranger, or you could be with others, in tune, aware, alive to the presence of the other in a way that Paul could only imagine in relation to things – to rocks, to the weather, to the air and the sky and the light. Between these two poles – between estrangement, on the one hand, and communion on the other – lay the common ground of availability, that lowest common denominator of the social. To begin with, he had imagined that these men who attended the meditation class were searching for a way out of that, for a possible detachment, or a final sense of community that would reconnect them with one another and with the world around them. After a while, though, he could see that they were just as available, just as indiscriminate in their way of being, as everyone else – that they went to meditation classes in much the same way as other people went to basket-weaving or judo.

These men mystified him. Why did they feel the need to be there, in that dim little room, every Wednesday night, rain or shine? What was it they thought they were doing? They didn't need to sit; they needed to *do* something – to practise some kind of very simple, basic 'right action'. Sitting there, in that scented room, he could taste his own thoughts, and he could smell theirs, an old, stale, fungal presence in the room, only half-masked by the incense and floor wax. This was Zen with a capital Z – the kind of Zen they wanted, an extension of the other good philosophies they had read about, only somehow more exclusive, ascetic, bare. They weren't there to take risks; they wanted nothing but reassurance. One night, listening to the rain, and to the measured breathing of the man next to him, Paul suddenly felt the absurdity of it all. He had to do something, to learn some new way of doing what he was doing. If right action meant anything, it meant ordinary action, just as meditation was ordinary action, an ordinary breath, one that showed that it didn't matter where you ended and the world began. It wasn't being, it was doing. It wasn't identity, it was self-forgetting. It wasn't surrender to some larger reality, or ecstasy, or union; most of all, it wasn't that little smile they all had, when they looked at you, or when they sat around later, talking and drinking their exotic teas. That saintly little smile, that gesture of selflessness. Every time he went there, he felt that what was going on in his head should have been happening in his body – or not even in his body, but invisibly, undetected, under the body, under the senses, an innate rightness, like the sense of balance, or the ability to ride a bicycle.

Paul looked out across the room. The other men – odd, he thought, suddenly, how they were all men – the other men were absorbed by the practice, by sitting in the correct position, breathing, being. A bus passed outside; Paul watched it come and go, the deep rumble suddenly rich and real compared to the aftersound of bells and the smell of incense, a deep rumble and a blur of colour on the windows. He could hear the rain; he could almost smell it. He stood up, walked quietly out of the room and down the dim staircase and out into the street. Minutes later, he was buying a ticket at the Arts cinema and making his way to his seat. The film that night – he had always remembered this – was *Andrei Rublev*.

From halfway through the first year, when he had first discovered it, the Arts had been his true salvation and principal escape. He would usually go in the afternoons, when there was less chance of a crowd. It was best on sunny days, when people had other things to do; he would buy his ticket early, then wait till the last minute, so he could pick a seat as far from the other people as possible. He liked it best when there was almost no one, maybe five or six, all sitting towards the back, leaving the wider, close-to-screen front section to him. It didn't matter what the programme was, but more often than not he would go to foreign-language films. It was strangely pleasurable to slip into that other world, to listen and watch those other people, whose clothes and gestures and language were so perfect and, at the same time, so remote from what he knew. With very little effort, he had trained himself not to read the subtitles, to concentrate on the images, on the atmosphere, on the voices of the actors. When he didn't know what was being said, when the language was utterly foreign to him – Japanese, or Russian, say – he would become acutely aware of the movement of language, and of how important silence was, how there were different qualities of pause and shift and delay, as rich in meaning as the words themselves. It always beguiled him utterly that, no matter what the scene, whether it was an interior at night, or a pair of lovers walking in a sunlit meadow, whatever transpired was always happening in the dark, as perfectly lit as if it were a dream, and just as concise, just as logical. Later, when the film was over, he would sit for as long as he could, watching the credits, listening to the score fade away. Finally, and with some reluctance, like a celebrant concluding a rite, he would get up and pass through one of the doors that the usher had opened on to the lit space of Market Passage, a last piece of theatre, a reversal of sorts when, for a moment, the world outside was a zone of artifice, and only the remembered film was entirely real. There were films he could hardly bear to leave behind, films like *Alphaville*, or *Le Grand Meaulnes*, or *Hour of the Wolf*, in much the same way as it hurt, sometimes, to wake, and leave behind the dream he'd been having, feeling it melt away in his mind, even while he still remembered it in vivid detail. Because it didn't matter how well you remembered, what mattered was to be present. It was as if he were leaving a life that would continue without him, a life that was running all the time, whether he was there to witness it or not. That world was the real world, the space to which he should have belonged. Waking up, stepping out of the cinema, coming in from a night-time or early morning walk along the Backs or through the side-streets, he felt he was being returned to a form of exile, to a place, a body, a person he had not chosen, and would have discarded if he could. Yet, oddly enough, there was pleasure, even, in that moment of transition, in that last moment of being alone with himself. In the cinema, or walking around with his camera in the dark, he forgot himself. Everything that mattered, everything that was authentic and honest and true, he knew, depended on that self-forgetting. It wasn't enough, just to be alone. You had to lose yourself. He would step out through the open doors into the street and it was a new beginning, a new start to a possible life, light and movement and people turning or stopping suddenly, the shadows in doorways like the memory of all the dreams and reveries of a long childhood, the childhood telescoped in his mind to almost nothing, all the sweet lost moments, the smell of the market and the sound of bells, people brushing by and the sunlight on his skin remembered, with the same vivid quality, from a childhood he never knew he'd had, or from somewhere he had dreamed, in all the forgotten dreams he had lost in waking to this world, leaving behind another, richer realm that continued at its own pace, with its own logic, whether he was there or not.

It was at the Arts that he had met Richard. It had been a particularly ill-attended afternoon show and, when the lights came up, they were the only two people in the cinema. As it turned out, absorbed in the film, Paul hadn't noticed that, when he'd arrived a couple of minutes late, two hours earlier, he had taken up a seat only a few places away from the only other customer. Now, as the doors swung open on to the bright street, they looked at one another and laughed.

'Not one of his more popular films,' Richard had said with a wry smile. He was about thirty, Paul thought, with unruly, sand-coloured hair, and jagged, angular features. He was also the tallest man Paul had ever seen, maybe six five or six, maybe taller.

'I suppose not,' Paul said.

'I quite liked it, though,' the stranger continued.

'So did I.' Paul was absurdly pleased that they agreed on this.

'Quietly assured.'

The ushers were waiting patiently to clear the theatre before the next showing.

'I suppose we'd better get out of here,' Richard said. 'Do you want to continue this conversation at Belinda's?'

Under other circumstances Paul would have avoided any kind of social situation after a movie. He felt cleansed, solitary, absolved of the personal for hours after a visit to the Arts, and he preferred to be alone. But there was something easy about this man, a spacious quality, a lack of urgency that allowed him to accept the invitation.

Now, more than a year later, Paul was heading over to Richard's to pick up a book the older man had recommended. It was a book about photography, by an American writer he had never read before. On the way, though, he thought he would try to find Penny, to see what she wanted to do later. Maybe they would go out. He felt guilty about Nancy; at some level, he wanted to erase the memory of the night, to relocate himself in the comfortable, easy world that Penny inhabited.

Paul found Penny in The Copper Kettle with her friend, Marjorie. From the first, he had disliked Marjorie in the quiet, somewhat resigned way that seems logical with people who dislike one openly, but Penny believed the reason for his awkwardness was that her friend was not only a strong, independent-minded woman, but, as a radical feminist, she wasn't afraid to speak her mind, and men, as Marjorie would frequently point out, *cannot stand* a woman who says what she thinks. For his part, however, what Paul disliked most about Marjorie was not so much her attitude to him as the way she treated Penny. He couldn't understand why Penny put up with the constant barrage of dogma to which her supposed friend subjected her. Today, the subject – not for the first time – was the rapist's latest attack.

The first two rapes had scarcely been reported; Paul couldn't remember the first, and the second had been a minor item, tucked away on the inner pages. As soon as a pattern had begun to emerge, however – as soon as it began to seem that the attacks were the work of a single individual – the papers began paying more attention. Now, months after the first rape, every sighting was front-page news. The rapes had gradually become more violent, with the knife as a new feature; at the same time, the police had no idea who the man was, and were beginning to clutch at straws in their attempts to solve the problem. At one point, a senior policeman who, from his picture, looked like an escapee from an old war movie, was advising women to invite their boyfriends to stay overnight in their bedsits or flats. He had told an *Evening News* reporter – without a hint of irony – that one of the best deterrents to rape was having a man about the house, adding that the vast majority of young people living away from home in bedsitters or flats were fully responsible in the way they conducted their lives – whatever that was supposed to mean. Stuff like this played right into the hands of people like Marjorie, who had turned up at Belinda's one February afternoon clutching a copy of *New Society*, and proceeded to read out the editorial, interrupting herself from time to time with tiny grunts and imprecations, while Penny looked on in admiration.

> Cambridge women are notoriously independent. They have walked and cycled alone at all hours of the day and night. But since the 'Cambridge rapist' appeared five months ago, they have changed. Chivalrous male chauvinists in town are having a field day. Women have turned to them for protection. There is now an updated version of the old proposition: 'Perhaps I ought to spend the night to protect you now that this man is at large.'

Marjorie snorted and gave Penny an amused, righteous glance. 'Protection,' she said. 'That's a good one.'

There are 8,000 young women in Cambridge in jobs, at the university or at other kinds of college. Some have bought watchdogs. Some have doubled up with their neighbours for the night, often with five or six to a bedroom. Bedside arsenals are common. One girl's includes a wrench, two pots of pepper, a cowbell

– hoots of derision from the women –

a torch and a whistle.

'How do they know all this?' Penny wondered.
Marjorie broke off, then found another choice titbit. 'Listen to this,' she said.

The man the police are looking for has assaulted six young women. It's some weeks now since the last attack. But last week lipsticked messages saying SLEEP TIGHT – THE RAPIST appeared on the windows of two hostels. So apprehension hasn't diminished much. Talk of the rapes is everywhere. Taxi-cab drivers reported the latest developments to students returning from the Christmas holidays. 'He's had six of them,' one cab driver told his girl passenger. 'He's not a bad-looking chap in the police photos. You'd think he'd be able to get himself a girl in the usual way.'

'My God,' Penny said.
Marjorie smiled grimly. 'Medieval, isn't it?' she said. By

now, they had completely forgotten Paul. 'It goes on,' Marjorie added. 'Listen.'

Only two of the women have seen the man, and their accounts differ. Many women at Cambridge say it is the abstract idea of a stranger in a crowd, making sadistic plans, that frightens them most. Being maliciously stalked is a common fantasy of dread. The fantasy has now come true.

'It's amazing. *The fantasy has now come true.*' She gave Paul a quick, searching look, then turned back to Penny. 'Don't they know it's *always* been true? That it's *not* a fantasy?'

Paul was experiencing his usual mixed feelings in Marjorie's company. Penny had introduced him to her some time back, and the woman had immediately put his back up. She quickly made it clear that she had no time for him, or what she imagined his views would be, on anything from politics to literature, though it soon became apparent he was supposed to derive some consolation for this from the fact that her disdain was in no way personal. It was something she felt for all men. She didn't dislike Paul as such, or so she thought. She simply judged him and found him wanting. Paul was amazed that Penny found her even remotely bearable, never mind interesting. It wasn't that he disagreed with what she said, far from it. Yet, though she made no explicit criticisms of Paul himself, there was no doubt that she was including him in all her judgements of men, that she considered him to be just as dangerous as the rapist – by association, if for no other reason. What hadn't occurred to her was that she, as much as anyone else, had succumbed to the dark allure of the rapist story, that her interest might be just as prurient, in its own way, as that

85

taxi driver's, or the sensation seekers who read every detail of the crimes in the *Evening News* with morbid interest.

That editorial had been three months ago, but the police were no nearer solving the crime and, if anything, the fascination with the rapist had increased. Talk of his crimes was everywhere. By now, almost everyone had his own sighting. Half-drunk, or stoned, on the way home from the pub or a party, a man would see a solitary figure cycling by, and he would catch a glimpse – nothing more, only the faintest suggestion – of the mask, the eyes glaring and hideous through the smooth leather. It always happened too quickly; the moment would come and go, leaving the witness alone, halfway across Jesus Green, or standing out under a dark sky on Grantchester Meadows, on a drunken walk home from The Blue Ball. It was a secret moment, a glancing touch, the merest taste of something; by the time he reached home, that man would remember almost nothing of what he had seen, or at least, nothing factual, nothing that would be of any use to a policeman or a reporter. Paul had always suspected that such episodes were fanciful, the product of an overactive imagination, or too much Abbot Ale, until, only a week or so back, he'd had his own – an incident so ordinary that it seemed to him afterwards either not to have happened at all, or to have been so undramatic as to be beyond telling.

He had been out with the camera, taking the dark path that skirted the edge of Sheep's Green, the one that led to the river. It had been a dark, windy night and, because of the late hour, he had imagined himself alone. When he'd heard a noise behind him, it had not occurred to him to think of the rapist; he was more concerned with the gangs of boys who wandered the city, looking for a lone student to beat up. Certainly, he had been surprised when, looking round, he had seen a woman – or a figure he thought must be a woman – standing nearby with her back to him, at the far end of the bridge, under the shadow of the trees. It was odd: he was sure she hadn't been there before; she must have come from the darkness of the far side, but he thought it strange that she should be out there, alone, so late at night. He couldn't see her face; all he could make out was her back, and one gloved hand resting on the parapet of the bridge; her hair was short, or tucked into her coat; she wore black trousers and boots. She wasn't very tall and, in spite of the heavy coat, Paul could see that she was quite slim. He had been standing still, observing her, for a minute or more, before he realised that he ought to make an obvious noise, to let her know he was there. There was something about her stillness that disturbed him. He began to feel something was wrong and took a step forward, one hand vaguely outstretched, though whether to help her or ward her off he wasn't quite sure. Part of him wanted to touch her, to break the spell, to shake off the sudden fear, for her or for himself, he could not decide, that had taken possession of his mind.

That was the last thing he could remember, when he thought about it afterwards. He stepped towards her, and she turned, but he had no clear picture of her face, only of a hideous disfigurement, a mask of a face, with wet, glittering eyes and a jagged mouth that looked as if it had been stitched shut. It reminded him of a photograph he had seen once, by a photographer whose name escaped him. It must have been an old picture – he remembered it as sepia-coloured, with an unsettling, Twenties softcore look about it: it showed a woman, naked to the waist, sitting alone in the back seat of a car, with what appeared to be a leather mask covering her face, her arms spread, her head tilted like a bird's. It had struck

87

him as intensely erotic, yet he had no idea why. Though the woman was masked, he imagined she was very beautiful – or rather, that it was because she was beautiful that her face was covered in this way. It had unsettled him for days; he was ashamed, almost, to realise that he was so drawn to this mask of a face. Yet he had been. Just as he had been drawn, at first, to that mask of a face he had glimpsed on Sheep's Green. And attraction was exactly what it was, he realised later, when he thought it through. The spell had only been broken when the figure turned away, and left him there, fixed to the spot, while she – or he – had made good her escape. Only at the last moment, when the creature was safely gone, had it occurred to him that what he had seen was a man; whether it had been the rapist or someone else, he could not have said. Yet, momentarily, it had thrilled him to think that he had caught a glimpse of the rapist.

Now, partly as a provocation, but also because he was tired of hearing Marjorie's triumphant, slightly whining voice, Paul couldn't help interrupting the conversation to tell them about Clive's map, and his plans for a vigilante exercise. As he spoke, he was aware that Penny was growing more and more irritated – not with his housemate's plans so much as the fact that Paul was repeating them in serious company – but Marjorie only listened, with a fixed scowl on her face, till he was finished.

'So,' she said. 'Your friend's going to save us all from the rapist. How ironic!'

'Ironic?'

Marjorie snorted. She snorted a good deal. She had the face for it: a critical, sharp-eyed, predator's face, ready to pounce on any sign of weakness or absurdity.

'Of course,' she said, responding to Paul's question, but directing her answer at Penny. 'I mean – it's not as if there's only one rapist. It's like these escort groups they've set up, so some *man* can come and walk you home after a party, or whatever. As if that man were somehow more trustworthy than any other man, just because he's volunteered to be there. If you ask me, I'd be very suspicious of any man who signed up for that kind of thing.'

She glanced at Paul. 'The best policy, in my opinion,' she continued, addressing herself to Penny, but obviously aware of Paul watching her as she spoke, 'is to assume all men are rapists, and take it from there.'

Paul laughed softly. 'I see,' he said. 'I'm assuming present company is not excepted.'

'How would I know?' Marjorie fixed him with an earnest look. 'I don't know anything about you. But let's say this – I'd feel no more comfortable having *you* walk around at night with me than I would any other man.'

'I see,' said Paul. He turned to Penny. 'And what do you think?'

Penny shook her head but, before she could say anything, Marjorie moved in.

'All we want is a world where a woman can walk anywhere she chooses, at any time of the day or night, and feel safe. Where she can go to bed at night and know she won't be woken up in the small hours by a man in a mask. Where she can have a drink with friends and not have to worry about what she wears, or says, or does being interpreted as consent to sex. Till then, all men are rapists.'

Paul nodded. There was no arguing with what she said. It wasn't the sentiments she expressed that disturbed him, it was the way she took it upon herself to judge him, along with all the others, as culpable by his very nature. Yet her argument was logical enough. The whole thing, the whole sorry mess of

89

men and women and sex, was fundamentally flawed. So why bother with it? Why not live apart from one another, why not maintain a respectful and wary distance? When he considered his relationship with Penny, it occurred to him that such a separation would not be so difficult to bear. He stood up.

'Well, I'd love to stop and chat,' he said. 'But I have to be going. Goodbye.'

Penny looked up, a pained surprise in her eyes. 'Don't be silly,' she said, quietly. 'Sit down and have some tea.'

Paul shook his head. 'I have to meet Richard,' he replied, a little shamefacedly. 'I'll see you later.'

Penny shrugged. Marjorie was watching them with undisguised amusement.

'He's got a book he wanted me to see,' he added, aware of how redundant the remark must have appeared, especially to Marjorie. 'Maybe see you later?'

'Maybe,' Penny said flatly.

'I'll ring you,' he said, aware of Marjorie watching him with a kind of amused, mock-concerned look on her face. 'Okay?'

Penny looked at his face but she didn't look him in the eye. She was also aware of Marjorie watching her, and her response was intended for her friend as much as for Paul. She made no attempt to seem even vaguely interested and, before she even spoke, Paul knew that he wouldn't be calling her after all.

'Okay,' she said. 'Bye.'

He backtracked along Trinity Street, then crossed King's Parade and headed out towards the Backs. Just before The Anchor, he turned into Laundress Lane and followed the riverside path through Coe Fen. He liked going to Newnham the back way, following the river up into the woods beyond Lammas Land, then tracing the narrow, overgrown path through the trees to the back of Owlstone Croft. It was dark on that last stretch of the track, heavy with the scent of cow parsley and muddy water; out here, between the dark river and the Croft, which had just been turned into a hostel for Tech students and nurses, he felt a shadowy, nervous kinship with the rapist, who had been seen in the vicinity more than once. Not that those sightings could necessarily be trusted: after all, as he made his way along the path that met Owlstone Road at the gate of the Croft, a lone male, moving slowly and carefully through the bushes, he could just as easily have been taken for the rapist himself. The thought sent a long shiver through his body, as he emerged from the shadows and into the light, though he couldn't have said why. It was simply the case that, no matter how uncomfortable it made him, he wanted to know how the rapist thought, how he moved, how he could act as he did. It wasn't ordinary curiosity that made him take this back way to Newnham, through the dark woods; it was something else, something more urgent.

Richard lived on Grantchester Road, in rooms rented from a family friend who spent most of her time in London. Usually, he had the house to himself; occasionally, the friend, an elderly woman who had once worked for the BBC, would turn up and stay a while, shutting herself away in an upstairs room where she listened to the radio and drank sweet sherry for days at a time. On the whole, it was a good arrangement: Newnham had to be the best place in Cambridge to live, with its village atmosphere and relative quiet; the house was spacious and deep, with a garden at the back and a bright, airy kitchen; out here, it was only a few minutes' walk to Grantchester Meadows, and the wide spaces of the fenland beyond. Not for the first time, Paul wished he could live this far up the river, away from the noise and the traffic, in one of these still, dim houses with their bay windows and worn, walnut-coloured interiors, their gardens backing on to the old cricket ground, with its ghostly pavilion, or the apple trees and pocket-handkerchief lawns to the rear of Chedworth Street. It was the most civilised place he had ever known; at the same time, without his knowing quite how to explain it, he had a sense, out here, of mystery, of private lives and long-held family secrets that no one would ever reveal.

The front door was never locked in the daytime. It was the last place in Cambridge, Richard said, where this old practice could still be observed without risk. Paul wasn't convinced that it was as safe as his friend believed and had suggested, with the rapist around, that it might be better to keep the door on the latch. Richard had laughed.

'I don't think the rapist is interested in me,' he said. In truth, Richard found the public fuss over the rapist more than a little absurd, not to mention dishonest.

'Isn't it odd,' he had said one day, over tea, 'the way this case is being treated? The way it obscures everything else? It's as if the rapist is all anybody can talk about. It doesn't matter that there are other rapes, or that men get beaten up and cut up with broken bottles and Stanley knives on the streets every other day. It doesn't matter that children are left to die in their own piss and vomit by neglectful parents. Nobody wants to look beyond the rapes.'

'Well,' Paul said. 'That's not really very surprising.'

Richard nodded. 'It's not surprising,' he said, 'but it's very convenient.'

'Convenient?'

'Sure,' Richard said. 'It stops us thinking about anything else that's happening. It keeps women in their place. It lets us think that we're okay, because — well, we might have our faults, but we're not like him, are we? We're not monsters.'

'Well,' Paul replied, '*we* aren't.'

'Do you know,' Richard continued, getting up to fetch more hot water, 'just a couple of days before the first of these particular attacks, two men were tried for the abduction and rape of a sixteen-year-old? The judge said it was the first instance in this country of something that has become known, in Australia, and other places, as "pack rape". They lured her into a car, then drove her out to the middle of nowhere and raped her.'

He paused to refill the kettle. 'These men were two ordinary guys,' he said. 'Cousins. Not monsters, just two lads having some fun. They're not so very extraordinary.'

'So what's your point?' Paul really didn't know what Richard was getting at. Just because people were fascinated by the rapist didn't mean they had forgotten the other crimes that were happening. It was just that the rapist had captured people's imagination.

Richard shook his head. 'So what happens when they catch this particular rapist?' he said. 'Will he be the monster everyone says he must be, or will he be just some guy, someone like you or me, or those lads who raped that young girl? Will we know any more about the causes of rape when they catch him, or will they just call him a madman and put him away somewhere? Will the social reasons for rape become any more apparent? I don't think so.'

'So what are you saying? All men are rapists?' Paul smiled. 'I know a couple of women who would agree with you on that one.'

Richard smiled grimly. 'That's the problem,' he said. 'Either everyone is innocent, and this man is a monster, or we're all guilty. Which belongs to an entirely muddle-headed kind of thinking. If this has nothing to do with sex, if it's about power, we shouldn't be looking at people from a sexual point of view. We should be trying to understand the desire for power.'

'But isn't that a male thing, too?'

'Absolutely not,' Richard said. He appeared almost shocked at this notion. 'The desire for power is symptomatic of weakness in both sexes. Only the weak want to have power over others.'

He smiled. 'This kind of thing gets me into trouble all the time,' he said. 'But I can't help it. For me, these men – those lads, the rapist, politicians, big businessmen – are simply advertising, by their actions, an extreme form of weakness. For me, the desire for power is, in the old-fashioned sense of the word, unmanly.'

This conversation had taken place a fortnight or so earlier, before the sixth attack, before the knife had actually been used. Paul had been surprised to find Richard so taken up with the case, or rather, with the public interest in the case; he had been a little taken aback, too, at how unhappy his friend had seemed. Usually, Richard was restless and full of new ideas, talking about some film he had seen, or some piece of music he had heard, or his research work. It was a surprise, not only to find him taking such a critical interest in the rapist case, but also to hear from him the same tired, clichéd views about rape and society that everyone else was habitually coming out with. It had been unsettling, after that last visit, to realise that his friend's views on the subject were not much different, or any more original, than Marjorie's.

Richard had what seemed to Paul a charmed life. He loved what he did, working on a taxonomy project with what he called 'minimum supervision'; he had a good place to live, at very low rent; he spent most of his time either alone in the house, or in the botany lab, or at the Arts or the Fitzwilliam, where his girlfriend, a shy, dark-haired, intensely beautiful A Level student named Gina, had a Saturday job. He had money enough to live the way he chose, and he was answerable to no one. He had travelled. Yet he always seemed uneasy, as if he was waiting for something else to happen, something unexpected. He was aware of the fact that other people, even some of his friends, were more than a little shocked by his relationship with Gina: at seventeen, she seemed far too young for him, yet he was completely indifferent to the disapproving glances and occasional whispers that greeted them both when they turned up at some Cambridge party. Though he pretended he didn't care what people thought, it was evident that he was worried, even a little frightened, about how they would respond to his behaviour.

Paul found his friend in the kitchen. The record player was on – it was the Fitzwilliam Quartet, playing the second Shostakovich String Quartet – and Richard was in the process of making tea.

'Perfect timing,' he said, as Paul came in. 'I've got lemon meringue pie. And those thingummies with the fruit in.'

As Richard had often remarked, the kitchen was the best feature of this old house, and he spent most of his time there. It had a long, wide, old-fashioned pine table where you could spread out with books and the papers and tea things or Sunday breakfast; you could open the windows to the garden and the room would fill with birdsong, or the smell of apple blossom and cut grass. Because it was a good day – still damp from the night's rain but warm and bright outside now – Richard had all the windows, as well as the back door, wide open, and he seemed happier than usual. The music was, to Paul's mind, not quite what he would have chosen, but when Richard got

95

into something he always made it into an obsession. Recent passions had included Rothko, Tarkovsky, Ibsen's later plays, some kind of flowering plant that Paul had never heard of and the Shostakovich Quartets. They sat quietly while the music finished.

By the time they had demolished half the pie, and two each of the fruit thingummies, the talk had drifted to girlfriends. Paul wanted to know whether Richard had any plans with regard to Gina.

'Of course not,' Richard answered. 'She's too young to get into something permanent.'

'Is that how she feels about it?'

'Not at the moment,' Richard replied. 'But she will.'

'Doesn't that bother you?'

'A little.' Richard gave a soft smile, and shook his head. 'The thing is, I have to exclude it from any consideration of what I want, or do. I look at Gina and I see all the reasons why I want to be with her, but they are my reasons. I know how romantic my thinking is.'

He poured some more tea. 'Scott Fitzgerald said a sentimentalist is someone who is afraid things won't last forever, whereas a romantic is someone who is terrified that they will. I'm a romantic. I see through it all, but it's me, nevertheless.'

'What about Gina?' Paul asked. 'Does she see through it all?'

'She will.'

'You're sure of that?'

'Pretty sure.'

'Sounds a bit ruthless to me.'

Richard nodded. 'I know what you're trying to say,' he said. 'But there's a bigger picture to consider than how either of us feels right here, right now. Being with Gina is more real for me than anything else, but I have to accept that it won't last. Which I do. I'd rather take this for as long as it works, knowing it will end, than have something permanent that has to be held together by an effort of will and possibly self-deceit.'

'Isn't that a little defeatist?'

'No.'

'Has it never occurred to you that Gina might want something else? Something more permanent?'

Richard laughed. 'You'll be suggesting I marry her next,' he said.

'Well,' Paul was surprised at how serious he felt about it. 'Why not?'

Richard shook his head. 'You know how I feel about that,' he said. 'As far as I'm concerned, marriage is a totally artificial, totally manipulated institution. For me, there is no more convincing argument for friendship between men and women than the average marriage. I know – I've watched my parents wriggle in that trap for longer than I care to remember.'

'Marriage is hell, eh?' Paul felt annoyed. He was thinking about Penny, about her basic assumption that what you did was meet someone, decide if you loved them enough, then you got a job and settled down, end of story. She hadn't outlined it in so many words, but she had come close. Yet what was so wrong with that, after all? The world must be peopled. He had grown up with the mute shambles of his own parents' marriage, but it didn't mean that things had to be so awful.

'I think it's rare for marriage to be hell,' Richard said. 'Purgatory, sometimes. But, more often than not, it's a form of limbo – not in the least unbearable, though depressing enough

97

when you stop to think about it. Marriage is a social tool, like education. The social world demands persons, to do its business. We want to live as spirits. There is a conflict there, and marriage is one of the ways the social world tries to ease, or at least cover up that conflict. All the things you do, you're not doing because you want to, but because you have to, for the sake of your marriage, or the kids, or the job, or whatever. You can't be controlled by those you hate, only by those you love.'

'Too easy,' Paul said.

Richard shook his head again. 'I know this is just talk,' he said. 'The social world is us, you and me. I know that. I am not a total disbeliever. On the contrary. But my beliefs – my values – have become detached. I mean it – they've become discontinuous with the social world. For me this might be sad, it might even seem tragic. I don't want to live alone, any more than the next man. But, for sound reasons, I am obliged to do so. I can do something about this – I can speak, and I can surrender my attachments. I belong, no matter how isolated I am.'

He smiled apologetically, and looked at Paul. 'Besides,' he said, 'out of the two of us, I'm not the real solitary.'

'Meaning?'

'Well, look at me. And look at you. I need people. In small doses, maybe, but I can't live without them. If I was stranded on a desert island, I would try to escape – even though I know the social world isn't worth it, I'd be building a raft within the week. I would want to return. This is where the things that matter to me are happening.'

He grinned. At such times he looked boyish and untouchable. 'But you,' he said, waving his hand vaguely in Paul's direction. 'You would stay where you were. If you had your camera, you'd take pictures, but it wouldn't matter to you that nobody saw them.'

'You think so?' Paul didn't know whether he felt wounded or pleased by this idea.

'Sure, I do,' Richard said. 'You think it's a virtue, to be in search of something, some perfect picture, some image for its own sake. That's what you're interested in. It's not that you want to communicate. You could take the perfect picture, and that would be enough. You wouldn't care if nobody saw it.'

Paul smiled sadly and shook his head. 'I don't think that's true,' he said, convinced that it probably was.

Richard gazed at him. There was an odd tenderness, a sudden concern, in his eyes. 'Maybe not,' he said. 'You have to remember that I don't know what I'm talking about.' He lifted the lid of the teapot and peered inside. 'More tea is needed,' he said. 'And a couple more fruit thingummies. Wouldn't you say?'

Paul nodded. Richard had already stood up and was filling the kettle at the sink, with his back turned. He said something else – some passing remark, to lighten the afternoon, to bring them back to earth – but Paul didn't take it in. All of a sudden he felt alone and, for the first time in years, he was aware of being quite simply and painfully unhappy, though he had no idea why.

As soon as he arrived, Paul could see that Nancy was in a bad mood. This wasn't new – sometimes things would happen at work that upset her, and she would be bothered about it for days afterwards; on this occasion, however, it seemed her anger was directed at Paul, though he had no idea what he might have done to deserve it, especially as he hadn't seen her for almost a week.

Nancy was in the living room of her two-room bedsit. She had been drinking for some time – an empty bottle of vodka lay on the floor, under the stereo, and, though she had reverted to Cinzano, it was obvious from the way she was behaving that she'd had a good part of it during the afternoon. As she made her way back to her chair, after slipping the latch and unceremoniously letting Paul in, she had staggered slightly, and when she spoke, she slurred her words.

'Come in,' she said. 'Make yourself at home.' There was an edge to her voice, an aggressive tone that was even harder than usual.

Paul wondered, not for the first time, what the hell he was doing here, and he had to resist the impulse to turn around and leave. 'You're drunk,' he said, simply.

'So what?' Nancy wobbled forward in her chair and poured herself another drink. 'Isn't that how you like me?'

'Not really,' Paul answered. There was only one glass on the table; it was obvious she had no intention of offering him anything. Instead, she filled her tumbler to brimming.

'Cheers,' she said, raising the glass to her lips and spilling the Cinzano over her hands, so that it dripped on to the table. 'Your health.'

Paul looked around. The room was a mess. Tapes and records lay scattered across the floor near the stereo; there were wet marks and stains on the carpet; in the little kitchenette that adjoined the living room, every surface was covered with empty glasses, foil takeaway trays and spills of what looked like Chinese food.

'Looks like you've been having a party,' Paul said, half to himself.

'So what if I have?' Nancy's voice was almost a snarl. 'What's it to you, anyway?'

100

'Nothing,' he murmured. 'Nothing at all.'

He waited. She sat low in her chair, looking up at him, angry and resentful, like a dog waiting to attack. Paul turned back towards the door. 'All right,' he said, 'I'm going. You're obviously not in any mood—'

'Oh no you don't,' she said. 'You're not just walking away . . . just like that . . .'

Paul turned, waited. She stared at him with a look of pure hatred in her face. 'What are you doing here, anyway?' She snatched at him wildly, clutching at his shirt as he jerked away, tearing the sleeve. 'What is it you want?'

Paul shook his head. 'I don't want anything,' he said, quietly.

Nancy laughed. 'Like fuck you don't,' she shouted. 'God! I'm sick of you coming round here, like you had some kind of . . .' She collapsed back into her chair, and grabbed her glass.

'Can you tell me,' Paul asked, 'what it is I'm supposed to have done?'

Nancy ignored the question. 'You know what you're like?' she said, quietly now, her voice almost sad. 'You're like a boy coming round to play, bouncing your ball all along the street. You don't see anybody else, you're so full of yourself and your own stupid little thoughts . . .'

She shook her head. Paul couldn't have said whether the look of contempt on her face was for him, or for herself.

'I think I'd better go,' he said, softly, edging towards the door.

It was the wrong thing to say. Before he could take another step, Nancy had leapt to her feet again, glass in hand, and showered him with Cinzano. At the same time, she launched herself at him.

'You fucking bastard,' she screamed. 'You're not getting

away that easily.' With one hand, she had a tight hold of his shirt, while the other clawed at his face. For the first time, Paul felt obliged to do something to defend himself against Nancy when she was having one of her outbursts. He grabbed the flailing hand and, at the same time, wrenched himself free. Then, with a quick, sharp twist, he turned her about, and pushed her away, so she tumbled to the floor, knocking the bottle off the low table. The chill liquid spilled over his feet, running into his tennis shoes. He turned quickly and walked to the door, but he did not leave right away. He still wanted to see if Nancy was all right. He didn't want to leave her, if she had been hurt in the fall. She lay still for a moment, then she struggled up into a sitting position. She didn't seem to be hurt.

'Are you okay?' Paul ventured.

She didn't answer. She looked around vaguely for her glass, saw the fallen Cinzano bottle, then, quietly at first, she began to laugh. Paul relaxed. She couldn't be hurt if she was laughing, he thought. Maybe she was coming out of it. Gradually, however, the laugh grew louder, becoming harder and colder and more bitter by degrees, till it became a thing in itself, not a sound that she was making, not an expression of amusement, or anger, or disgust, but something involuntary, a form of possession, a vital force that she could not have controlled if she wanted to. At the same time, Paul was aware of her giving in, not willing so much as surrendering to it, letting herself fall, losing herself in this alien sound.

'Okay,' he said, making the effort to stay calm, to be reasonable. 'Stop it now.'

But she hadn't stopped. She couldn't. He had waited a long time — several minutes — and she had just sat there, laughing, lost in herself, beyond caring and beyond help. Deciding there was nothing he could do, Paul had finally made it to the door,

102

and stepped out into the hallway. Another nurse – a woman he had met months ago, at the same party where he had first found Nancy – passed him on the stairs and, noticing his troubled look, asked if he was okay.

'I'm fine,' he said. 'I'm all right.'

Then he was outside, in the grey of evening, walking home in the slow summer rain.

The next morning, he woke with a start. There had been a noise; someone was at the door and, for a moment, still half-sleeping, he wondered if it was Nancy, come to tell him she was sorry about what had happened. He looked at the tiny travelling clock on the table by the window, the one his father had given him as a going-to-college present. It was 11.45. Somewhere outside – in the graveyard over the garden wall, or in the apple tree at the edge of the garden – a bird was singing, a thin, clear song that sounded as if it had been carefully sifted through ozone and rain. Then the noise came again, louder this time, a hard, determined banging at the front door. He swung out of bed and pulled on his jeans and the shirt he'd been wearing the night before, all the time hoping that Clive or Steve would answer. Even after the walk home in the rain, the shirt still smelled of Cinzano.

The house was empty and still. In the hallway, at the foot of the stairs, Clive's bag, unzipped and crammed full of muddy sports kit, lay discarded, emitting a faint rain-and-grass-and-sweat odour. There was no sign of the big man, though, and the front room, where Steve occasionally hid out during the day, watching kids' TV, was quiet. Before Paul could even reach the bottom of the stairs, the banging at the front door was resumed. Barefoot, with the shirt on at a squint, he threw open the door and was struck by the sudden light. Upstairs, at the back of the house, the air had seemed grey and heavy, still saturated with rain, but here, on the street side, the sky was bright, a high white glare. Before him, dressed as if for church, or an interview, in a blue suit and red-striped tie and very shiny black shoes, stood a tall, thick-set man, his face set in an angry scowl; slightly to one side, as if she didn't want to be there, and would have slunk away if she could, a young girl, about eleven or twelve years old, whose name he thought might be Angela, hovered uncertainly, obviously afraid of the man, but also bound to him by some common interest or concern. Before Paul could speak, the man turned to the girl.

'Is this him?'

The girl shook her head.

'Are you sure?'

The girl stared at Paul, as if she was wondering whether she should change her mind, then shook her head more forcefully. Paul turned to the man.

'What is it?' he asked. 'What's wrong?' He noticed that the man, in spite of his newly pressed suit and tie, was still unshaven.

The man ignored him. 'You better not be mucking me about,' he said to the girl. 'If this is him—'

'It's not him,' the girl said, with a slight whine.

The man turned to Paul. 'Where's Steve?' he demanded.

'Steve?'

'Yeah.' The man's face hardened; he was frustrated that he hadn't found who he was looking for, and he was ready to move on to the next phase in a process that was probably familiar to him – the phase where he lashed out at whoever was handy.

'He's not here at the moment,' Paul said. 'I don't know where he is. But I'll tell him—'

The man stepped forward, just enough so his face was inches from Paul's. 'You'll tell him nothing,' he said.

The girl was scared now. 'Da-ad,' she whined. 'It's not him. Leave him alone. He's all right.'

The man swung around and confronted his daughter. 'Do you know him, too?'

The girl was silent, while her father hovered, his face almost as threatening, almost as close to hers, as it had been to Paul's a moment before.

'Well?'

The girl shook her head. 'I want to go home,' she said.

As father and daughter conferred, Paul's eye was caught by a movement off to his right and he turned. The man – who had not forgotten him for a moment, in spite of his sudden switch of attention to the girl – turned around and caught sight of the woman whom Paul had just noticed, edging along the street cautiously, her eyes fixed on the man and Angela. The man reared up and stepped back.

'Get back in the house,' he shouted. 'I told you to stay put.'

The woman faltered, but her eyes never left her husband. 'Come on, Mike,' she said. 'Come home. People are watching.'

Sure enough, faces had appeared at the doors and windows along the street. At the corner, just a few yards behind the mother, another, older woman, in a blue raincoat, stood watching. It was enough for the man. Where reason had made no impact, the possibility of gossip overcame his still simmering anger. He turned away. At the same time, the little girl gave Paul a shy, quizzical look.

'Bye,' she said, quietly. Paul wasn't sure whether this was meant as some kind of muted apology, or a provocation, or an involuntary and quite innocent figment of habitual politesse.

105

He stepped back and pushed the door to quietly, making sure it clicked shut. For the first time since he had come downstairs, he remembered himself: barefoot, in a stale shirt, his hair a mess, his mouth dry and sticky. Though he didn't know what the man had wanted – other than that it had something to do with Steve – he felt strangely accused, as if he really had been guilty of some offence against that pretty child; or if not of that, then of some other, unspecified crime, which he had coolly and knowingly committed, then forgotten.

CAMBRIDGE, 1975

Animals loved him. It wasn't a pet thing, like some people had, which was basically a mercenary arrangement on both sides. It was something closer and, at the same time, more respectful: a recognition; more of a secret kinship than an understanding. The animals that lived with him – he didn't think of them as objects he owned, they were just there, the same as he was – those animals weren't neat and tidy and clipped into shape like the poodles, or the little beige lapdogs in waistcoats that he'd seen on the Cambridge streets. He didn't shampoo them, either, or put flea collars around their necks. Instead, he kept them close to nature, so he could watch and listen and learn all about them. He wanted to see what they were like, when they felt they were alone, when they didn't know they were being observed. Most of all, he wanted to be *like* them, to be just as watchful and alive and perpetually on the alert as they were.

Sometimes it surprised him, what he'd learned. He remembered the time the police had picked him up for some burglary or whatever. They had locked him in the cells and he had started to leap around, to bang up against the walls and scream and gibber and throw himself against the door, the way a monkey would do, when you locked it in a cage. Then, after a bit of that, he'd sat down in a corner and wrapped his hands around his face and head, like a baby chimp does when it's unhappy or scared. The coppers were really taken aback by this; for a while, he had even thought they would let him go and he'd run back and forth, screeching and swinging his arms about and jumping up and down on the spot, then crawling off into a corner and hiding his face for a while, till he was sure it was no go, that he was just wasting his energy. Other times, he'd watched the cats when they were out hunting, the way they moved so slowly, so carefully, eyes fixed on their prey, never looking away from what they were after. He was impressed by what appeared to be their infinite patience – and he observed how effortlessly they blended into the background, how every ounce of their energy was tuned to being hidden, to being camouflaged.

That was how he'd come up with the idea of being a woman. If the police were after a rapist, it stood to reason they would be looking for a man. So what better disguise when he went hunting than a woman's hair, a woman's clothes, a woman's carefully made-up face? If he was moving along at a fair enough speed on the bike, or walking in the dark, away from the obvious sources of light, nobody would be able to tell the difference: he was lithe, slim and, even though he said it himself, he moved as easily and gracefully as any woman. More so, even. For, to any observer with the sense to know what he was looking for, he moved like an animal, like a cat or a weasel out hunting. And, as any fool knew, it was the female of any species that made the best hunter. So, really, there was a kind of justice in it, too.

To begin with, he had been nervous, going out in women's clothes and a wig, his body scented, his face discreetly made up. He didn't know if he could necessarily pull it off. After a while, though, he had started to enjoy himself. It felt good, being a woman, with his particular secret tucked away at the back of her mind. It felt good the way a big cat must feel good, with its razor-sharp claws sheathed in the soft velvet of skin and fur. But it felt even better when he undressed, in the back garden, or in a passageway between the houses, and slipped on the mask. He'd made it himself, from an old shopping bag, and he was pleased with how it had come out. It was a leather bag he had used, an animal's skin, flayed off its body and cut into strips so it would look like something ordinary, something innocent, but he had changed it in various ways. He'd cut it up again so it looked like a face; he'd made a hole for the mouth, then he'd sewn in a big, saw-toothed zip, with jagged little silver teeth, for biting. He'd made narrow slits for the eyes, then he'd highlighted them in white, so he would look like a wolf, or a big cat, when he came out of the dark and the girl saw him for the first time. There was nothing more important, he thought, than that first impression you made, when you came into a room.

Afterwards, he would take off the mask and fold it carefully. He would put the dress and the wig back on and cycle home, and nobody would know. He'd be cycling through the town, under the lights, with the knife and the mask in his bag, and nobody would know who he was. He would disappear into the dark at the end of Adams Road, or out past the vet school, and when he went to work next day, it would be in all the papers, how some *animal* had struck in the night and claimed another victim. That was what they called him, every time: an animal; not just the papers, but the girls, too, they always seemed to come up with *animal*, thinking it was the worst thing they could say, the worst insult they could throw at him. At work, the others would talk about it, and he'd stop to listen. Then, when they turned to him, he would nod and say, yes, isn't it terrible, what can you do, he's just *an animal*, that's all there is to it.

Whereas, in reality, he could be anything he chose. Anything at all. Whatever he liked, he could become. It was up to him. It was his choice.

ACTS OF CHARITY

It had been a while since Richard had come round with an invitation to a party. It was one of his many oddities: most of the time he liked to be alone, or sitting in the Arts among strangers, watching a movie in the dark – he said watching a film with people was just as companionable as any dinner party, maybe more so, in most cases – but every now and then he would announce that there was to be a party, somewhere in Chesterton, or up on Madingley Road, or just down the road from Paul's house, on Tenison Avenue, or Panton Street. At first, it had come as something of a surprise to discover that Richard liked this kind of thing, but it had soon become apparent that there were people who only knew Richard from the parties. As the months passed, Paul gradually came to see that his friend had gone to some lengths to separate his life out into different compartments. Sometimes he would introduce a friend or acquaintance from one world to the life of another sphere; usually, however, he kept people apart, just as he drew clear lines between the person he allowed himself to be at parties and the person he was at other times, in the clear light of day, or in the quiet of his rooms in Newnham. What mattered most to him – as Paul discovered when he asked why Richard never gave parties himself – was the division between one area of his life and another. It was as if he was two or three different people.

'I'm not a host,' his friend had said. 'I'm a guest. It's like going on holiday. Same as it is for you.'

He was right, of course. Paul enjoyed the parties, as far as they went, but he didn't miss them in the long gaps between Richard's sociable spells. He never sought them out himself, just as, these days, he hardly ever drank when he wasn't at Nancy's. He had his own, detached life, just as Richard had. Tonight, as they walked in at the door of the party to which Richard had been invited, he was struck by the fact that, though he had been to seven or eight parties by now, he didn't know a single person in the room. Yet Richard knew almost everyone. Some he greeted as old friends, others as acquaintances; when they got to the kitchen and stepped out through a set of narrow French doors into the garden, Richard found Gina waiting for him on the patio with a long drink in one hand and a cigarette in the other, as if the whole thing had been prearranged. Gina was the most beautiful girl Paul had ever seen: though she was only seventeen years old, she dressed and looked older. Tonight, she was wearing a dark-blue dress and black high-heeled shoes, to the obvious dismay, or disapproval, of some of the other women on the patio, who obviously believed that the clothes and the make-up and the way Gina behaved was cheap and demeaning to women. To his great amusement, they blamed Richard for bringing a young girl – a schoolgirl, in fact – to these parties. Paul had heard the whispered remarks, he had seen the looks; once, when he had brought Penny along, she had made no secret of her feelings about Gina.

'I think it's sad,' she had said, 'that a girl like that has to dress up in that way to please men.'

'Maybe she does it to please herself,' Paul had suggested, more than a little amused by Penny's moment of pique. She herself dressed, he had decided, to please the little phantom mother she carried with her everywhere, the one who helped her choose her knee-high boots and summer dresses.

'I doubt it,' Penny said. 'I'm sure it has much more to do with Richard.'

Paul hadn't argued; but the next time Richard had invited him to a party, he had gone alone. He liked to watch Richard and Gina together, to slip away to the edge of whatever was happening and listen for Gina's bright, musical laugh, or to listen to Richard talk, when he got into one of his many arguments. Not for the first time, this evening's disagreement concerned the rapist. A group of women from the Tech had brought it up – it was something of an unpleasant surprise to recognise Marjorie amongst them – and they were arguing with a young Irish student named Matthew, whom Richard apparently knew well. As the discussion flowed back and forth, Richard looked on, interested, while Gina proceeded to tune herself out, sipping at her drink and sharing a joint with a tall thin girl in a Chinese-style dress.

Eventually, Richard couldn't hold back any longer. One of the Tech women had been talking about the rapes, and about the way they had been reported in the paper, as indicative of men's attitudes to women and, in response to some provocation by the Irish boy, had repeated the now commonplace slogan: ALL MEN ARE RAPISTS. It was too much for Richard.

'You've said that already,' he said. 'It's just not very helpful. You're just repeating slogans.'

'It's not a slogan, it's a fact.' The woman, who had thick

113

black curls held back by a brightly coloured cotton scarf, permitted herself to be indignant.

'I'd be interested to know if you really think that,' Matthew interrupted. "Do you think that every man, every single one, is a rapist?'

'Potentially.'

Matthew was annoyed. 'So I'm a rapist,' he said. 'He's a rapist—'

The dark-haired woman shook her head. 'I don't know,' she said. 'I don't know any of you at all. So what do you think my safest assumption might be?'

Richard looked thoughtful. 'I think there's another question here,' he said. 'A question for men to consider.' He looked at Matthew. 'Maybe it's not so much that every man is a rapist, or even that he is a potential rapist – for someone else. But every man has to be aware of himself as a potential rapist. We're all of us angry, and we've all been trained to think of sex in terms of conquest. A man has to bear in mind how conditioned he is by that. And the denial of his pleasure – making a battle, making a conquest of it – is essential to this society. The rapist possibly even thinks of himself as a rebel against that denial, as taking what he wants on his own terms. But we could all fall into that trap. The answer is to step out of that equation and think in other terms. We need a new way of thinking about sex. We need a new way of thinking about ourselves as social persons.'

The dark-haired woman looked exasperated, 'So you agree, then?' she said.

Richard nodded. 'I agree that men need to think about it in different terms. The whole game has to change. But women have to think in different terms, too. You have to look and see

114

how you are the instruments of order, in the way you behave with men.'

'Oh, I see.' For the woman from the Tech, this was a return to familiar territory. 'So it's all the woman's fault?'

'It's nobody's fault,' Richard said, with too obvious patience. 'People are only doing what is expected of them. Everyone needs to stop just reacting and take stock. We all have to change.'

'Well, women are trying to change. I don't see much change from men.'

'Maybe you're not looking,' Matthew chipped in.

Richard smiled. 'Anyway, isn't there something artificial about all this?' he said, breaking in quietly.

'Artificial?'

'Yes. Exactly that,' Richard replied, in the same very quiet voice. 'Artificial.'

'I don't know what you mean,' the woman said. Making a point of not looking him in the face, she addressed her words to the general company.

'Well,' Richard said, 'we've been going around for months pretending there was something odd going on. But there was nothing odd about it. It was just an extreme case of what's going on all the time.'

'I see.' The dark-haired woman had given up on the conversation, leaving her friend, a small, thin, red-haired woman, who might have been a mature student, to step in 'So you think it's normal that a madman is breaking into women's houses and raping them?'

'But he's not a madman, is he? He's just another man. You've probably seen him. You could have passed him in the street, but you wouldn't know him if you did. He looks just like one of us.'

'That's exactly the point that Annie was making,' the mature student said. 'We just don't know. We can't trust any man.'

Richard nodded. 'It isn't that sensible,' he said, without obvious irony, 'to trust *anyone*.'

'But you have to admit that this man is abnormal,' Matthew said.

'That's the whole point,' the dark-haired woman interposed. 'He isn't abnormal. He's just a typical man.'

Richard smiled and shook his head. 'Typical?' he said. 'What's typical? You'll be talking about human nature next.' He caught Paul's eye and raised his voice slightly. There was something theatrical about Richard's manner when he got involved in these conversations – a touch of Socrates in the *agora* – that left Paul feeling just a little uncomfortable. 'Did you know Aqualung got beaten up yesterday?' he asked.

'No.' Paul was shocked but not surprised. 'What happened?'

'Grad-bashers, I suppose,' Richard said, his voice falling back into its usual register. 'Or skinheads. Whoever. It's not the first time it's happened. It won't be the last.'

'But Aqualung isn't a student,' Paul said. He had a fleeting image of Aqualung in his mind's eye – that lost, innocent face, that vague air of betrayal – and he felt a stab of absurd guilt, as though he himself had somehow failed to protect the guy.

'Does it matter? Thing is, it won't be in the papers.' Richard glanced at the dark-haired Tech student. 'Nobody's going to go around making a fuss about it. A girl got raped in Huntingdon just last week. That's not on the front page either. The Cambridge Rapist is the star, not his victims, or any other victim. You get on the front page if you're a victim of the star attraction. Otherwise, you're just a statistic.'

116

The Irish boy was watching them closely. He sensed there was something he had missed. 'Who's Aqualung?' he asked.

Richard looked grave. 'A person of no consequence,' he said.

The conversation had broken up after that. The woman from the Tech looked unhappy and offended: it was obvious she felt Richard had derailed her argument out of typical male spite and superiority, while Matthew grew pensive and drifted away from the group on the patio. On the surface, it had been an ordinary, rambling, half-stoned conversation about nothing, but, under it all, Paul had the uncomfortable sensation that Richard's remarks were meant for him. At the same time, he had no idea why.

Later, though, as the party had started to thin out, Paul found his friend and the Irish boy in deep conversation over a vodka bottle in the front room. They were sitting facing one another on the floor by the stereo; both were quite drunk and more than a little stoned, and the boy looked somewhat the worse for wear. As far as Paul knew, Gina was still out in the garden somewhere.

'Hey,' Richard called when Paul came in, 'come and join us.' He picked up the vodka bottle and waved it in Paul's direction. 'Have a drink.'

Paul sat down and let Richard refill the empty glass he had been clutching for the last hour. If there was one guarantee in life, it was that Richard would always be the one who still had something to drink at the end of a party.

'Meet Matthew,' Richard said. 'Matthew thinks feminist philosophy is going to change everything for the better. He even thinks men are going to benefit—'

'We are,' Matthew said, slurring a little. 'Everybody benefits from change. It's just that they can't see it, because

117

they're used to what they've got. Feminism is the next revolution—'

'No it isn't,' Richard said. 'It's just another -ism and, like any -ism, it's based on a sociological way of thinking which is fundamentally *wrong*. Because sociology is basically wrong. It's tainted with wishful thinking – on the one hand, with a naïve faith in human predictability and potential for improvement en masse, on the other with a vain idea that sociology is a scientific – that is, truly descriptive – discipline. But the idea of a science of human behaviour is absurd.'

'Why is it absurd?'

Richard shook his head. 'We don't think about ourselves descriptively, not in that way.' Richard was rambling a little, and he was aware of the fact; at the same time, he seemed to be quite sincere in what he was saying. 'Sociology isn't a science,' he continued. 'It pretends to be, but it isn't. Maybe it's not this straightforward, but a real science makes generalisations which work in a rule-of-thumb way for individual cases. But sociology makes generalisations which *never* apply to individuals. We have to understand that. We have to nip sociology in the bud.'

Matthew laughed. 'It's a bit late for that,' he said.

Richard shook his head gravely. Paul couldn't tell how serious he was now. 'It had better not be,' he said. 'Because sociology is dangerous.'

'Oh, really?' Matthew said, a little too loudly. 'Really? Okay – give me an example. Give me an example of how sociology is dangerous.' He raised himself a little, then slumped back to the floor. Richard gave him an amused, quizzical look, then carried on speaking, as the boy unscrewed the vodka bottle and refilled his glass.

'Well,' Richard said, 'how about this male/female thing.

Sociology builds up this abstract, generalised description of how men and women operate, and it's complete nonsense, because it only works in a social context, whereas – at that level – people are individuals, not social units. If you take people as individuals, you could make the generalisation that women and men have traditionally had different goals in life. That's probably fair. Traditionally, men have wanted to play, women have wanted to settle down. When a man sees a woman he likes, he wants her to stay pretty well as she is, for as long as the thing lasts. Whereas a woman has to see potential for change – shorthand version: she has to think the man is ready to settle down. For a time, while she is young enough, a woman seems to want other things, but this is a necessary development, to convince the man that, like him, she wants to play. It's not a deception, it's just an adaptation, a phase of development. It's like some plants – some junipers, for example. They have two kinds of foliage – juvenile and mature – which look quite different, and fulfil different purposes during the overall life and growth of the plant. Or various insects, passing through their different phases. It's a phase, when women seem loose and free and ready to take risks; at the time that is what they want. But as soon as they are ready, they begin to effect the changes, to make the demands, to pin you down. Whereas a man . . . Underneath it all, men stay as they always were. They want to go out, they want to go in pursuit. They want to scavenge and forage. That's what art comes from; that's where war originates.' He grinned. 'You think I'm talking rot, don't you?' he said to Paul.

'Absolutely,' Paul replied, feeling a little sullenly that some part of what Richard was saying – not the part about art and war, but some of the rest – carried more weight with him than he would have wished. He was also aware that Richard was, as

119

usual, talking obliquely about something else. About himself, perhaps.

'But I'm not, though,' Richard continued, almost wistfully. 'It's just that what I'm saying is not acceptable, just as it's unacceptable to say that young men are bound to go around attacking people like Aqualung, or that there will always be the odd Cambridge rapist turning up from time to time. People want to believe in progress, in what ought to be, what could be. They forget how things are.'

'Which is a good thing,' Matthew interjected drunkenly, looking vaguely annoyed.

'Sure,' Richard said. 'Any individual can rise above the basic pattern, but exceptions do not make the pattern, they only confirm it. It's not something we should say out loud, but we have to take into account all the basic stuff – which includes what I just said. Sure, there are women who want to break out of the changing and settling-down mode, but don't be deceived into thinking that this will help you in any way. The whole structure of a capital-based society depends on keeping enough of us invested in marriage and the nuclear family, and women are the glue that holds all that together. They won't be allowed to free themselves, any more than we've been allowed the so-called sexual liberation everyone keeps talking about. If you want to be free, you had better decide what that means for you, and do it by yourself. Nobody is going to help you. All these groups running around shouting may change appearances, but the basic structures will shift and develop to accommodate them. We can't have a revolution – sexual, or political, or spiritual or whatever. All we can have is change.'

'And change is good,' Matthew said, coming full circle, in his own mind at least. He had found something convincing, a solid thing to cling to, in all this talk, and he wasn't about to let go.

Richard laughed. 'Good or bad,' he said, 'it doesn't matter. Change is all we've got. For the time being, anyway.'

He looked up. Paul hadn't really been listening for a while; he had been watching Matthew, amused by his drunken antics, by the way he swayed back and forth, his eyes losing and regaining their focus, his speech slurring. Now, though, he became aware of something – a silence, an attention from Richard that forced him to turn and look back towards the open door to the patio. It was Gina. She was standing in the doorway, listening, watching. She might have been there for some time, but when she saw that they were aware of her she turned and disappeared quickly back into the garden.

Richard cursed softly and turned to Paul. 'How long was she standing there?' he asked.

Paul shook his head. 'I don't know,' he said. He looked at Matthew, but the boy had no idea what was going on.

'Shit.' Richard struggled to his feet and headed for the door. 'I'd better see if she's all right.'

Paul nodded. 'She'll be fine,' he said – but Richard was already gone and the boy Matthew had slipped sideways on to the floor, his hands folded one over the other, his face peaceful and composed, like a child's. A gust of cool air touched Paul's face as Richard passed through the open door, and for one perfect, solitary moment, he felt as if time had stopped running, as if all the conversations had stopped. As if, half-drunk, alone, quiet in himself, he could go on sitting there, in that empty room, for all eternity.

An hour later, the party was winding down. Matthew was still asleep on the floor; Richard and Gina had made things up and were slumped together on the sofa, listening to the music. The guy whose party it had been – a quiet, happy-looking man whose name Paul didn't know – was acting as disc jockey, changing records after one or two tracks, searching for that perfect moment when the party reaches its turning point, when the night becomes something else.

This quiet time, at the end, was the part Paul liked best; this moment when most of the people were gone, and the music ran on in its own quiet realm – slow jazz, Indian music, anything that belonged to the night. After a while, he had gone back to the kitchen and sat at the table by the door, where he could look out at the garden. The French doors had been left open here, and the cool air from the garden gusted in from time to time, cutting through the smoke and the aftertaste of wine, a clear, dark essence that seemed to come from far away, from somewhere along the train lines that ran northwards along Devonshire Road, out and away to fields and stockyards and lit motorways. The man who had thrown the party had put *Blue* on the turntable with the arm folded back, then gone off to bed, nodding to Paul happily as he went; now the words, which he had left as a gift for anyone still awake to hear, came wafting out to where Paul sat, suddenly aware that he was the only one left awake, the only one who was listening.

Only a dark cocoon before I get my gorgeous wings
And fly away . . .

He had always loved that song. Gina called it Richard's Song – which it was, of course, though it belonged to a different Richard, from another time and place – but Paul had always taken it personally, moved and, when he wasn't drunk, a little embarrassed at the way the words reached in for something that only sentiment could touch, something private that couldn't have been said out loud without seeming laughable. It was too lush, too expressive, but it was true, in its own way, on nights like these, when you were the last person awake at a party, and you were getting ready to get up and leave, to go out into the dark city and walk home, through the chiming streets, alone.

When he got home, some time after three, he found Clive sitting alone in the kitchen, with a bottle of Martell. It was unusual to find him up at this time of night; it was even more unusual to find him drinking alone; Clive was very much the social drinker, one of the lads. A regular at the Sports and Social Club, he would drink beer with his mates, then go to one of the Indian or Greek restaurants in town, where they would all make a lot of noise and insult the waiters. From time to time, they did something stupid – like the night Clive and two of his team-mates had played knock-door-run on the way home and got into an altercation with an unappreciative householder – but it never ended badly, no matter what they got up to. They were the rugby crowd, after all, and people turned a blind eye to their shenanigans. Usually, their stupid pranks were regarded as a bit of harmless fun: chatting up unaccompanied women, making fun of the effete barman who occasionally worked at the club, having food fights or belching competitions in Indian restaurants. So it came as something of a surprise to Paul when he found his housemate at home, his face streaked with blood and dirt, on his fifth or sixth straight brandy.

'What's up?' he asked. 'Did you get into a fight?'
'Sort of.'

'Oh.' Paul sat down. 'There's blood on your face.'

'Is there?' Clive emptied his glass with one swift movement. 'It's not mine,' he said.

'I don't suppose it is,' Paul answered. He was puzzled. Clive had been in fights before, but they hadn't put him in this kind of mood. Maybe he was in trouble this time, Paul thought. Maybe he had done more damage than usual, and the police had got involved.

'So whose blood is it?'

'Some bloke's.'

It took a while for Clive to open up, but eventually he told what had happened. It seemed that he and his vigilante gang – mostly other blokes from the rugby team – had gone out looking for the rapist after the club, concentrating their search on the area around Chesterton Road which, according to Clive's map, was where he was most likely to strike next. They had been a bit drunk, and a few of the lads had half-bottles of rum or brandy on them; they had wandered around for a while near the swimming pool, where they'd seen a bloke on a bike looking suspicious; then they had split into pairs and posted themselves out on Jesus Green, keeping an eye on the paths, the bridge to Chesterton Road, and the open area on the far side, near Midsummer Common. That was where Clive and his team-mate Gareth had seen another suspicious-looking guy with some kind of ski hat or mask on, making his way along Victoria Avenue. They had called out to him to stop, but he had run away as soon as he saw them.

'I'm not surprised,' Paul said. He was beginning to see where this was going. 'I mean – wouldn't you?'

Clive looked unhappy. 'I suppose,' he said.

The thought hadn't occurred to him at the time, though. In fact, it had seemed obvious, when the man, whose face was still hidden, had made good his escape, that he had something to hide. So Clive and Gareth had sounded their whistles and set off in pursuit.

'Whistles?'

'Yes.' Clive poured himself another brandy. 'You know. Like the police have.'

'So what happened?'

Clive's story was pretty confusing, but as far as Paul could tell, it appeared that he and Gareth had caught up with the bloke, who had panicked and, in the ensuing struggle, had lashed out, hitting Gareth in the mouth. It had taken the two of them quite an effort to overpower the guy, but they had finally got him down and pulled of the mask. Clive had already begun to realise the bloke wasn't the rapist – he was too tall, he thought, and there was something about him that wasn't right – when two of the other lads had arrived, alerted by the whistles and, seeing the struggle, had jumped in.

'That was where it all went pear-shaped,' Clive said. He took a long, choking swig of brandy and slapped the glass down.

'Don't you think you've had enough of that?' Paul said.

Clive nodded. Then he raised the glass again and finished off what was left, before replacing the screw top on the bottle.

'It wasn't what was supposed to happen,' he said. 'We had it all planned out.'

Somehow or other, the plan had gone wrong. The man wouldn't stop struggling, and he wouldn't answer any of the questions Clive was firing off at him. And before he knew it, things had got out of hand. The mask was one of those tight, close-fitting nylon affairs that terrorists and suchlike wear, with stitched holes for the mouth and eyes; there was no doubting that this in itself was suspicious. It all added up. Even if he wasn't the rapist, he was up to no good.

'So what happened?' Paul didn't want to know, but felt compelled to ask.

'I don't know,' Clive said. 'I think he's all right. I managed to get Gareth to stop and . . . I think he's not that badly hurt.' A look of panic crossed his face. 'I couldn't really do anything,' he said. 'We had to get away.'

'So you left him there?'

'Yes.'

'He didn't get up?'

'No.'

'He was still on the ground?'

'Yes.'

'Did anybody else see you?'

Clive shook his head. 'I don't think so,' he said.

Paul thought. He didn't want to be involved in this, but he couldn't just let it go. The supposed rapist could be lying out there on Midsummer Common with some kind of serious injury, with nobody to help him. It was only ten minutes away on the bike.

'All right,' he said. 'I'm going to go and check.'

Clive gave him a surprised, hopeful look.

'I'll be back soon,' Paul continued. All of a sudden, he realised that he would rather be outside, cycling around in the dark, than spend another moment with Clive. 'Wait here,' he said. 'And don't drink any more.'

Clive nodded. 'It was partly his fault,' he said. 'I mean, what was he doing out there at that time of night in a mask?' The big man was bewildered. 'He has to be *some* kind of pervert.'

Somewhere, in one of the houses on East Road, a dog was

barking. It was the only sound of the night-time that Paul
disliked; there was something ugly and banal about it. He
liked the sound of rain, or the swish of traffic; he liked to hear
music in the distance, or the singsong of voices across a field.
Once, he had started setting up his tripod on the Backs and he
had been so absorbed that it had been some minutes before
he'd noticed the couple, just ten or twelve yards away, making
love under a star-filled sky. At exactly the same moment, they
had become aware of him – as if his sudden attention had
drawn them out of their rapt state – and they had waited a
moment, sizing him up, weighing the danger, before continuing, their voices muffled, but still audible, while he pulled his
stuff together and moved away. That sound – their muffled
whispers, the soft, low noises they had made in the night – had
lingered in his mind for days afterwards, and he had felt an
oddly satisfying goodwill towards them, as if they had
deliberately included him in their lovemaking.

Now, as he cycled towards the spot where Clive and his
vigilantes had abandoned their victim, the noise of the dog
followed him, seeming to come, first from one side, then from
another. It was a clear, cool night; the lights were still lit along
Maid's Causeway and Victoria Avenue, and there was no one
else about. He quickly reached the place, just beyond the
public toilets on the Common, where the incident had taken
place. Clive had said that he and the others had left the man at
the point where the paths crossed, not far from the road, or if
not there, then just beyond, a few feet into the darkness, out
of the street light's acidic glare. When Paul reached the spot,
however, there was no one. It was immediately obvious
where the fight had happened, but a litter of coins on the path,
which had evidently spilled from the pockets of the assailants
or perhaps their victim, and a trail of blood, leading from the

scatter of coins on the tarmac path away across the grass and into the darkness, were all that remained. The supposed pervert had gone. Paul hoped he was not too badly hurt and, at the same time, wondered who he had been, and what hunger had driven him out into the night, in a ski mask, to risk what had happened, or worse. Surely, even if he wasn't the rapist, he had something to hide and, if so, there was probably very little likelihood of his going to the police. As usual, Clive had been lucky.

He was still there, standing astride his bike, wondering who the man had been and why he had been out there at that time of night in such an unlikely getup, when a voice hailed him from the direction of Victoria Avenue, in the region of the toilets.

'Hey. You.'

He turned sharply. Three young men were clambering over the railings at the edge of the green and were heading in his direction. In his concern for the stranger in the ski mask, he had forgotten the risks of being out there, near a public toilet no less, at that time of the night: the Victoria Avenue public conveniences were a notorious meeting point for men, and so had long ago been abandoned as a rendezvous, and had become a more usual haunt for skinheads, gay-bashers and other weirdos. Quickly, he hopped back on to his bike and pedalled away as fast as he could in the direction of the river, the voices calling after him through the dark.

'Hey, you. Bum boy.'

'Hey, poof. Come here.'

He could hear them running on the hard tarmac now, as he picked up speed. If they had any brains at all, they would take a chance and try to cut him off where the path met the river and forked, one track leading back towards the town, the other out and away, towards the houses at Riverside, and the lit through-road on Elizabeth Way. He couldn't believe how stupid he had been, not to have even noticed them coming; now, he had to take the same kind of gamble, and hope he was faster or luckier than they were. Chances were they had been drinking and wouldn't have much heart for the chase, but he couldn't count on that. As the river appeared in front of him, he glanced back; the men were still running, still on the path. It would have been easier if they had committed themselves and cut across already, in one direction or the other, but he had no choice now: calculating that it was a harder and wider angle in the Elizabeth Way direction, he turned right and headed out towards Riverside. It was dark here, and he couldn't see too well, but he reckoned that would work against them as much as it did him. He was glad he hadn't brought his camera bag, as he usually did when he went out at night. He had thought about it when he was leaving the house, then thought better of it, for the masked man's sake. The surprising thing was, in all the time he'd been coming out at night, he had never run into this kind of situation.

A voice rang out behind him, as he caught sight of a light from Riverside.

'Aw, fuck it!'

The men had stopped running. They hadn't even thought to cut across; they had just chased after his tail light like idiots. As he sped away, their voices came, ugly and defeated on the night air.

'Run for it, bum boy.'

'You're claimed, cunt.'

'Fucking poof!'

A moment later he was cycling along Riverside and

129

crossing under the Elizabeth Way bridge. It took him twenty minutes to get home, by way of River Lane, crossing into New Street and heading back up to East Road. By the time he got back, the kitchen light was still burning, but Clive had gone to bed, leaving the brandy bottle and a pair of new rugby socks on the kitchen table.

Over the next few days, Clive made himself scarce. At the same time, Steve seemed to have disappeared. Paul came and went in constant anticipation of another visit from the irate father, or the police, but a week passed and nothing happened. One morning, after a late session with the camera, Paul found Clive in the kitchen, wearing his freshly scrubbed, one-of-the-lads look. He was reading a copy of *Playboy*, balancing the magazine against a giant ketchup bottle, while he noisily demolished a bowl of cornflakes. When Paul appeared, the big man grinned.

'Hiya,' he said. 'Late night?'

Paul nodded, but he didn't say anything as he filled the kettle and fetched some milk out of the fridge.

'I've just got back,' Clive said. 'I went home for a couple of days.'

'Oh.' Paul stayed noncommittal. He didn't want to be bothered with this. He put two spoonfuls of tea into the brown pot, the one that had the smaller chip on the spout.

'I needed a break,' Clive continued.

'Don't we all,' Paul muttered, grudgingly. He felt petty, but he couldn't help it. He already knew, without waiting for the end of this conversation, that Clive wasn't going to ask him about the man on Midsummer Common. It was forgotten, just another of those drunken escapades that were, by common consent, quietly excised from the record. It was a matter of honour: nothing a man did when he'd been drinking could be held against him.

'Where's Steve?' Clive finished his cornflakes and fetched a cup from the draining board. 'Is that tea?'

Paul sat down and pointedly examined the cover of Clive's magazine. 'Swotting, I see,' he said, ignoring the first of Clive's questions. He didn't want to get into another big Steve thing. Clive grinned.

'It's got some really interesting articles,' he said. 'That's the only reason I buy it. Scout's honour.'

Paul nodded. 'Quality writing,' he said. 'So rare these days.' He considered warning Clive about the possibility of a further unwelcome visit from the besuited Mike and his womenfolk, but he thought better of it and let it pass. He didn't want to see where the rugby player's code of male honour would go with that particular piece of information.

Later that afternoon, he went in search of Penny. As usual these days he found her in Belinda's, having tea with Marjorie. He'd begun to wonder what was going on between the two of them – if there was something more than an ordinary friendship, some kind of crush on Marjorie's part, say. It seemed unlikely; Marjorie certainly didn't act as if she was in thrall to Penny or, for that matter, to anybody else. Paul couldn't imagine her feeling romantic about anyone, male or female. Still, her being there was bad timing, and, standing in the doorway, he hesitated a moment, feeling too tall and clumsy and unneeded. The girls were at a table towards the back of the room and neither appeared to have seen him come in; for a moment, he even thought of stepping back out into the street, so he wouldn't have to join them.

At that very moment, Penny looked up. She had a

conspiratorial look on her face, a half-smile touched with satisfied contempt which dissolved when she saw him into a blank, neutral gaze. With nothing for it but to go on, he approached their table.

'May I join you?' he said, addressing the question to Marjorie more than Penny. It annoyed him, this deference – almost a form of guilt – that she induced in him. Even if Penny insisted that Marjorie didn't dislike him personally, it was no consolation for the other woman's behaviour. As it happened, Paul didn't care who Marjorie liked, or what she thought; he was simply angry with himself for allowing her to have such an unsettling effect on him, an effect he knew Penny sensed, not as discomfort, but as a form of assent, a tacit, even unconscious acknowledgement that Marjorie was right – about what was immaterial – and that he was somehow *wrong*.

'Hello,' Penny murmured, moving slightly to accommodate him as he sat down. 'I didn't expect to see you today.'

'Sorry.' Paul didn't know why he was apologising. 'I wasn't looking for you. I thought you were working.'

Marjorie was studying him the way she might study a strange animal that someone had brought in on a leash and set down on the table, a monkey, say, or a trained seal.

'Look,' Paul said, 'if I'm butting in, I'll go—'

'Nonsense,' Marjorie said. 'We were just talking about the news.'

'The news?'

'You didn't hear?' Marjorie smiled grimly. 'Well, I don't suppose it would matter as much to you as it does to us.'

'What news?'

'The rapist,' Penny said. 'He's been caught.'

'Oh.' Paul tried to twist his face into the appropriate

132

expression, somewhere between happiness and the necessary solemnity. 'That's good.'

'One down,' Marjorie said curtly. 'Several million to go.' She stood up. 'Anyway, I have to get off.'

'Don't leave on my account,' Paul said, trying for what felt like an impossible evenness of tone.

Marjorie grimaced. 'I have a meeting,' she said. 'Bye, Penny.'

After she was safely gone, Penny gave Paul a cold, aggrieved look. 'What's wrong with you?' she said.

'Nothing.' Paul studied her face. It was apparent, all of a sudden, that the distance between them had become well-nigh impassable. It was odd: these affairs – these *relationships* – were supposed to be inexact and unscientific, matters of the heart, or of the spirit, yet at moments like this, as things came to what suddenly seemed an inevitable end, everything was decided by a simple calculation of distance and tone of voice and facial expression. When you reached this point, you should just stand up and walk out; words were unnecessary, explanations redundant. Yet you couldn't help staying, you couldn't avoid going through the motions. Nobody ever said what they really thought. Everything worked by pretexts.

'Did you ever wonder why strong women like Marjorie make men like you feel so uncomfortable?' Penny said.

'No mystery,' Paul answered mildly.

'No?'

'She's rude,' Paul said. 'And bigoted. People feel uncomfortable around bigots.'

'She's a feminist,' Penny said.

'No she's not,' Paul replied, feeling himself being drawn needlessly into an argument he didn't want to have. 'She just hates men. There's a difference.'

'It's not surprising,' Penny said, bitterness creeping into her voice. 'With her history—'

'What do you know about her history?' Paul demanded, suddenly angry but managing to keep his voice down. 'Other than what she's told you?'

Penny stiffened. She was openly upset now, but it was a decision to let it show, part of the process, another piece of theatre.

'Look,' Paul said, 'I don't want to argue about Marjorie. I don't even want to talk about her.'

'Okay.' Penny sat back and folded her arms. 'What do you want to talk about?'

There it was: the oldest conversation-stopper in the book. No matter what he said, it would be wrong. But if he said nothing, it would be his fault that they never really talked any more. Paul smiled sadly, and looked at the floor. 'Why do we do this?' he murmured.

'What?' Penny's voice was hard, getting ready for indignant.

At that precise moment, like a ministering angel, one of Belinda's girls, the tall pretty one whose name, he seemed to remember, was Jacqui, descended upon their table and began clearing away Marjorie's crockery. Paul gave her a sideways, mock-grateful look.

'Thank you,' he said, in best café-style *sotto voce*.

Jacqui smiled and moved away. She was a friend of Gina's, which was the main reason Paul remembered her; it wasn't the first time, though, that he had noticed how attractive she was. Penny allowed herself a tight, contemptuous smile.

'And why is it men like you always fall for the waitress?' she said.

'How do you mean, men like me?'

'It's that little choice you're always making. What's the easy way? How do I minimise this?'

'I've no idea what you're talking about.'

'No? I came round to your house the other night.'

'Oh?'

'You were out,' she said. 'But Clive was in.'

'Really?' Paul wondered if she was lying. 'I must have been at Richard's.'

'That's all right.' Penny smiled brightly. 'Clive entertained me.'

'Lucky you.'

Penny gave a soft laugh and shook her head. 'He's a real character, is Clive,' she said, giving him a triumphant, meaningful look. 'We had an interesting evening.'

'Ah.' So this was what his housemate had been avoiding that morning. Paul's mind raced. He hadn't seen Clive since the attack on Ski Mask, but he could have been around for much of the next day. He had probably hidden out at the club, getting his story straight with Gareth and the others, before heading home. If he had, he could have been back by the time Penny came around.

Penny watched him. He was supposed to be upset now, or indignant, but he didn't feel anything at all. He wasn't even sure Penny's insinuation was true.

'Well?' Penny bent forward and leaned her elbows on the table. 'Don't you want to know what happened?'

'Not really.'

'Well, I'll tell you anyway,' she said. 'We had a drink, and your friend kissed me. He wanted to know why I was wasting my time with a bloke like you. Said you have a bit on the side, some nurse, apparently. He thinks you don't deserve me.' She paused meaningfully. 'Well? Is that true? Do you have a bit on the side?'

It was a rhetorical question; Penny didn't even wait for a reply.

'Don't worry,' she said. 'I'm not expecting you to do anything. You don't have to go home and beat him up, or anything like that. In fact, I had quite a good time. Clive's quite funny when he's drunk, isn't he?'

Paul smiled. 'He's a real hoot,' he said.

'Well, I was drunk, too. So I didn't mind. Especially considering your bit on the side.' She laughed. 'You know what he said about you?' she asked.

'I'm not that interested, to be honest.' It was, he thought, time to end all this. Get up. Leave. Walk away. No hard feelings. Go while the going was good.

'You know when you see a man walking home along a country road at night? The kind of man who's missed his last bus and hasn't got enough for a taxi, so he's walking home alone, in the dark? He says that's who you remind him of. That man.' Penny studied him, watching for some kind of reaction. 'That's what he said,' she added, unnecessarily.

'I see.' Paul was surprised at how much Penny was enjoying this. At the same time, he was putting together the other puzzle: all the little clues and giveaways that he should have picked up at the time. He had imagined Clive as a friend, more or less; or, if not a friend, then neutral, at least. Now he saw that this new hostility wasn't new at all, that it had been there, quietly brewing all along.

'Well,' he said, 'that's that, then. I'm glad you told me.'

Penny shook her head softly. 'Is that all you have to say?' She sounded like Mrs Greer, from his school days. *Is that all you have to say? How do you plan to get away with it this time? Explain yourself.*

'Pretty much.' Paul stood up. 'Goodbye, Penny,' he said.

She looked surprised, but only for a moment. The look of contempt quickly returned. 'That's right,' she said. 'Run away.'

'Seems like a good idea,' he said, as disgusted with himself as he was with her, or Clive. As he headed for the door, he noticed Jacqui; she was standing at the far end of the counter, cradling what looked like a glass of iced tea in her cupped hands. It was evident that she had been watching them, but when Paul caught her eye she didn't turn away, or seem in the least embarrassed or guilty. Instead, she nodded her head slightly, and smiled as if to say that he was doing the right thing – or at least, that was how he read it, as he slipped out and away, into the warmth and the light of the afternoon.

He didn't really want a confrontation. He had never much liked Clive, but he'd never felt sufficiently exercised about the man's idiocies to actively dislike him either. Besides, he didn't want problems with the house: Steve had obviously done something to upset the neighbours, and, with the distinct possibility that he had done a runner looming large in his thinking, Paul didn't really want to risk losing Clive's last week of full rent and – more importantly – his share of the retainer for Mrs Yarr. If Paul had any chance of staying on over the summer – and there was a good chance he could arrange it, if Clive and Steve paid their retainers, and Mrs Yazz kept to the agreement they had discussed – he couldn't afford to alienate Clive. He was only mildly surprised at how little he felt when he considered Clive's betrayal; it wasn't much of a shock, when he considered it. Clive had always let it be known how much he liked Penny, in that half-joking way that was as much veiled warning as poor-taste humour. How he knew about Nancy – if that sorry affair had been what he meant by 'a bit on the side' – was another matter. In fact, what troubled Paul most was the idea that he had let something slip, that his private life was in any way less private than he had imagined.

He hadn't wanted a confrontation, and he'd been praying that Clive would be out as he headed back home, but the big man was in the kitchen, eating a takeaway curry directly from the foil containers, his elbows propped on the table, the copy of *Playboy* from earlier propped on the ketchup bottle, its pages blotched with greasy thumbprints. He was surrounded by the usual debris: wet spills of boiled rice, odd streaks of reddish or off-brown curry sauce, a scrunched-up flyer from the college Christian Association that he had used to mop up one of the larger spills. At the far end of the table, on top of a pile of old papers, lay a pile of soiled rugby shorts which Paul hoped he was planning to wash some time in the foreseeable future. It was always a mystery where all this soiled kit came from: as far as Paul knew, the rugby team hadn't played a serious match for a good two or three weeks, yet the foul-smelling, mud-streaked shirts and shorts and the socks – particularly the socks – continued to appear, in various states, in the hallway, or the bathroom or, more often than not, the kitchen. It only made Clive's hearty, innocent, hail-fellow-well-met greeting more difficult to take.

'Still studying, I see,' Paul said, with a nod towards the *Playboy*. 'I'm not sure your new love would approve of your chosen reading material.'

Clive looked confused for a suitable moment, then nodded.

'So she told you,' he said. 'Well, I can't say I'm proud. But it's not all my fault. You only had yourself to blame.'

'How do you work that one out?'

'Look, I didn't mean for you to find out like this,' Clive said, setting down his fork. The smell of curry struck Paul as more than a little inappropriate to the occasion. 'I was meaning to talk to you myself.'

'Well,' Paul said, suddenly fascinated by Clive's meal, 'you had your chance this morning.'

'I know.' Clive pushed the foil container to one side. 'It's just – well, you know how much I like her. And you obviously don't give a damn. I don't think there's anything wrong with . . .' He broke off. 'Christ! Will you stop staring at that curry.'

Paul laughed softly. 'Sorry,' he said. 'It's just that . . . I don't think I've ever seen food that particular colour before—'

'What the fuck!' Clive shook his head sadly. 'It's just beef curry, for Christ's sake.'

'Anyway.' Paul looked up. 'It doesn't matter. I just wanted you to know, you have my blessing. If you want to – you know – move in, or whatever—'

Now Clive was annoyed. 'Your blessing?' He spat a tiny fragment of boiled rice across the kitchen. 'I don't need your fucking blessing.'

Paul nodded. 'Fine,' he said. 'All I'm saying is—'

Clive was ready to fly off the handle. Presumably, Paul's offhand manner struck him as insufficiently serious. He had probably been expecting something else – reasoned capitulation, perhaps, some gentlemanly admission of defeat. He was deprived, however, of the appropriate expression of his righteous anger by a loud knocking at the door.

'Oh, shit.' Paul's heart sank. It was Mike. How would he explain this to Clive. He stood up quickly. 'I'll get it,' he said.

Clive didn't speak, but returned to his curry.

It wasn't Mike, however. It was his daughter, Angela.

'You'd better come and get that bloke,' she said. 'Before somebody sees him.'

'What is it?' Paul stepped into the street and pulled the door to behind him. 'What bloke?'

'Your mate,' she said, impatiently. 'He's going about with no clothes on.' Her face became set and businesslike. She was obviously embarrassed. 'If my dad comes home, he's going to kill him.'

'Where is he?'

Angela pointed towards the graveyard at the end of the street. 'He climbed over the wall,' she said. 'He tried to touch me. I shouted at him. He ran away.'

'What do you mean, he tried to touch you?'

Angela looked at her feet. 'You know,' she said. 'Like on the telly.' She looked up. She had obviously had a fright, but now, to Paul's surprise, she seemed genuinely concerned for Steve. 'He's got no clothes on,' she repeated softly.

Paul nodded. He wanted to reassure her. As if it was the most natural thing in the world, he walked to the graveyard wall and peered over. It looked deserted. It took him a moment to make Steve out, where he lay, stark naked, under a tall holly bush. He turned back to the girl.

'Okay,' he said. 'I'll take care of him. All right?'

Angela nodded.

'You go on home now. I'll take care of him.'

She nodded again, but she didn't move. 'You should call the loony bin,' she said.

'I'll do that,' Paul said. He noticed a couple of other girls, about Angela's age, watching them from the far end of the street. 'Your friends are waiting for you.'

Angela turned. 'That's just Claire,' she said. 'She's too scared to come down here. I'm not, though.'

'You're very brave,' Paul said. At this, finally satisfied, the girl smiled and ran back to the far end of the street where her friends were waiting.

As soon as she was gone, Paul clambered over the wall. Steve was on his back, his eyes fixed on the sky; he seemed oblivious to his surroundings. Slowly, Paul walked over to where he lay, weaving a path through the headstones. It was evening now; the sky was softening; the air had begun to fade from lime-green to grey above the trees. Laid out naked, under the holly tree, Steve looked terribly white and thin, like one of those dead Christs in early German or Flemish paintings. He did not move as Paul approached. Though his eyes were open, he seemed not to see that someone was there, or who it was.

'Hey,' Paul called softly. 'Steve. How are you doing, mate?' He was aware of how ridiculous he sounded, how insincere. Steve didn't move. 'Come on,' Paul said. 'Let's get you back inside. It's turning cold.'

Steve's eyes flickered but he didn't speak.

'Do you want me to call somebody?' Paul ventured. He thought he caught a glimmer of recognition in Steve's face, but it was too late. From the far side of the graveyard, where the gate to the street was, a plump little man in a track suit and trainers was approaching, looking worried and curious.

'Is he all right?' he called. He had probably been watching for some time, but had only plucked up enough courage to come over when he saw somebody else was there.

'He's fine,' Paul said.

141

'He doesn't look fine.' The man was close enough now to see Steve's gaunt, haggard face. 'I was just coming back from my run,' he said. 'And my wife said, there's a funny-looking man out there in the graveyard. So I came out to see if he was okay.' The man shook his head softly and blinked several times. 'He's got no clothes on,' he added helpfully.

'He's not well,' Paul muttered.

'My wife's called the ambulance,' the man said. 'They'll be here soon.' He looked back towards the gate. 'Are you a friend of his?'

Paul shook his head. 'Not really,' he said. He wondered how much of this Steve could understand.

'You'd better leave him then,' the man said. 'The ambulance will be here soon.'

Paul looked at the naked figure on the grass. Steve's eyes were closed now; he looked like someone who feigns sleep in the vain hope that he will be left alone.

'I'll wait here,' the man said. 'Till the ambulance comes.'

Paul nodded. 'Okay.' He started back for the house. At the far end of the graveyard, he could see a woman watching them and, behind her, someone in uniform had appeared. The man in the track suit turned.

'That's them now,' he said. 'You get on. It'll be all right.' He smiled kindly. 'He'll be taken care of, don't you worry.'

As soon as Clive left for the pub, Paul ran upstairs and tried Steve's door. It was unlocked. He could hear something inside: a thin, patient rustling, like the sound a leaf makes, blown along a country road at night. Paul took a deep breath and pushed the door to.

The first thing he noticed were the cages. You couldn't help noticing them; there were a dozen or more, placed

142

around the room, but mostly set out on the large table by the open window. Almost all appeared to be empty but fuzzed with a dark stain at the centre that Paul didn't understand until something moved in the cage closest to where he stood, motionless in the open doorway, and he saw that each of these stains, one, sometimes two to a cage, was a living thing. There were rabbits, guinea pigs, hamsters, various kinds of ornamental mice – the type of animals that children usually keep as pets, but they looked to Paul unfinished and vague, not quite plump or silky enough, not quite rounded. Most of them were still alive, but all were in a bad way, some close to death, others obviously distressed. Half-starved, gaunt, somehow emptied of light and substance, they lay helpless and inert amongst the handfuls of dirty straw that Steve had used to line the cages. Everywhere – not only inside the cages, but on the floor under the big table and elsewhere – lay the animals' spoor, some of it old and dry, some fresh. In one cage, whose occupants were both very obviously dead, there was a small pool of dried blood. Elsewhere, the animals were in various stages of decay, on the one hand, or agony, on the other; it was evident that they had been in this condition for some time.

Now Paul understood the smell that Clive had complained about.

As this tableau gradually sank in, Paul remembered all the animals of his own childhood, all the found, broken things he had carried home to keep in shoe boxes or makeshift cages, in the vain hope of nursing them back to life, and he felt a sudden rush of pity for every living thing, human and animal, fish or fowl, alive and well, hurt or dying. Once he'd had a budgerigar, a plump, ugly bird called Jackie; it had lived happily for a couple of years, then had caught a chill and died

143

pathetically on the living-room floor, next to the fire, where Paul had set it down to warm it. He remembered standing there, in the front room with his father, watching the bird flutter and flail for a while, then tip sideways, one concertina wing spread out, showing the green and yellow feathers, and he had been struck by how helpless they were, how there was nothing they could do to save it. There had been a cat too, and though he had never taken to the creature, its patient death, presumably of old age, had upset him for days afterwards. Why, he wondered, was everything so soft? Why were animals so vulnerable? Maybe Steve had asked himself the same questions, only he had reversed the process: instead of bringing home the crippled and the near-dead, he had filled his room with small, quick, vital things, to see how they died. For there was no doubting the meaning of this room: it was set up as a form of theatre, as a spectacle. As Paul slowly realised that the cages were arranged in such a way that every one of them was visible from the bed in the far corner of the room, he remembered something Steve had told him weeks ago, something about how things looked when they were dying. At the time, he had ignored what the guy was telling him: it had struck him as nothing more than a piece of bravado. Now, he saw that all those little packages Steve had been carrying back and forth had been dead animals that he was getting rid of, or replacements for those that had died. He had lain there on the bed, watching, listening, taking it all in. The thought that he had slept there, night after night, amidst those fading mouths and dulling bodies, left Paul sickened and disgusted. On the other hand, he was beginning to realise that he would have to do something about all this. There was little chance of Steve coming home in the near future and sorting it out, and Clive was unlikely to be any help, even if Paul did let

144

him know what was going on. At the same time, he couldn't risk Mrs Yazz finding out what had been going on in her house.

As he planned what to do, he remembered a question he had asked in Scripture class, when he was twelve or so. They had been talking about the idea of redemption, and the teacher, who was a nun, had said something about the original sin, and how Jesus had died to redeem us from the sin of Adam and Eve. He had always wanted to ask about that, about original sin, but he had sensed, every time he began leading up to it, that this was a question you didn't ask. Still, it seemed crazy to him that these people, whom God had created in His own image, would be cast out of the garden just for wanting knowledge. He knew the answer to the question, if he had framed it, would have had something to do with disobedience, but that still didn't explain why God had made the Tree of Knowledge and set it there, in plain view, to draw them into a temptation it would have been almost impossible to resist. The question he did ask, though, was subtler, and seemed, the moment he asked it, more cunning that it ought to have been – as if the years of doctrine and mystery had made him into something he was not. As soon as he had spoken, surprising even himself, he could tell from the look on Sister Catherine's face that, in her eyes at least, he had betrayed himself as a schemer, a trickster, a boy knowingly in league with the Devil.

The question was this: when Adam and Eve were cast out of the garden, were the animals also cast out? He had been thinking about Noah, and how he had to take the animals with him on to the Ark, and he had wondered if the animals which Adam had named, the original ones, would have stayed behind in Eden, or would they have had to go, through no fault of their own, into the Vale of Tears? Sister Catherine had no answer. She told him he had misunderstood the story – which was her standard reply to everything for which she had no set rejoinder. She seemed angry, even, that he had raised the question.

Now, as he took in the enormity of what he had to do, that question returned to him. Surely, he thought, the animals had been innocent of sin. Surely God would not have let them be cast into the darkness, because of what humans had done. It was all he could think about, when he finally set to work, checking which cages contained live animals, and which only corpses. All in all, there were eight dead, seven still alive. Most of the live ones were weak and frail; if he let them go – in the graveyard, say – they would only suffer more. They would starve, or they would be found by other animals and their last hours would be yet another squalid ordeal. All he could do – the thought came to him in a sickening rush of logic – the only solution, was to kill them off as humanely as possible. He had read somewhere that drowning was a relatively quick and painless end; he wasn't altogether convinced, but it was better than poison, and he knew he couldn't trust himself to kill a live rabbit with his bare hands. So it was that, over the next hour, praying all the time that Clive would not come home and disturb him, he filled the bath to the brim, then carried the last remaining survivors of Steve's bizarre menagerie, still in their cages, to the bathroom, where he lowered them into the water and held them under, till the animals stopped moving, all the time thinking about Eden, and the hopeless innocence of the creatures, as if it was something he remembered personally, something he had known and lost, and would always regret.

146

CAMBRIDGE, 1975

On the first and last morning, he wakes early, in the cool, grey hiatus of dawn. The blankets on his narrow iron bed have spilled on to the floor, leaving him almost naked, covered only by a rumpled, more or less white sheet. It takes him a moment to realise where he is: instead of the usual sounds and smells – birdsong, a certain freshness of the air, the scent of cut grass – there is a city outside: a whole aching city, just beyond the tiny, high window of the cell. He can hear it, at a slight distance, behind the other, less familiar noise, which could be a fan, or perhaps a generator, tucked into the wall somewhere below the room where he is lying. If he could, he would look to see where he is: he can't say how high up this might be, or what floor he is on; he can't tell what is above or below him, or where the noise of traffic is coming from – and these are things he likes to know, these are the important things. You have to know exactly where you are, you have to be able to see what options you have, no matter what the circumstances. He can take a guess, of course, but that's not the point. It doesn't matter that a room like this will almost certainly give on to a narrow, dank yard, or a rear-of-the-building car park, walled in on both sides and looking out over another, less austere space, the courtyard of a cheap bed and breakfast, say, or a pub, a rainy space full of plastic furniture and folded

147

parasols, or a narrow gap between high stone walls, where someone has recently unloaded a stack of soft-drink crates.

All night, they had talked to him, voices coming and going in the dark, or in the lit room where he had sat quietly, waiting for something else to happen, waiting to resume his own version of events. It was time now – he knew that – but it had taken a while to pull his life together, to see the pattern, to recognise the completeness of what he had done. The night before had felt like an interruption at first – the lights, the bodies of the men around him, the sound of his own breathing, and the oddly muted blows that had rained down on his back and arms – but, standing or sitting in those other rooms, and finally, lying here, he had begun to assemble a definitive history, a total account of all that he had done. It had never occurred to them – to the newspapers, or the police, or the people he had heard at work, discussing 'the case' – it had never once occurred to them that he was part of the overall plan of things, or that he had taken his own risks, walking alone in the dark, or going from house to house, watching and listening and, at the same time, aware of his own special danger. Because he had been in danger, always: side-streets; city; night; a man walking in the rain, watching, listening, choosing. It wasn't the danger you saw on television, or read about in a book. This was something else, something to do with a different sense of loss, of the moment when he too would become conscious, not only of himself walking those dark, deserted streets, but also of that invisible assembly of movement and steps and even breathing that matched him in every way, but was not himself – like that invisible presence the Arctic explorers described when they came home from being lost, walking for hours or days in the snow and the dark with a single, unseen companion. It would be impossible to

148

talk about this to anyone else and make himself understood, but he had known all along that this other was always waiting to arrive.

Now, sooner or later – in the next hour, over the next few days, and for months after that – they would bring their questions, and they would wait for him to give answers. When and where; how and why. Why, most of all. They would be angry with him, or they would try to understand; sometimes they would be sad for what he had done. He would tell them what they wanted to know – because it didn't matter, it was nothing more or less than what they expected. What he would never tell them – what they would never ask – was the only thing that mattered. No matter what the facts of the case turned out to be – and they were still not altogether fixed, they still remained to be decided – what mattered was that he knew things about those women that no one else would ever know: more than their names and faces, more than the details that would not be repeated in court, more than the facts of the case. He knew their fear; he knew the intimate smell and feel of it; he could recall how it was different for each of them, the way a perfume is different, depending on who wears it, and he could replay it all, over and over, as often as he liked. Knowledge is power. That was something those people said, but they didn't understand what they were saying. Not the way he did. No matter how long they lived, or what they did to themselves to forget that one night when they wakened in the dark and realised that he had come, those women would never be able to claim full and exclusive knowledge of themselves again. They would have to share their bodies, and their voices, and their dreams with him, till the day they died. No matter what happened, nobody could ever take that away from him.

But there was also something else, something more important that he could never have told. When he thought about it, he knew how it worked, but he couldn't have told it to someone else, even if they had been ready to listen. Maybe there weren't words for it. If he could have done, he would have explained – not because he wanted them to know so much, but because it had made sense to him, it had begun to sound finished, when he had begun to say out loud what it was he had done. What he had felt, what he had known. And he wanted to tell about the end, because that was the most important part – not the anticipation, not the time he had spent with those women, not even the power he had felt, in his hands and his chest, when they were helpless, and he could do whatever he wanted. Maybe there was a pleasure in those things, but the best part, the real pleasure, had been in that final moment, especially with the last two or three, when he had left them, holding his knife to the girl's soft, white throat and whispering, close to her ear, that she had better be still, that he would kill her if she moved. Then, as she lay, still, terrified, not even daring to breathe, he had slipped away silently, leaving her there. It was something he had only thought of halfway through, but that moment, that vanishing trick, was everything to him now. It didn't even matter that they had caught him – by accident, as it turned out, which was something of a consolation. It didn't matter to those girls that he was behind bars now, because they would always remember that moment when he vanished, as if by magic. For the thought would always be there, at the back of their minds, maybe even for as long as they lived: the thought that, if he could disappear at will, just like that, without a sound, he could come again, just as easily, just as quietly. The police could say what they liked, the newspapers could write stuff about locking him up forever and throwing away the key, but those girls would know the truth of it. No matter how hard they tried to forget, they knew that he was not gone, that he was waiting to return, in some form or another, days, or weeks, or even years later, when everyone else had forgotten him. Because that moment when he had vanished would never end. It would come again. All he had to do was wait.

FULBOURN

Because He was alone in the day room, and because He knew that nothing else would happen, or nothing more than evenings like this one, long and slow and exact as if someone had measured out the time in neat, precise units, the way they measured out the medication – most of all, because the night was coming, and they had just given Him His chlorpromazine, He was telling Himself a story. It wasn't the story He had intended to tell, but the thing about being in this place was, no matter how hard He tried, He couldn't keep to the one thing, He couldn't decide for Himself what He really thought. His mind would set off on another tack altogether, and He could even *see* things – that was how strong it was. What He wanted the story to say was how much He liked the night, that there was something magical about the dark that had to do with the cool of it, with the odd gust of wind through the trees, or the lights and the scents on the road that led back to the city, white headlamps and the smell of diesel, all the late-night stores and lights in upstairs windows above grocers' shops, all the interiors packed full of vegetables and fruits, marmalade jars, swimming costumes, buckets of sand. Out there, the night in a story could be anything you liked: a fairground, or a long drive through summer meadows, or walking home with a girl after school. But here, the night was nothing like that.

Here, the night was distance, not time. Here, when darkness fell, He could think of nothing but the inseparable gap between this place and every other place in the world. When visiting time was over, He would remember – five, six, ten, twenty, or a hundred times each night – that He was in the place for the mad, four miles away from the city and, at the same time, infinitely distant, in a house that was impossible to leave unless you crossed an eternity of slow evenings like this, when the trees moved gradually closer together, and the fields dwindled into themselves, inventing the darkness, making it up. You couldn't cross that distance by the country road that ran out through stands of cow parsley into the suburbs, past men in cricket whites and children on new bicycles standing at the end of their street as if they intended staying there forever. You couldn't cross it by following the avenue of lime trees to the edge of the cemetery, or the path across the meadows after a mowing, the thick stubble of it waiting for dewfalls and the first stars. In fact, you couldn't cross it at all. If you came here, it was already decided that you were mad, and you couldn't go anywhere by choice; you had to stay for as long as nobody in the city wanted you back.

It wasn't an accident that He had come to be here. It had been planned long ago, when He was very young. He remembered when He was a little boy, and His mother would fill the hot-water bottle, standing over the sink to pour the almost boiling water, then swaying the bottle back and forth, to let the steam escape. When she had finished screwing down the stopper and checking it was tight, He would take it to bed with him, for the warmth and the blue of it, that smell of warm rubber becoming just one of the smells He knew as home. Other smells were jam and new cakes and the smell of washing, but it was always a warm smell at home, just as the

153

world outside was mostly cold-smelling, rain and snow and wind from the hills when He walked back from school in the dark, with that pain in the palms of His hands, or blood running from His nose, where someone had hit Him for no reason. He was glad when He stopped going to school, though by then, of course, it was too late because everything had already been decided. The teachers had asked Him questions He didn't understand and the other boys made fun of Him, or tripped Him up in the corridors when the teacher's back was turned, so He would be the one who got into trouble. Once a boy called Witherspoon had followed Him along the road and, when they were out of sight of the school, that boy, that Witherspoon, who would be cursed now, for all eternity, had pushed Him over a hedge. Suddenly, He was lying in somebody's garden, and a dog was barking at Him, but He couldn't get away, because all the wind had gone out of Him.

He'd been scared to tell anybody about what was happening. He told his mum He'd fallen over, all the times He came home with a bloody nose or scabbed knees, and she must have believed Him, otherwise she wouldn't have made Him go there every single day. He had imagined that school would go on forever, getting worse all the time, but in the end it was school that had sent Him away, and He was surprised when He didn't have to go there any more. Things hadn't happened the way they said, or not exactly, but He was glad to leave. His mum went to see the headmaster and when she came home she was crying. She asked Him what He had done, and how Michael Walker had got those marks on his neck, but when He tried to explain she said it didn't matter, she didn't want to hear about it. Then she said He wouldn't be going to that school again. He would be staying home till Christmas, then He would be going to a different place. On Christmas Day it snowed, and they had paper hats and then they ate turkey and stuffing. That year, He didn't have to go to the Christmas party, where the girls had put jelly down His shirt and laughed at Him. When dinner was over, He sat by the window while His mum did the dishes. Every now and then, He glanced upwards, to see if the angels were there. That was where you saw them, up in the sky, and if you looked to the East, you saw a special kind of star. He didn't know which way East was, though, and He didn't want to ask His mum, in case she got annoyed with Him.

The first of the animals was a hamster. It was so warm in His hands, He just wanted to hold it all the time. It had these wet-looking eyes and a small wet mouth; its fur was light brown, and it was always warm. Obviously, He hadn't meant for it to die. He must have done something wrong, but He didn't know what it was. He started to realise it was sick one afternoon, just after Christmas, but it didn't die for almost a week. He had watched it as much as He could all that time, but He hadn't been sorry when it finally expired. He'd had other animals after that – a rabbit, gerbils, a guinea pig – but they had all died quite quickly. His mum was always surprised when they did that, but He wasn't. Animals were supposed to die. That was how it was meant to happen.

Once, when He was walking in the park, He saw a little girl sitting on the ground near the bandstand, with her back to Him. Her little pleated skirt was spread out on the pink and grey flagstones, her long blonde hair hung down over her face. He was curious to know what she was doing, so He walked up behind her; the girl didn't look up, but she knew He was there. He had expected her to be playing with some toy, or scrawling names on the flagstones; instead, He saw that she

155

had a jar on the ground beside her, which was half-full of worms. It must have been full to begin with, for more worms were spilled out over the pavement, some whole, some cut neatly into two or three pieces. The girl was in the midst of dissecting one when He looked over her shoulder: with the thumb and the forefinger of her right hand, she held the creature in place, while the left hand slit the pink-brown flesh with a penknife.

She had not looked up all along, but she knew He was watching. Before He could say anything, she spoke. In a soft, gentle voice, like a teacher doing a demonstration of a science experiment, or a cookery lesson, she said, 'I'm cutting them.'

'Why?' He asked.

She looked up at last. He could see that she was very pretty. 'It makes them grow,' she said.

He nodded. For a moment, His eyes remained fixed on the sections of pink and brown flesh, then He walked away quickly, without looking back.

They kept telling Him that nobody had to stay. Anybody could leave if he really wanted to go, but that was a trick. Every time you tried to get away, you were caught by one of the guardians, and punished in some subtle way. It wasn't an ordinary punishment, though. Most of the time, you didn't even know you were being punished. The first time He had tried to leave, He'd gone quite far before He met a man in a black coat, standing in the middle of a huge patch of nettles with a sack in his hand. The man looked familiar: he was thin and dark in the face, with long black hair tucked up under his cap and a thick, black moustache. The man was stooping down, peering into the undergrowth, as if he was looking for something, but as soon as he noticed that he was being

156

observed, he stood up straight. After a moment, he lifted his bag from out of the nettles and held it up.

'Do you want to see?' he asked; then, without waiting for an answer, he started out of the nettle pool, towards the path. He looked like he belonged to the woods; he wasn't even a man at all, but something else, from outside time; he had risen up out of the earth one day, like those people in fairy stories. His long black coat seemed so close-fitting, so natural on him, that it might have been part of his body, and the scarf around his neck looked like it was made of fur or hair. When he stepped clear of the nettles, he put down his bag and held it open.

Inside, there were three hedgehogs. They were still alive; He could see their tiny pig-like faces and the tiny feet, small and pinky-brown, straining against the side of the sack. The only time He had seen a hedgehog, it had been curled up tight in a ball, and all He had seen were the spines, but the three in the bag were scrambling around, clambering over one another, trying to find a way out.

He looked up. The man's eyes were large and wet, like a dog's.

'What are they for?' He said.

The man closed the bag again and smiled. 'Don't you know?' he asked.

He shook his head,

'They're for eating,' the man said, still smiling.

For a moment, He thought the man was joking. Then He realised it was true. For the first time, He noticed that the man's face was covered with little holes, all across his cheeks and his nose. Then slowly, like sugar dissolving in a cup, the man began to melt into the air, till there was nothing left except the sack, all crumpled up in a puddle, and spotted with water and mud.

Next day, another man came to see Him. He didn't remember this man from anywhere specific, but He felt sure He had seen him before. The man said his name was Paul. He asked a lot of questions, then he went away. After the man Paul was gone, He started telling Himself a story, but it didn't come out right. It had started quite well, though: it was a Saturday, in early summer, and a young boy was carrying a large mirror in a pine-wood frame through a busy market town. As he reaches the corner of the market square, the boy happens to glance down at the surface of the glass and he sees, not the sky above his head, not the steeple behind him, not the black lacework of trees in the churchyard, not even his own face but, if only for a moment, without time for the sensation fully to sink in, a small hole in nature, an emptiness, a loose stitch which, if pulled, might unravel the universe and show its underlying blackness, a blackness like decay, or like the small local darkness that falls each and every time an animal dies.

THE INSECT STATION

All of a sudden, the house was empty. Clive had gone back to Croydon for the summer, and Steve was in hospital. Mrs Yazz had suggested to Paul that he could stay on for as long as he wanted, at reduced rent, if he would look after things, and didn't mind the painters coming and going. She had told him, weeks before, that she was planning to redecorate the whole of the ground floor over the summer, but she didn't mind if Paul stayed in his room if he didn't mind the smell. Because of the decorating, it seemed important to get the place cleared up as quickly as possible. While Clive prepared to go – the big man was sulking now, as if he was the one who had been wronged – Paul had been obliged to clean out the dim, foul-smelling menagerie at the back of the house surreptitiously, taking the cages, with their dead, void bodies out into the night one by one, and dumping them in rubbish bins all over the city, so no one could trace them back to their origin. He didn't want Mrs Yazz to find out what had been going on in her house, but as he cleared the room he realised, with some surprise, that there was another reason for taking it on. The truth was, he suddenly felt guilty about Steve, sitting out there in the madhouse, thinking about little girls and staring at the day-room wall – he was a human being, after all, and there was no knowing what hell he had suffered, as he presumably

159

tried, and failed, to accommodate his strange hunger. As far as Paul knew, Steve had committed no crime. Somewhat reluctantly, yet driven by a curiosity which shamed him, he had traced his co-tenant and visited him out at Fulbourn a couple of times, but he had been unable to clarify Steve's intentions with regard to the animals. Had he meant to let them die? Had he taken pleasure in watching, as they faded away, becoming no more than phantoms, mere stains on the air, huddled in the fetid nooks and angles of their cheap cages, their eyes huge with hunger and fear? Was it a desire for power that had prompted this demented experiment? Was it curiosity? On that first visit, Paul had been hoping for some kind of answer – but confronted by the thin, heavily medicated spectre he found in the hospital day room, he had not been able to frame the question that he needed to ask. All he really knew was that the cages had to be got rid of before Mrs Yazz's workmen arrived. He had no doubt that, even if he wasn't the one at fault, she would have held him responsible for the state of her house, as the rent-collector and go-between, and would probably have forced him to leave. That would have left him no choice but to head back home, which was the last thing he wanted to do. Richard had found him a job for a few weeks, helping out at one of the biology field stations, and, with the reduced rent, he would be able to stay on for most of the summer. To keep the peace, he would make a token visit home towards the end of August, but at least he wouldn't have to spend the long summer months in his mother's house. He was surprised at how much this meant to him.

Meanwhile, Penny had stopped round for a last visit – a clumsy and somewhat bitter occasion which left Paul feeling guilty and foolish. He had no idea what had transpired between her and Clive, and he had no real interest in finding out, so they had sat in the kitchen, drinking tea, with nothing to say, for half an hour before she finally left. He had asked about her plans for the summer but she hadn't really answered his questions. Perhaps she had sensed his indifference, and this small withholding of information was all she had left to deny him, though she had probably sensed his growing detachment from her long before he had realised, with the usual surprise at how little he understood about his dealings with others, that he hadn't ever liked her very much. He assumed she was heading home to Sussex, though the thought crossed his mind that she might have been stopping off in Croydon on the way. It didn't really matter. At the same time, he was annoyed with himself when, as she rose to leave, he was struck again by the idea that there was something he had failed to understand, some key question that he had not even had the presence of mind to ask. It wasn't until much later, when she was safely gone, and he was alone in Steve's room, sweeping up the last of the straw and droppings that had spilled from the now vanished cages, that it occurred to him that some drama had been enacted – some sudden, perhaps violent, or at least forceful, event, not so much a seduction as a form of insinuation, a drunken and only half-willing assent, out of panic and disgust on Penny's part, to Clive's purposeful, self-righteous desire. He remembered the attention, the almost embarrassing scrutiny, over the months that she had been coming to the house, that Clive had lavished upon Penny – all the stupid remarks about how wonderful she was, and how undeserving Paul had been of such a gorgeous woman – and he wondered if some kind of near-rape hadn't taken place. As soon as the thought formed, however, he put it out of his mind, telling himself that this was just another piece of self-deception; that he was, in fact, flattering himself, in the usual roundabout way, in imagining anything other than the likely course of events – too much wine, a conversation in which things were said that would not otherwise have come to light, a growing frustration, on Penny's part, with Paul's self-absorption, a guilty and pleasurable recognition on Clive's of the opportunity for the most banal form of male betrayal.

It had been a difficult week, but then he had started working and everything had changed. It was a clear, bright summer's morning when he cycled out to Zoology Field Station 3, where he was to meet a man called Tony who would show him what he had to do and pretty much leave him alone from then on. It was to be a simple, undemanding job: Paul would keep the cases clean, tend the gardens, damp down the glasshouses where the special food crops were grown, and sow fresh seed when required. The money wasn't great, but it would be enough to get by. It was only for six weeks, but it was definitely better than going back to another summer of gloom and unspoken accusations from his mother, and that sense of vague frustration and pity for his father which usually plagued him through visits home. The way things were working out, he could be away all day, and Mrs Yazz's painters were usually finished by the time he got back. The silence and the stillness of the house, on these long summer evenings next to the graveyard, was eerie and reassuring, with the others gone, and no further likelihood of a visit from Penny or – hopefully – from anyone else. In a more or less cursory manner, he had tried to contact Nancy a couple of times, but either she hadn't received his messages or she didn't want to see him. Not that it mattered. In his own mind, whatever it was they had shared – whatever sad web of fantasy

162

and self-deception – was over and done with. For now, at least, he was happy to be left alone.

The field station was out on the edge of town, just off the Huntingdon Road. Though there were houses nearby, the land itself was completely closed off to the south and east on the city side, while its north and west aspects, which bordered on wide fields of grain, were shielded by tall hedges of thorn and marcescent beech, which made the place seem remote and quiet, and entirely separate from the rest of the world, a charmed circle, with its own time, its own weather. Paul's new boss was a gentle, somewhat pedantic man, obviously proud of his knowledge and skill with the insects. Tony Barton was tall and thin, dressed in a grimy white lab coat which, even at a distance, smelled of chemicals and damp. From the first, Paul noted in him an extraordinary diffidence: though he was the man in charge and – as Paul was to learn – something of a legend in the Zoology Department for his skill with the insects, he didn't act like a boss, or seem in any way sure of what their working relationship required of him. As Paul pulled up on his Hercules, Tony was there at the gate to meet him; he was carrying an old-fashioned shopping basket, with a thermos flask poking out at the top, and had just left his own bike, perched precariously against the whitewashed wall of one of the outer buildings.

'Hello,' he said. 'I'm Tony.'

Paul hopped down from his bike and took the man's proffered hand. 'I'm Paul,' he said, awkward at having to state the obvious.

'Thought you might be,' Tony said. 'You can leave your bike here. You don't need to lock it.'

Paul set his bike gingerly against the wall.

163

'Nobody even knows we exist out here,' Tony said. 'So it's quite safe.'

They stood a moment, regarding one another, unsure what to do next. Finally Tony grinned. 'Well,' he said. 'Let's start with the grand tour. Then we'll have a cup of tea.'

Paul nodded. 'That's great,' he said, feeling awkward again. From the first, he'd been struck by a kind of remoteness in Tony's bearing, a distance which he sensed would be impossible to cross, a distance intrinsic to the man himself, though it also had to do with the field station, with the sheer seclusion and quiet of the place.

The tour was short and, though they both felt awkward with their roles, Paul found it oddly enjoyable. First, they crossed the narrow lawn and stepped into the main building. At the far end, Paul could see the office, but between them and the inner door was a long, narrow frame greenhouse, full of glass cases set out in rows on lab benches. This room was filled with a heavy, sweet scent; it was so powerful, and so oddly reminiscent of something – of childhood perhaps – that he almost stopped on the threshold to close his eyes and savour it. He resisted the temptation, however, and followed Tony in, pausing at each case as they went, so Tony could identify the insects it contained, and offer some initial advice about care and maintenance. As he spoke, Paul became aware of the noise: not a buzz or a hum so much as a murmur, a sound that seemed vaguely intelligent and purposeful, like some language being spoken that he didn't understand.

'This is my favourite room,' Tony said. 'We keep stick insects here, and some other stuff. Over there is where we were trying to breed swallowtails.' He pointed at a large, empty case full of dried leaves and flower stems. 'But mostly it's locusts,' he continued. 'We use a lot of locusts.'

164

Paul peered into the nearest case; it was packed full of busy, green insects, like grasshoppers, only larger and greener. Tony leaned in and put his head close to the glass.

'Listen,' he said.

Paul lowered his head, but he could hear nothing more than that low murmur.

'I sometimes bring my lunch in here,' Tony said, smiling softly. 'It's very restful. And it's fascinating to watch them, when they shed their skins. They're not skins really, they're exoskeletons. But you know what I mean.'

Paul nodded.

'Look, there's one,' Tony said, stroking the glass with an outstretched finger. 'See how it turns itself upside down, and struggles out from its skin. It's making gravity work for it. There's an intelligence there, wouldn't you say?'

Paul bent dutifully and peered again into the glass case.

'See how bright it is when it's new,' Tony said, his voice hushed with wonder, like the narrator on a television nature programme.

Paul nodded. He wasn't quite sure what he was looking for at first; then he saw, quite clearly, as if he had known what to look for all along, that some of the insects were brighter and newer than the others, almost grass-green, shiny and wet-looking, as if they had just that moment been reborn.

'Wouldn't it be nice if people could do that?' Tony laughed softly, apologetically. 'Well, Something like that. You know.'

'Yes,' Paul answered, feeling it was necessary to say something, no matter how lame. 'I know what you mean.'

Tony gave him a sceptical look and smiled.

'I'm sorry. I get a bit carried away sometimes,' he said. 'I know it sounds a bit daft, but I love these insects. They constantly surprise me.'

He moved on. At the far end of the glasshouse, in a dark alcove between the locust room and the office, he pointed out a series of small cream-coloured metal containers with steel handles, for all the world like half-sized fridges.

'These are where we keep the pods,' he said. 'You don't touch these, okay? Department rules. They're very sensitive. Okay?'

Paul nodded. 'What are they?' he asked.

'They're like incubators, you could say,' Tony said. He looked for a moment like a proud but troubled child who has been burdened with some unexpected responsibility, and must be sure he keeps control of a younger and less trusted brother. 'Anyway, I look after these. Nothing for you to worry about.'

He moved on into the office. It was bright here, far brighter than Paul had expected, and it smelled faintly of something like mothballs.

'This is the office. Would you like some tea?'

Before Paul could answer, Tony had flipped the lid off a small electric kettle and was filling it at a wide old-fashioned sink, the kind you find in old plant nurseries, or botany labs. Standing there, in the gold sunlight, Paul wondered what the tea would taste like, whether it would be tainted with chemicals and sap, and with the thick, deep smell of the breeding insects. Tony smiled and shook his head.

'I'm not used to company,' he said. 'I've been on my own here for a long time.' He put two tea bags into two earthenware mugs. 'I don't have any sugar.'

'That's all right,' Paul said. 'Just a drop of milk is fine.'

Tony smiled. 'I don't have milk either,' he said.

Over the next few days, Paul learned all he needed to know about his new job. As well as the locust room, attached to the office, there were five other buildings: a low hut with brick footings like a prefab, but with no obvious windows: this was where the cockroaches lived; an aluminium-framed glass-house, much wider and taller than the locust room, where the various trays of wheat and grass were kept lush and baize-green in a constant atmosphere of fine mist and warmth; and a long, narrow building, like a small hangar, with separate doors giving on to a series of dark, low rooms full of boxes, old cases, clay pots and plastic seed trays in high stacks, and rows of tools on wall racks. Tony called this the tool shed. At one end, built of the same materials and in the same style as the tool shed, but set slightly apart, was the first of what Paul came to think of as the mystery rooms. This building was kept locked at all times and could never be entered by unauthorised personnel, a fact that Tony impressed upon him with something close to vehemence. It was smaller than the tool shed and, like most of the other buildings on site, had small, high windows. The fact that this room was forbidden was mildly intriguing, but it was the last of the buildings – the other mystery room – that engaged Paul's imagination from the moment he first set foot inside. The Manducca Room. This was one of the only three or four buildings in the country where manduccas, or tobacco moths, were kept; government regulations ordained that they had to be kept apart at all times, in mysterious isolation. The manducca room was, in fact, a room within a room: an outer brick shell, with no windows and a single, narrow door, was set around a separate inner structure, similarly locked and windowless, where the moths were kept. Even though they were separated from the outside world by two walls, even though entry could only be gained via two locked doors, the manduccas were further enclosed by thick gauze nets, which someone had festooned around a wide

167

table, under a single pale-gold bulb. Tony explained that the moths were dangerous, not only to tobacco, which was their usual food-plant, but also to potatoes and tomatoes, which accounted for the heavy protective measures that government and the Zoology Department had imposed. The manduccas could only be moved on site, or even disturbed, with written permission from the Professor of Zoology; they could only be transported to another site by order of a government minister. Fluttering around in their gauze prison, bathed in a constant gold light, these huge, soft insects, unlike any Paul had ever seen, were lovingly tended by Tony, who was even more protective of their lit sanctuary than he was of the locust pods. On his second day at the insect station, however, Paul was allowed to see them and, after an interminable lecture from Tony on procedures, and what to do if a single one of the creatures escaped, he was told he might bring the moths their food on those days when Tony was not on site. The moths lived almost entirely on deadly nightshade, which was cultivated in a long, shady bed at the far end of the garden.

It was an easy job. Paul kept the garden, made sure the glasshouses were properly ventilated and watered down, fed the insects, swept out the dead skins from the locust cases, and filled the rest of his time with general cleaning and tidying, from washing bottles to weeding the deadly nightshade beds. He dumped old peat from the used seed trays into a compost bin behind the glasshouses, and sowed fresh seed, starting new batches of wheat and grass every other day to meet the demands of his charges. The locusts, in particular, were voracious. He had always thought of them in biblical terms; now, at close quarters, he was beginning to see how interesting, even beautiful, they were. He particularly liked to watch as they shed their skins – the way a single insect would find a way to set itself apart in the crowded case, and begin the process, hanging head-down on the glass wall and struggling free, eventually emerging as a new, quite perfect version of itself, leaving the ghost of its old form behind, a dull husk that would remain, clinging to the glass for whole minutes, before it collapsed and dropped to the floor of the case. After a while – when Tony had decided he was to be trusted, and had begun leaving him alone, most days, for hours at a time – he had started having his breaks in the locust room, sitting amidst the deep, green scent of new wheat and the hum of the massed insects in their cases, watching them renew themselves endlessly, as he drank his tea, or ate the sandwiches he had prepared early that morning, before Mrs Yazz's men had arrived.

Tony came and went. He had other, more specialist work to do, and he didn't talk much. Once or twice, Paul saw him disappear into the mystery room beyond the tool sheds, but he never let Paul see what was in there and he never spoke about it when he re-emerged, locking the door carefully behind him. Nevertheless, Paul couldn't help noticing that Tony looked uncomfortable, even unhappy, as he left the hut – which had to be no more than six or eight feet square inside – and it provoked his curiosity about the place. Usually, Tony seemed contented in his job; there were even times when this odd, quiet man reminded Paul of his father. He had the same detachment, the same quiet, intense manner when he worked, the same pleasure in the small task, the same curiosity and attention to detail. And it was true that his father would have enjoyed this work as much as Tony did; he would have felt at home with the stillness of the place, and its apparent isolation; he would have been happy looking after the insects. What set men like Tony and his father apart, Paul thought, was that

169

they didn't need other people to be contented; they were comfortable with *things* – materials and tools, animals and plants, stones and water were as significant to such men as other human beings, perhaps even more so. Sitting in the locust room, eating his packed lunch, Paul remembered the time his father had found a nest of baby spiders in a berberis shrub he was about to clip in the garden and had immediately stopped work, letting the bush stand unpruned for weeks, so the animals could grow and move away. That afternoon, he had called Paul out to see them – fifty or more tiny spiderlings with ochre and brown markings, hanging in a sleeve of gossamer amidst the protective thorns of the barberry; when he saw that Paul was interested in his find, his father had fetched a magnifying glass from his shed, and they had studied the animals, finding the details of the markings and the face that were invisible to the naked eye. Yet it was only now, thinking back to that day, when he couldn't have been more than five or six years old, that Paul understood how well his father had managed things. Another man might have made an education out of the moment; he would have had Paul study the spiders, make notes, look them up in a book at the library; but his dad hadn't done that. He had just made a space for Paul's own observations. Looking back, years later, Paul was surprised at how strong and clear the memory was, how it tapped down to something deep in his mind, some area of separation and stillness that he had not been aware of till now, a sense, not of pride, but of something deeper and purer, a kind of aseity, a reservoir of affection, not only for Tony and his father, but also, more surprisingly, for himself.

Meanwhile, outside work, he lived a slow, uneventful life. With everyone gone for the summer, the house seemed oddly quiet and remote, and there were times when he felt happier there than he had ever been anywhere. It was as if some essence, some taint from the field station had infected him, and was turning him into another version of Tony, detached, silent, distant from everything that was going on around him. He had quickly fallen into a routine. In the mornings, he would rise early, before the workmen came, and cycle up to the field station, where two or three days out of every five he was alone with his charges. Sometimes he stayed on in the evenings to watch the locusts, or to sit in the office, listening to the quiet that seemed to extend for miles around him. When he cycled home at the end of the day, shrouded in the peculiar scent of the insects, he felt like an alien in the world he had imagined he knew so well.

Weekends were much the same. The city had been transformed for the summer into a new, unfamiliar place, home to gaggles of French schoolchildren, to helpless Italian and Swiss language students trying to master bikes or punts for the first time in their lives, to Japanese and American tourists who wandered the streets in droves with their big, fancy cameras, in search of the special angle, the instant of revelation, that would fix the moment in their minds forever. For Paul, there was something poignant about this quest, though he wasn't altogether sure why. The pictures he took bore no resemblance to the tourists' snapshots, his motives were entirely different, he knew that time could not be frozen, that nothing could be more dissimilar than memory and photography. He remembered an old saying – he thought it was Chinese, but he wasn't certain: *he who remembers, forgets.* Something along those lines. Memory had its own dynamic: something crucial could lie hidden for years, then emerge, when the time was right, yet it didn't matter if the memory was exact, it wasn't necessary that it be a replica of the event that had happened years before. On the contrary, what mattered was the alchemical process that had been going on under the surface in the intervening years – what mattered, in other words, was the transformation itself, the secret process by which the memory appeared to move away, to betray the remembered event, but in fact fulfilled another purpose altogether, some purpose beyond recollection, a purpose that belonged to the present, and not the past: renewal, say, or revelation. What mattered was the transformation. Fidelity had nothing to do with it.

So why take pictures at all? The Japanese tourists, who had saved for years to make this one trip, and would probably never come again, the Italian kids who were away from home for the first time, falling in love or getting drunk or just walking, alone and unsupervised, in the Botanics or around the market, the American art lovers passing through on their way to some place else, stopping just long enough to do the Fitzwilliam and Kettle's Yard – all of them had every reason to want to record the moment. They had worked for this, they had saved and planned and travelled miles through occasionally hostile terrain. They probably knew they were on a wild goose chase – it would take an absurd arrogance, Paul thought, to look down on them. They probably were all too aware of the fact that the camera captured nothing, that it recorded nothing but an illusion. They probably even understood that, in their eagerness for a record that would fix them forever in front of the Fitzwilliam steps, or King's Chapel, they were losing the experience of the moment, deferring it to a later date, in order to share it with their family and friends. But then, that was what mattered to them: not to be there, amongst strangers, not to have an experience that didn't matter, with people who didn't count, but to be seen to be having that experience by the people they cared about, to share it, to capture it and bring it home. Paul had wondered, from time to time, why men and women with top-of-the-range equipment, with beautiful new cameras and powerful lenses that he couldn't afford, and would have put to quite different uses – why they, who must have known better, would photograph a wife or a husband, or a friend, tiny and insignificant, in front of a huge public building. They must have known how absurd the human figure would look, isolated in the corner of the frame, dwarfed by the classical pillars or the high windows and spires. Yet, in the end, he had come to realise that this was the whole point: what mattered wasn't the image of the chapel; what mattered was the fact of being there, of being seen. It was a way of becoming visible, in a series of significant places, and so constructing a story, which could be told, again and again, in the years to come.

As it happened, Paul usually took fewer pictures in the summer, because of the light. Spring and autumn were better suited to his purposes. This year, however, with the work at the field station, he began to see a whole new set of possibilities – possibilities that had much less to do with light than with the suggestion of something present, but not quite visible – like the photographs he had taken in the streets around his house, or the bakery, or the empty greens and meadows at first light. For the first time it was interesting to take photographs in plain daylight, of the various insect houses, and their ordinary surroundings, or even of the interiors, with their sunlit or darkened cases set out in rows, the locusts or stick insects or various lepidoptera not quite in focus, lit boxes of energy and motion, like versions of some abstract or unspecified life. One day, when Tony was off-site,

Paul sneaked out the key to the manducca house and, with his tripod and his bag of lenses, let himself into the dim, nightshade-scented room. He had no intention of photographing the moths themselves, or even of disturbing them: what he wanted was the veiled space within which they were obliged to dwell, a space whose shape was quite different from the manducca room itself, lit by its single bulb, the heavy nets cascading from the roof, filled with light and moving shadows. From the photograph, no one would be able to tell what form of life lived in that space, but that was entirely the point. The moths moved about in their private light, like spirits, and if Paul's plan was successful, if he managed to take the picture he wanted, it was their spirits, not their physical presence that he would – not capture, like an anthropologist capturing a pygmy's soul, but reveal, the way beauty is revealed in a magic trick, or a circus act. It was a form of magic he was after now, a form of alchemy. In a way, he was no different from those tourists with their expensive Leicas. He was trying to tell a story which could be repeated, and so alter the facts of his temporal life – to become a participant, or a celebrant, rather than a witness. The detached observer he had originally intended to be was a remote and improbable fantasy to him now. With the insect station pictures – matter of fact, even banal in the execution – he had become a different kind of photographer, and – though it felt silly and grandiose to take the idea seriously – a different kind of person.

For the first time, he was taking the pictures he wanted to take, photographs that, in some mysterious way, matched his thinking. For months now, he had been mulling over the story of Orpheus – not so much the tale of his descent into Hades, or the recovery of Eurydice, as that element of the myth which said that Orpheus could make things – rocks,

174

trees, even animals — come into being merely by singing. It seemed true to him, this story: more true, more fundamental than the rest of the tale. It wasn't that Orpheus actually created animals and plants out of nothing, like the Christian God, it was obvious that this was not the intention of the myth. It was more that the essential creative act was one of seeing, and making seen, for the first time, the true nature of the world, a world that had seemed given, and finished, and entirely nameable until that moment. Until Orpheus sang, the animals were mere objects, named and forgotten and shrouded in the contempt bred of familiarity; afterwards, however, they were new, they had become strange. They were themselves once again, and not the creatures men had taken for granted. Even rocks, or trees, or rivers were affected by Orpheus' speech: all of these things emerged, alive and shining, made other in the poet's song. In the same way, things emerged in photographs by Kertész, say, or Carleton Watkins, or Raymond Moore. People said photography wasn't a real art, but that was a social thing, a form of absurd snobbery, a received opinion that they were too lazy to examine. In the myth of Orpheus, Paul saw the key to the argument that anything could be an art, so long as it performed this Orphic function, this liberation of the thing — the rock, the horse, the Nissen hut, the road junction — from its object-state, from its deadening familiarity, from the fixity of its name and supposed definition. He wasn't sure when he had decided this, but at some point he had come to believe that photography was, or could be, this Orphic art form, the art that brought us back to the things themselves. Language was too difficult; it was too socialised. People would get lost in the words, in the possible semantics; it was too much of an invitation to the ego to write or to speak. What was needed was an essentially silent work. Better to simply

175

connect with things in themselves, and to show the connection – a meaningless, almost involuntary communion with things as they happened to be; if anything could free things from their names, as Orpheus had done, it would be a certain form of photograph, a way of picturing the world from which all invested meaning had been stripped away, a neutral, and so natural act. The point of the exercise was a continual re-estrangement from the given. There were times when he believed this – and there were other, clearer moments when such theory melted away and he was left alone with the act of seeing, a point at which silence really was possible, a detachment from himself and from things, a letting go, an admission of powerlessness which seemed, for minutes at a time, the key to what he wanted to do.

Over the next few weeks, life continued in a kind of vacuum. He saw nobody; he did nothing; he went nowhere, other than work and an occasional trip to the swimming pool on Parkside. At night, he felt happy in the empty house; he would stay up late, or rise early in the morning, when it was still dark, and stand in the back room looking out over the graveyard. There was no news of Steve, though Clive wrote a curt letter towards the end of July to say he would not be coming back after the holidays. A day later, a postcard arrived from Penny. She was friendly, almost chatty, in the little space she had allotted herself for this one communication, but the only information she conveyed was that she needed him to return a book she had lent him. There was an address, which he did not recognise, to which the book could be sent.

It was getting warmer. The papers had forgotten about the rapist; people had started leaving their windows open again. There was an almost party atmosphere after the months of fear. It felt odd, being alone, coming home or waking to an empty house, with all this fuss and life going on around him; at the same time, Paul realised he had never been so happy. He remembered an experiment he had read about, where people were kept in isolation, in quiet, neutral rooms, fed only the most basic foodstuffs, exposed to the absolute minimum of external stimuli; the theory was that they would become paranoid and withdrawn, that they would lapse into madness, without the basic contact with the world that ordinary people take for granted. Yet Paul could think of nothing he would have enjoyed more, for a while at least: more often than not, he felt he was too exposed, too available; there was never time to slow down and register things, to take stock, to be who he was. Spending the days alone – doing his chores at the insect station, or reading, or listening to music – he began to detach himself from the noise and clamour of the world; his nights became richer; he started sleeping for six or seven hours at a time. Now his dreams were intense and vivid and, at the same time, impeccable in their logic: orderly visions of motorway journeys or the house of the self, or perhaps some memory of childhood: the not-known-then suddenly revealed; things slipping into place and becoming comprehensible. He would wake and the room would be fixed in moonlight like the world in an early collotype; the garden would be bright and still; the houses along the street would be utterly silent, as if they had suddenly emptied, leaving him alone in a rational world. There were times, as he lay there in the cool of the dawn, when he felt this was the only world that was real, that the rest was an illusion or, at best, a compromise. He had the impression that this world was a distinct space, a place where a man could stay forever, if he only had the will and the discipline. It was a world that had its own laws, its own order.

In such a world, you could go beyond conventional logic, without going against it. You travelled with that logic to a certain point, then the road petered out, and you had to find another way of going on, of moving forward. It wasn't that the order of the universe was incomplete – there was nothing supernatural or mystical about this world. All you could say about it was that it existed somewhere beyond the ordinary maps. Somewhere in his mind, it had a name, an appropriate designation, but for a long time he couldn't work out what it was. It was familiar and strange, empty and full, private and, at the same time, wholly impersonal. It had nothing to do with anybody else and – at the same time – beyond doubt and beyond verification, he knew that it was his father's world.

He hadn't seen anyone for days. He was sealed into his own silent world of pictures and slow cycle rides across town to the field station. At night, he looked through his old contact sheets and prints, or he sat for hours with the two slim volumes of Raymond Moore photographs he had managed to acquire, studying a single picture for hours at a time. Then, towards the end of July, Richard came round to the house and announced that he was going to a party.

'You have to come, too,' he said. 'This is my last party. Well, the last in Cambridge anyway.'

'What do you mean, your last?' Paul had noticed something different about Richard as soon as he had opened the door. His friend seemed tense and nervous, almost manic.

Richard smiled softly and shook his head. 'I'm leaving,' he said. 'I've had enough of Cambridge.'

'Leaving?' Paul was dumbfounded. Richard had always seemed as much a part of Cambridge as Parker's Piece, or the University Library. 'Where are you going?'

178

'Spain,' he said. 'I'm going to Spain. Probably. Or maybe somewhere else. But first – we're going to a party.'

'Well. This is a bit sudden—'

'I'll explain on the way. Come on. I said I'd meet Gina there, and I'm already late.'

The party was being held in a large house off Grange Road. Paul remembered that he had been there before, some time towards the end of his first year, but he couldn't remember the occasion. Richard would have taken him, in those early days when they had first known one another: all he recalled of the place was a sense of mysterious luxury – mysterious, because it was a student house, inhabited by a solitary, odd-looking boy named Alex – and a vivid image of the garden, which ran from a series of French windows at the back of the house to a small apple and cherry orchard, lit on the occasion of his first visit with hundreds of coloured lights. As far as he could recall, it had been his first party in Cambridge, a first glimpse of an entirely other way of life: people out on the lawn drinking champagne, others going off into the orchard in pairs, their faces illumined by the fairy lights, the boy Alex, at the centre of the lawn, setting off a hot-air balloon that rose into the night sky, a tight packet of gas and fire, floating away into the distance. At the time, he had not known that this was as much theatre to these people as it was to him; he had thought it was just how they lived, that they took their charmed existence for granted.

Almost as soon as they arrived, Richard disappeared – to look for Gina, Paul supposed. Alone, he scanned the room, which was already crowded with elegant, self-conscious people, mostly around Paul's age, though there were a few older men amongst the crowd. He was looking for Alex. He remembered him as slender, rather effete, with thick dark hair

179

and a cold bruise of a mouth, like a character out of a Cocteau film, defined utterly by his strangeness and by the vague suggestion of gorgeous – and wholly artificial – vice that surrounded his pale, thin body like an aura. On their first fleeting encounter – a shouted introduction in a crowded room – he had assumed the boy was gay; later, however, it turned out that he was something of a ladies' man. Indeed, in spite, or perhaps because of his appearance, women found him very attractive. Or so Richard had said. Paul had found this difficult to understand: he had, on admittedly brief acquaintance, come to think of Alex as an exotic, but essentially sexless creature, an odd, wholly accidental being, like some cross between a rare animal and a circus clown. Now, he found himself looking for the strange boy, going from one room to the next, searching him out, though he had no idea why.

Finding Alex took a little while. Finally, Paul saw him with two girls in identical white dresses and a tall, slender boy with a shaven head, standing at the edge of the lawn, looking up at the sky. Someone had let off a hot-air balloon: bigger and more colourful than the one than Paul had seen at the last party, it was suspended above the orchard, just ten feet or so above the trees. Alex looked excited.

'It's too heavy,' he said to the others. 'It's going to fall.'

'Nonsense.' The boy with the shaven head laughed. 'They don't just fall.'

'Of course they do,' Alex replied. 'They have to come down somewhere.'

'Not until they've exhausted their fuel supply.' The boy with the shaven head lit a cigarette, illuminating the little group. Even from a distance, Paul could see that Alex was wearing some kind of black eye make-up; he was dressed in a turquoise shirt, with tight white trousers and turquoise deck

180

shoes; beside him, the other boy, who was a little older and more conventionally handsome, seemed almost austere. One of the girls looked familiar, though Paul couldn't recall where he had seen her before, but it was the other one, the taller of the two, a serene, dark-haired girl of about twenty, who caught his eye, as the foursome stood watching the balloon hover, then finally rise and swim away into the dark. He waited by the drinks table on the patio by the French window till they turned and walked back towards the house.

'We need another drink,' Alex said, as they reached the table. The party were just a few feet away now but Alex hadn't recognised Paul, who had stepped aside into the shadows by a large potted shrub. Instead, the boy found a bottle of wine and started charging the girls' glasses. Just as Paul worked out that the shorter of the two girls, the one he had recognised, was in fact Jacqui from Belinda's, Richard appeared at the French doors. He was alone.

'Hi, Alex,' he said. 'Do you know where Gina is?'

Alex shook his head. 'I haven't seen her,' he said. 'Have a drink.'

Richard shook his head. 'I was supposed to meet her here,' he said. He was obviously anxious about something.

'She's not coming.'

Richard looked over at Jacqui, who was watching him with a half-amused, half-annoyed expression. 'What do you mean, she's not coming?' he said.

'I mean, she's not coming,' said Jacqui, quietly. From his vantage point in the shadows, Paul could see that she was enjoying the moment. 'She's staying home.'

Richard looked worried. 'She said she would meet me here,' he said.

'I think that was before she found out about your little trip.'

'What?'

'You heard.' Jacqui smiled sweetly. 'You shouldn't go talking about your plans to all and sundry.' She turned to the others and laughed. 'Careless talk costs lives,' she said quietly. The boy with the shaven head laughed with her, but Paul could see that Alex was not amused.

'Shut up, Jacqui,' he said. 'Can't you see that he's upset.'

'No kidding.' Jacqui's tone was withering. 'Well, I'd say what goes around, comes around.' She grabbed the shaven-headed boy's arm and started off towards the orchard. 'Come on, Marcus,' she said. 'I need some air.'

As the pair walked away across the lawn, Paul took a few steps further into the dark. He hoped Richard hadn't seen him. At the same time, he was still transfixed by the dark-haired girl. She had not spoken, but she looked as unhappy about the scene Jacqui had created as Alex obviously was. By the light from the house, Paul could see her face more clearly now, and he was taken off-guard by what he saw. Though he was sure he had never met this girl before, it was as if he knew her, as if he had known her all his life, and then before that, from some other place, some other time. The thought struck him as absurd even as it came to him, yet he couldn't shake it off. He could not take his eyes off her. Even as Alex tried to reassure Richard, even as the three went back inside, he was watching her, willing her to turn and see him there, standing at the edge of the light – to see him just once, and somehow recognise him as he had recognised her.

'It's all right,' Alex was saying. 'We'll go inside and call her at home. You can talk to her.'

Richard said something in reply, but Paul couldn't make out what it was. A moment later they were gone, and he was alone in the dark, his mind floating away, like the hot-air balloon, on its own small flame, into the emptiness of the sky.

A couple of hours later, the party was beginning to run down. Paul had wandered back and forth, pretending to look for Richard, or hovering at the edge of a conversation, or a piece of adolescent theatre, hoping to get a chance to speak to the girl he had seen in the garden. Once or twice, amidst the crowd, he had caught her eye, and once she had smiled at him, though Paul had no idea whether this was a sign of the recognition he was looking for, or just the general good humour that the occasion demanded. In spite of the fact that he spent the next couple of hours in her immediate vicinity, however, he was unable to speak to her. Either she was with Alex, or someone else, or she was moving away across the room, going to greet someone, or disappearing into one of the bedrooms. Meanwhile, he drifted. He didn't know anyone at the party and, as he listened in on, or caught snatches of conversation, he was glad of that. Eventually, he found Richard in a small room off the hall: his friend was drunk, sitting alone in an armchair in the corner by a standard lamp, with a large-format book spread out on his knees.

'What are you reading?' he asked.

Richard looked up quickly. His eyes were bleary, but he was smiling softly – whether in greeting, or at some thought he'd been having, Paul wasn't sure. 'I'm not reading,' he said. 'I'm looking at the pictures.'

'Oh.' Paul stepped forward. Even from where he was standing, with the book upside down and at an angle, he could make out a photograph by Richard Avedon. It was the famous picture of Avedon's sister Louise, on the shore at Long Beach, taken when the artist was still only a boy.

'Did you know,' Richard continued, his voice slurring just a little, 'did you know that Avedon loved his sister so much that he took a picture of her and taped the negative to his arm, so that the sun would burn her image into his skin?'

Paul nodded. 'I've read that story, too,' he said.

Richard smiled sadly. 'Of course,' he said. 'Still, I'll bet you've never burned someone's picture into your skin. I'll bet you never did that.'

'You're right,' Paul said. 'I never did that.' He couldn't recall ever seeing Richard this drunk.

'Neither have I,' Richard said. He was staring at the photograph. 'But now that I think about it, I wish I had.'

Paul shook his head. This self-indulgent mood was beginning to annoy him. 'Maybe you ought to get home,' he said.

Richard looked up. Paul couldn't help seeing the hurt in his face.

'Gina didn't come,' Richard said. 'Alex wanted me to call her, but I couldn't. Apparently, she found out that I'm going away.'

'I see. You didn't tell her yourself, then?'

Richard shook his head. 'I wanted to,' he said. 'But I couldn't.' He stood up suddenly, and the book slipped to the floor. 'I'm going to see her,' he said. 'I have to explain.' He took a few random steps in Paul's direction, then stopped. There were tears in his eyes. 'I really love her,' he said.

Paul nodded. 'I know,' he said, hoping he sounded more sympathetic than he felt. He wasn't at all sure what Richard thought he was doing. All of a sudden, he was planning to just up sticks and go to Spain, or somewhere – this was all the explanation he had given Paul, as they had made their way to the party earlier in the evening – and now he was surprised that Gina was upset about it. Yet he wasn't really upset, he was

184

just maudlin, and annoyed at having been caught out. Not for the first time the thought passed through Paul's mind that Richard had planned to just go, and to say nothing. All of a sudden, that seemed his style.

'I just don't love her that much,' Richard continued, and Paul was amazed as the man who, a moment ago, had appeared so unhappy, flopped back into the chair from which he had just risen, his face contorted with laughter.

'What a joke,' he said, gasping out the words. He couldn't stop laughing. He was even rocking in his chair. 'Look at me. You don't think any of this is serious, do you?'

Paul watched and waited. He didn't know what to say.

'All right, all right, all right.' Richard sat up straight and tried to steady himself. 'All right.' He stood up again. 'What say we go and see if we can't find ourselves another drink?' he said, his voice clear now, his face composed. He crossed the room and put his hand on Paul's shoulder. 'This could be our last drink together. We ought to make the most of it. Don't you think?'

Paul shook his head sadly. 'Let's do that,' he said, with an attempt at a smile. He didn't want to be angry, or upset. He just wanted to get back to the party.

Paul didn't find the dark-haired girl till the party was almost over. Richard was in the sitting room, talking to Alex and another man, while Jacqui and the shaven-headed boy sat listening, like a pair of sullen monkeys, huddled up together on the sofa. Alex was stoned, but he was happy and – to Paul's surprise – Richard seemed happy, too. He was talking about photography and love and the picture by Avedon, but he was making it funny now – funny and a little absurd, a piece of surrealist nonsense about photography and mirrors and the

185

ways in which one person went about stealing another's soul. After a few minutes of this nonsense, Paul got up and went out into the garden.

It was a beautiful night. The sky was full of stars – though it occurred to Paul, as he crossed the lawn, that they might as easily have been hot-air balloons, receding into the distance, from parties just like this one, all over the country. He was wondering where the balloon had gone, the one that Alex and his friends had launched earlier, when he saw the dark-haired girl standing under a tree at the edge of the orchard. She was looking up too, but not at the sky. She was gazing up into the tree.

'Are you going to climb it?'

Paul was aware of how silly he sounded but it didn't matter. All that mattered was that, unexpectedly, he was here alone with this beautiful girl.

The girl smiled and shook her head. 'There's something up there,' she said. She had a soft, barely perceptible Irish accent. 'I saw it.'

Paul was close to her now. He looked up into the branches of the apple tree. 'It's probably a bird,' he said.

The girl shook her head. 'I don't think so,' she said. 'It was bigger.'

'A cat, then?'

'Bigger than that.'

Paul nodded. 'Maybe it's an elephant,' he said. He peered up into the dark. 'They get lost sometimes.' He caught hold of a branch and pulled himself up. 'When they do, they take shelter in trees.' The tree creaked a little under his weight. He could see the fruits, tight and green and hard, amongst the thick, dark leaves. He took a moment to look around, then dropped back to earth. 'Can't see anything,' he said.

'Maybe it's hiding.'

'Maybe.'

'Or camouflaged.'

'Could be.' Paul remembered that there was a children's joke about this, though he couldn't recall the details. Something about elephants in trees with painted toenails. Now, by the light from the house, he could see the girl more clearly. She was smiling, but he wasn't sure if she was just being polite. He hoped she wasn't. At the same time, he felt a slight rush of panic. At any moment, he knew, this girl would disappear. She would go back into the house, or someone would come to find her, and he would never see her again.

'Do you know how the elephant got its name?' he said, quickly.

'No.'

'It's an old story,' Paul continued. 'It seems God told Adam to go out and name all the animals. Which he did. He took a clipboard and a sheet of paper, and walked around the garden, choosing names for everything he saw. Giraffe. Wild boar. Hedgehog. Rattlesnake . . .'

The girl smiled indulgently. She probably thought he was a complete idiot.

'When he had finished, Adam went to God and presented him with the list. He was quite pleased with himself, actually. And God was pleased, too. He liked most of the names. There was just one that bothered him. "What about this last one," God said. "Why did you call it an *elephant*?" And Adam said, "Because it looks like an elephant."'

The girl smiled. 'I've heard it before,' she said.

'So have I,' Paul answered, without missing a beat. 'Only it was funnier when I heard it. My name is Paul,' he added, surprising himself. 'I'm a friend of Richard's.'

187

The girl nodded. 'Hannah,' she said. 'I'm a friend of Alex's.'

'Ah.'

Hannah laughed. 'What do you mean – ah?' she said.

'Nothing. Just ah.'

'I see.' Hannah peered up into the tree. 'Well, anyway,' she said. 'It's gone now. Whatever it was.'

At that very moment, a light appeared on the far side of the lawn. Hannah turned. It was Jacqui.

'They're looking for me, I think,' Hannah said.

Paul nodded.

'So.' Hannah stood watching him. 'I'd better go.'

'Okay.' Paul felt like a fool. He could see that Jacqui was already making her way towards them across the lawn. If he could only say something more. If he could only speak. But now, as the moment fizzled away, he couldn't think of anything.

'Hannah?' Jacqui sounded sober and mildly annoyed. 'Where are you?'

With a last look at Paul, a look that seemed both amused and puzzled, Hannah turned and crossed the lawn, meeting the other girl halfway. Paul stayed where he was. Jacqui seemed not to have noticed him and, after a moment, the two women went indoors.

Paul waited a while, then followed. Inside, there was no sign of the girls, or of the shaven-headed boy, but Alex was there, standing in the middle of the room while Richard, who was also on his feet, made ready to leave. 'The wanderer returns,' he cried, as Paul came in from the dark. 'You coming?'

Paul nodded and, after the usual farewells and thanks, they

set off into the dark. As they walked, Paul set about teasing out of Richard what he could about Hannah.

'Who is she?'

'Who – Hannah?' Richard seemed amused. 'You're out of luck there,' he said. 'She's Alex's fiancée.'

'His what?' Paul tried to sound calm. 'I didn't know Alex had a fiancée.'

'Well, that's Alex for you.' Richard shook his head. 'He's a dark horse.' He laughed. 'Still, I wouldn't let that get in your way.'

'Meaning?'

'Nothing.' Richard gave him a quick, searching glance. 'Only it occurred to me that Hannah would be exactly your type. Nice-looking. Intelligent. Unattainable.' He allowed himself a sufficient pause, before continuing. 'Should suit you down to the ground, I wouldn't wonder,' he concluded, with a mocking and – or was it just Paul's imagination – a somewhat melancholy grin.

Maybe Tony had decided his assistant was coming in late, or having a day off, that morning, a week after the party, when Paul finally got to see inside the room beyond the tool sheds. As it happened, he had set out earlier than usual: it was a fine morning, with just a hint of summer mist on the Backs as he headed out to the field station; he had it in mind to take a few pictures before he started work – outdoor photographs of the sheds and glasshouses, and maybe the locust room as it looked first thing, with the early morning sunlight filtering in through the leaves of the hedge trees. He was half-embarrassed by the idea. In some ways, it felt like cheating – too much of what he had in mind resembled photographs he had seen by Moore – but he'd thought to give it a try, to see if he could learn

189

something by going through the same procedures, thinking in the same pictures, the way artists were supposed to sit for years in museums and galleries, copying the works of the masters. And maybe it really was that simple, to begin with. To learn the technique, maybe what you had to do was imitate the best models you knew; not necessarily the recognised greats, but people like Moore, or Kertész, people who had already been where he wanted to go.

He had been delayed, however, when he punctured a tyre halfway along Queen Street and, with no repair kit in his bag, he had been obliged to chain the bike to a fence-post and walk the rest of the way. It wasn't that far, but it set him back a good fifteen minutes or so. When he finally arrived at the field station, there was no sign of Tony, so, determined to make the most of his time, Paul carried on working for as long as he could. He had walked around the perimeter of the site, along the hedge that bordered the fields, looking inward, finding angles, seeking out odd pools of light or shade for about half an hour, then he had found something interesting at the back of the cockroach house and forgotten the time. In the meantime, Tony had obviously turned up and, seeing no bike propped against the wall of the tool sheds, had naturally assumed that Paul had not yet arrived. It was his practice to deal with the mystery room and the incubators when his assistant was off-site – Paul had already figured out that much; on this occasion, however, he was uncharacteristically careless. When Paul had finished at the back of the cockroach building and emerged into the sunlight of the main lawn, he found the door of the mystery room unlocked and slightly ajar. A minute later, or five minutes earlier, he wouldn't have had the opportunity to see inside – it turned out that Tony had actually seen him from the office window as he crossed the lawn and had hurried to intercept him, but he was too slow. By the time he got there, Paul had had enough of a glimpse inside to see what was going on.

The room was even smaller than he had imagined and, unlike the other rooms, it was almost empty. There were no cases, no tools, only a single narrow structure like a lab bench, about three feet high, bolted to the floor in the middle of the room. The bench was old, worn smooth at the edges and blotched and ring-stained all over its surface; it ran almost the length of the room. Across the top, three narrow wooden boards had been fixed with screws, about a foot apart, and on each board a rabbit sat perfectly motionless, staring up at Paul with wide, desperate eyes. Later, when he went through the scene in his mind, trying to find some other explanation than the most obvious one, what struck Paul as the worst part of it was that the rabbits were of the large, flop-eared, cuddly kind that children kept, one of them black and white, with a very pink nose, the other two reddish brown with white muzzles. The animals were breathing hard, their eyes large and wet and somehow darker than they ought to have been, their plump sides heaving against the leather straps which circled them at the midriff and neck, and pinned them to the boards, to which the straps were attached with large metal buckles. The room was visible for no more than thirty seconds, but that was enough not only to see how helpless and terrified the creatures were, but also to surmise what was being done to them – or one of them, at least – before Tony stepped up and slammed the door shut. The black and white rabbit, the one with the pink nose, had a small, rectangular patch shaved clean on its flank, a clean, greyish patch of skin, bisected by what appeared to be a small, very clean incision. It was all Paul saw before the door clicked shut, but it was enough.

191

Tony was angry and guilty at once. It was his fault that Paul had seen anything, and he knew it – which was all the more reason for him to go on the offensive.

'What are you doing?' he said, his normally soft voice rising unnaturally. 'You know this building is out of bounds.'

Paul didn't speak. He could see Tony was worried about what he might do or say, about the possible repercussions if this got about. At the same time, there was no doubting that the man didn't like this side of the job – a chore he had been living with, presumably, for weeks, or even months – any more than Paul did, which was why he was so angry. He probably suspected Paul of just waiting for this opportunity to discover his secret. Yet, the truth was that, distracted by thoughts about the photographs he had been taking, Paul had responded automatically to the open door: he had thought someone else had come on-site, while he had been messing about with the camera, and either forced or picked the lock. His first impulse had been to close the door, without even looking in. Over the weeks, he had decided it was none of his business anyway; he had developed an almost filial loyalty to Tony and, besides, he couldn't have imagined it was anything bad. Certainly nothing like this. But he couldn't say this. It felt like an excuse: like a small boy who has accidentally done wrong, trying to justify himself; now, having seen what he had seen, he didn't feel he needed to excuse himself. He was disgusted. He just wanted to get his stuff together and go home.

Back in the office, Tony made the usual pot of tea and reverted to his normal, soft-spoken, kindly manner. The experiment, he said, was fully sanctioned by the Zoology Department; it was part of a long-term study of insect–borne

192

diseases being conducted by one of the senior researchers and might one day bring real benefits to humankind. In its present form, the experiment was not dangerous to humans; Tony stressed that Paul should not worry about himself, a thought which had not, until that moment, even occurred to him. Nevertheless, the subjects had to be kept isolated, in order that the research might not be compromised. Paul had never heard Tony speak like this. The terminology was not his, it was officialspeak, a form of words that Tony had adopted – and had probably even rehearsed – for just such an occasion, just as he had adopted the grimy white lab coat that he always wore, as being somehow appropriate to the scientific nature of the job. Paul didn't know how much of this story to believe – especially the part about the benefits to humankind – but he was surprised to realise that he didn't really care. As he'd stood in the doorway, his camera frozen in his hands, the image of Steve's bedroom had returned to him: the dead and dying animals, the stench of decay, the darkness of the cages where the few surviving creatures lay, gasping out their last breath. There was no doubt in his mind that this experiment and Steve's menagerie of horrors were part of the same human story, the same ugly continuum. These animals – like pets, like the exotic creatures in zoos and television nature programmes – all these animals were objects, nothing but things to be used, whether for pleasure or profit, as the need or the whim arose. For the first time – and he saw, with a sudden shock, as if someone had just this moment told him that he was the unknowing participant in a crime – for the first time since he had come to the insect station, he stopped to ask himself just what all these locusts and cockroaches and tobacco moths they were breeding were actually *for*. What function could they fulfil in a zoology department, other than the most obvious one?

Tony had made the tea and poured him a cup. Now he had stopped talking and was sitting at the big desk where he kept his papers. Paul remembered that, once, when he had been looking for something, he had noticed that the drawers of this desk, like the rabbit room, had been locked.

'You've had a bit of a surprise,' Tony said.

Paul nodded. He felt sick and unhappy.

'Maybe you should take the rest of the day off,' Tony continued. 'Go home, take it easy. I'll take care of things here.'

Paul couldn't argue. When he tried to speak, he found he had no words for this man who, until ten minutes ago, he had come to think of as a friend.

'Go on,' Tony said. 'I'll see you tomorrow.'

And with a nod, Paul had gone, back out into the sunshine, past the tool shed, past the locked room where the rabbits lay, and away into the noise and heat and bustle of the city.

He finally met Hannah again two days later, on a wet Saturday afternoon, on Gonville Place, opposite the YMCA. He had been in town, buying film, and was on his way home when a sudden windy squall blew up. It would have made most sense just to run for the shelter of the Y; instead, he stood in under one of the big silver limes at the edge of the Piece. It was something he liked doing, and not just when it rained. In summer, the scent of the flowers was rich and heady; the trees would be full of bees, or literally dripping with honeydew; on wet days, there was a cool sweetness under the branches that always took him back to childhood, to afternoons he had spent in one of his hiding places, under a stand of sycamores

194

out along the coast path. Besides, when the weather turned wet, or cold, the Piece would clear, and he experienced an odd satisfaction, seeing that wide, green space in the middle of the town, suddenly void and still, like an empty theatre. He had photographed it on several occasions, but he had never captured the sense of space. At night, with the lamps lit, it worked better, but he still had not worked out how to take pictures in the daytime, when there was nothing for the eye to fix upon, when what he wanted was exactly that lack of a focal point. It was the same on the few occasions he had been out on the fens; time and again, the same question had come up: how do you picture absence? How do you photograph the space where a tree has just been cut down and hauled away, and convey both the disappearance of the tree and the new space after a felling?

He had been standing a while, lost in thought, before he became aware of Hannah. She could have been there for some time, maybe a minute or more, for all he knew: when she first spoke, she was close to him, only a foot or two away, and there was a stillness about her, as if she had always been present: an elemental, a part of the tree's very life, like the perfume of the flowers, or the sound of the rain in the leaves.

'Looking for elephants?' she said at last, when she saw that he had finally realised he was not alone.

'Sorry.' He felt suddenly foolish and awkward. 'I didn't see you.'

She was even more beautiful, he thought, than she had seemed at the party. Her long, dark hair was tied up in a loose bun behind her head, but a few strands had gone astray; her eyes were dark, almost ink-black; from the set of her mouth he guessed, not only that she was amused by something, but that he was the source of her amusement. Or perhaps she was just happy to see him.

'You were miles away.' She smiled. 'I didn't know if I should disturb you or not.' A thin smoor of rain had settled on her hair. 'Are you all right?'

'I'm fine,' he said, beginning to recover himself. There had been a moment – and he had no doubt that Hannah had been aware of this – when his confusion, a mingling of sudden joy that he had found her again, and an awkwardness at being so close to her, so aware of her skin, of the scent of the rain in her hair, and, most of all, the almost gravitational pull of her body, had been obvious. It was only now that he realised just how desperately he had been looking for her since the party. And now, having found her, he still couldn't think of anything to say.

Hannah laughed. 'Are you sure you're all right?' she asked, with an evident lack of concern. In a moment, she would say goodbye, nice to see you again, and go on her way.

'I'm fine,' he said. 'I was just . . .' His mind pedalled wildly. 'It started raining again and . . . I thought I'd go for a coffee at the Y. Would you like a coffee? Do you have time?'

'Sure.'

'Great.'

The Y was almost empty, which was surprising. Usually, it was crowded with foreign language students, bright, vivacious groups of Italian girls, or young men from Africa or the Far East, grouped loosely around the tables, calling back and forth, laughing, moving freely from one seat to another, grooming and hugging one another, like the animals in a nature documentary, unabashed, affectionate, wholly un-British. At one time, before Penny had decided she didn't like the place, Paul had come here often, for a coffee or just to sit and watch:

196

he was always surprised at how casually intimate these people seemed with one another, how little they minded the invasion of their space, how easily they could touch.

'Have you seen Richard recently?' Hannah asked him, when they had settled down to coffee.

'Not since the party,' he answered. 'Why?'

'I just wondered,' she said. 'We haven't seen him either, and we wondered if he had gone yet.'

'Gone?'

'Yes.' She gave him a surprised, quizzical look. 'Didn't he tell you he was leaving?'

'Oh, that,' Paul said. 'I don't think he's going for a while yet.'

'No? Alex told me he was leaving some time this month.'

The mention of Alex came as an unwelcome reminder of Hannah's near-marital status, and Paul glanced involuntarily at her ring finger. It was bare.

'Alex is your fiancé, right?' he said, feeling awkward again.

Hannah laughed. 'Who told you that?' she asked.

'Richard,' Paul answered, quietly.

'Oh.' She shook her head, and took another sip of her coffee. 'Well, that's Richard for you.'

Paul waited while she set her cup down carefully and brushed a strand of wet hair back off her face.

'We're not engaged,' she said. 'That's just one of Richard's little jokes. He wanted us to get married, so he could be best man.'

'I see.'

'Really?' She gave him an amused, almost critical look. 'And what do you see?'

Now he really did feel awkward. Having pulled himself together, after the surprise of meeting her, he had been

197

determined not to be too obvious. At the same time, he wanted to tell her everything about how he felt – how he had looked for her ever since the party, how he had quizzed Richard about her – not because he expected something to happen between them, but because he could hardly bear to sit here, drinking coffee and saying nothing. He shook his head.

'I mean,' he began, not sure where this would go. 'I suppose I thought of you and Alex as together—'

'We are together.'

'And Richard said you were his fiancée. Which is none of my business anyway. So.'

He gave up. She was waiting for him to say something else, but he didn't know whether she expected an explanation, or perhaps for him to say how he really felt about her. Surely she knew. That night, in the garden at Alex's house, it had to have been obvious. Or maybe she was just playing with him. She and Alex were together, she had said it, in so many words. They just weren't engaged.

'So.' She slid her coffee cup to one side and settled back in her chair. 'What are you doing here? I thought you'd have gone home by now.' It was obvious that she could see right through him, but she was making an effort to gloss over the awkwardness. And if she was with Alex, engaged or not, it was only common courtesy at least to try to hide his attraction to her.

'I'm working,' he replied. He told her about the field station, about the locusts and the tobacco moths, and enjoyed her theatrical mock-shiver when he described the cockroach house; then, when she asked why he hadn't gone home, he told her about that, though he didn't say too much about his mother. Meanwhile, she sidestepped his questions in much the same, noncommittal fashion as she had discussed her supposed engagement. Her family were in Dublin, she said, but she liked Cambridge better; Alex had the house, and it was as easy to stay here as it was to go back. She had a room on the other side of Midsummer Common, and she liked it there. She had been worried for a while, when the rapist was still on the loose, about the walk back from town over the Common, and Alex had suggested she stay with him – there was plenty of room, after all – but she preferred to be on her own. Paul listened. It was curious, how frank she was and, at the same time, how little she gave away. From the way she spoke, he couldn't have said if she was madly in love with Alex, or was just barely tolerating him. As soon as she said one thing, she immediately undermined it: she and Alex were together, but she didn't speak about him as if he mattered one way or another. If anything, she seemed fonder of Richard. And she appeared to be genuinely interested in Paul, in what he did, in what he thought, in how he felt. At one point, she asked him what kind of photographs he took.

'How did you know about that?' Paul wanted to know.

'Oh.' She looked caught out. 'Richard told me.'

So she and Richard had been talking about him, presumably at the party, if Hannah hadn't seen him since. Maybe Richard had told her what he had said that evening, as they were walking home. He shook his head.

'I try,' he said. 'I haven't really got very far. I know what I want, but I can't seem to get it just so.

She smiled enigmatically. 'That sounds familiar,' she said.

Paul waited for more, but it didn't come. Then, for something to say, he asked her what photographers she liked, and if she knew Raymond Moore. She didn't. Aware of how naïve, of how absurdly enthusiastic he sounded, he told her about the statement, about the idea of the encounter. She seemed interested in this. It was another hour before she looked at her watch and, with an expression of genuine surprise, told him she would have to go.

'I should have been somewhere ages ago,' she said. 'But it was nice to see you.' She stood up.

'It was nice talking to you,' Paul said. He experienced that familiar wave of panic. 'Maybe we could do this again.'

She looked down at him. 'Maybe,' she said. She hesitated a moment – and Paul actually imagined she was about to sit down, to forget her appointment and stay. He stood up. He didn't want anything, now, other than to touch her. Nothing else mattered. If he could just touch her, if he could only tell her, straight out, how he felt. But then, how did he feel? He didn't know. What words were there for this? Besides, she had already guessed. Finally, after a long moment, standing together in the middle of the room, surrounded by empty tables and chairs, she made a decision. She took a small reporter's pad and a felt pen from her bag, and wrote something in it.

'Call me,' she said. She tore the page from her notebook and handed it to him. 'Any time after Tuesday.'

He took the paper and nodded stupidly. Before he could say anything else, she had turned and walked away, quickly: a woman late for an appointment, who has been unavoidably detained.

He found Mrs Yazz in the kitchen, waiting for him. The work on the downstairs rooms was almost finished, though the hall was still full of cover sheets and paint tins, and there was a large, fold-out toolbox like the one his father had, in the gap under the stairs. Mrs Yazz looked serious; she obviously had something on her mind. Paul's first thought was that she wanted him to leave for the remainder of the summer, so she could get the men into the rest of the house. It had to be something important for her to let herself in: though he had always known she had a spare set of keys to the house, she had never used them till now. If she needed to see him for any reason, she would either call while he was at home, or pop a note through the door, asking him to come around to her house, which was two minutes away, in the next street. So as soon as he saw her, sitting at the table with her hands crossed in front of her, as if she had just turned aside from prayer, Paul knew it was serious. She was still in her coat, though she had taken off her plastic rain hat and mac, which were hanging on the kitchen door to dry.

When he had first met her, Paul had concluded that Mrs Yazz was a typical Cambridge landlady; though, on later acquaintance, she seemed less ruthless than most. She and her husband had started years ago, when they first arrived from Poland, with a single bed and breakfast; gradually, through sheer hard work and self-denial, they had acquired several more properties in the area around Mill Road. When her husband had fallen ill, they had given up the B&B, and Mrs Yazz had taken sole responsibility for the management of the other houses. Her husband had died slowly, from some kind of wasting illness, but Mrs Yazz had kept things going, and had even added another two houses to her list of properties. Now, some ten or more years after her husband's death, she had become something of a mythical figure among students at the Tech and elsewhere. She had no children of her own, but she had a wide network of young friends – that, at least, was how she saw them – through the house lets and, though she was strict about money and standards of behaviour and housekeeping, she would often refer to the young men who passed through her life as 'her boys', occasionally becoming quite sentimental about certain of her former tenants. This affection was always retrospective, however; the chosen always belonged to the past, when they had moved on and could do no harm. Though she had lived in Cambridge for almost thirty years, she still had a strong Polish accent and a thin vocabulary, to the extent that it was sometimes impossible to make out exactly what she was saying. This infuriated her, and Paul had quickly learned to pretend he understood her every word. Now, however – and this was always the case when she knew she had something important to convey – her diction was clear, even a little sharp, her words exact and to the point.

'Finally you are home,' she said, rising and folding her arms, as Paul entered, still damp from the rain. He had run back from the Y in the rain and he was still a little breathless.

'Yes,' he replied, confused by her presence in the kitchen, and her odd, solemn manner. 'I was having coffee with a friend—'

'No time for that,' Mrs Yazz interrupted, though with no trace of her usual impatience. Indeed, for the first time, Paul was struck by a softness in her voice, a tone at once careful and kindly that worried him.

'What is it?' he asked.

'You have to go home,' Mrs Yazz said quickly. She looked awkward and unhappy. 'Your father is unwell.'

'What?' Paul studied her face. There was something she had not said. 'What do you mean unwell?'

'You must talk to your mother,' Mrs Yazz said, averting her gaze. 'You will call her, from my house.'

'Is it serious?'

The woman gave him a soft, bemused look, and nodded.

'Your mother telephoned me,' she said. 'She told me you must telephone, as soon as you are home.'

She shook her head. She had been given more information than this, but she wanted Paul to hear it from someone else.

'Your mother will explain,' she said, sadly.

Finally, Paul understood. His head filled with sound and light, as he took in what his landlady was trying not to convey, in so many words, and he felt sorry for her, sorry for his father, sorry for everyone. He sat down at the table.

'He's dead,' he said – and he was struck by the simplicity of it, by the clarity of the realisation. It was the last thing in the world he had expected to happen, yet now, as the knowledge sank in, he was not particularly surprised.

Mrs Yazz was on the point of tears. 'You call your mother,' she said. 'From my house.'

He looked at her face. She was crying now, the tears running down her grey, softly rouged cheeks, and he felt guilty, as if it were his fault, as if he was the one who had done something to upset her.

A minute later, they were outside, Mrs Yazz in her rain mac, carrying her plastic hat, Paul still in his damp clothes, crossing the road and turning into the next street. It had stopped raining. Mrs Yazz had insisted he use her phone to call home, though he would have preferred to use a call box. He wanted to be alone with this now, but he could hardly refuse her offer, after what had happened.

The phone was in the hallway, perched on a walnut table, surrounded by an arrangement of tiny ceramic dogs. Mrs Yazz left him alone and went off to the kitchen to make tea, while he dialled the number and waited. It rang a long time before his mother answered. When she picked up, her voice sounded thin and hard.

'Yes?'

'It's Paul,' he said, then stopped. He couldn't think of anything else to say.

'Oh.' Her voice softened. He thought she had probably been crying. 'She found you, then . . .'

'Yes.'

'Listen,' she continued. 'Something has happened. There's been an accident.'

'Yes.'

'It's your father.'

'Yes.'

She seemed unable to say what it was she had to tell him.

'Mrs Yazstremski told me he was ill,' he said, prompting her. He wanted this done with.

'What?' She sounded surprised by this. He tried again.

'Mrs Yazstremski said Dad wasn't well.'

'No.' His mother was definitely crying now. 'He's not ill. He's—' She broke off and pulled herself together. When she spoke again, her voice was cold, hard, steadied.

'He's dead,' she said. 'He died last night.'

'What?' He could tell there was something she wasn't telling him.

'He's dead,' she repeated dully, but it was as much as she could manage. Paul could hear her crying, sobbing now, her breathing broken and desperate. He wondered if anyone was with her. Finally, after a long time, she spoke again.

'He went to bed early last night.' She was blurting it out now, getting it said, getting it over with. 'He had a headache, he said. I looked in, but he seemed all right. I thought he was just sleeping.'

Paul's head was racing. He didn't understand this. How could a man just die in his bed, suddenly, without a sound, without anybody knowing. There had to be something she wasn't telling him.

'Listen,' he said, 'I'm coming home. All right? I'm coming home as soon as I can. Just wait till I get there, okay?'

His mother wasn't really listening now. 'Okay,' she said. 'I'll see you later.'

'Is there someone there?' he asked. 'Is someone there with you?'

'Mrs MacMillan is here,' she said.

'Okay. I'm on my way.'

He waited for her to speak, but she was silent. A moment later she put down the receiver, and he was listening to the empty phone line.

He left first thing the next morning. In the past, he had enjoyed these journeys, in spite of the changes and delays, especially when the trains were not too busy. There was something about life in transit that suited him; he enjoyed being between trains, sitting on a deserted platform, listening to the rain as it beat down and poured off the station roof on to the tracks, or between places, travelling across the open country in a deserted carriage, watching the land flash by, the dark woods, the open fields, horses in paddocks, empty farmyards. He remembered the time he had made this trip through a sodden, partly flooded landscape; he'd stood at the window in the corridor, taking pictures from the train of the waterlogged fields, of trees half-submerged in muddy water and stranded livestock gathered together on the high ground, and he'd had a sense, not merely of cleansing, but of renewal, of things mixed up, of a voice moving upon the waters. He had wanted the photographs he had taken to fix this vision, this notion of renewal; he had wanted them to say that the flood was as much a part of the ordinary, natural run of things as anything else. At the same time, he had wanted to capture the secret pleasure he took in all this water, in spite of the destruction. There was something amphibian, some vestige of catfish or frog, in a mind that loved mornings like these, when flood water stood on the fields, and any rut or dip was filled with vivid rain. There was even a secret pleasure in the words: teeming, spill, flood; in the amber or milky-brown of hill-water; in the sound of a stream, or a ditch.

Now, however, he thought about his father as the train hurtled across the empty land. Years ago, on journeys like this, his dad had been in the habit of playing a little game, on the long drives back from England, where you had to watch for the Borders and, when the time came, if you were the first person to see the sign for Scotland, you called it out. If Paul called first, he would get a reward: some sweets, or a small gift of some kind. His mother had always found this game annoying. Yet, as they crossed the Borders, the time had gone faster, and it had seemed much more like home for that piece of silliness – the brown hills, the rivers, the little ruined barns and farm buildings by the side of the road – all of it seemed familiar and strangely beautiful. And maybe, Paul thought, it was more than that. When you call a landscape beautiful, it usually just means it's pretty, or picturesque; yet what his father had always liked – he knew this all of a sudden, as if he had been quietly working it out for years, somewhere at the back of his mind – what his father had loved was something more exact and, at the same time, much subtler than mere prettiness. It was a sense of the world's being right, of things being just. For his dad, there had been times when everything simply sat true, like a good piece of carpentry. There could be beauty in a ruin, a familiar, almost cinematic beauty in the

206

haunted space beneath a broken roof, or an empty window-pane where the darkness had formed like moss, a beauty tinged with nostalgia for the earth itself, in the muddled grain of floorboards thick with dust and broken glass, but what his dad preferred was the ordinary, unglamorous beauty of a settled place, of a town or a village on the way to somewhere else, a lonely farmhouse glimpsed from a passing train, piles of turnips or mangolds in the yard, wet straw, a stain of light in an upper window, packed ice rutted and scarred with tyre tracks. What his dad liked was to drive past a school at lief-time, when the children ran outdoors to politics and barter; most of all, he liked the lull of glimpsed rooms, where someone had left a door ajar, and something quickened, just for a moment, at the borderline of habitation, one remove from seen.

Now, as the train made its way north, across a land blessed by summer, Paul saw it all anew with his father's eyes — animals in the fields, settlements, roads running away from the railway through the bright countryside — and, for the first time, he felt connected to things, not merely an observer, but a participant, a strand in the fabric of time, cradling his single small grief, as the afternoon wore on, and business continued as usual, in the world of others.

ACTS OF GRACE

Nothing is more elusive than the memory of the recent dead. All of a sudden, their lives are captured and rounded off, locked in an unexpected stasis, sealed and inscrutable, like a historical event. The place they once occupied becomes a space for others to inhabit: other voices, other thoughts and dreams, other bodies, taking their place, using their possessions, erasing them with stories that can never be completed. It can take hours, or days, or even months, but the moment comes when they shift into the past tense, and no matter how hard we try to recall them, no matter how difficult it is to let them go, they are done with. By the time Paul had heard all the details of his father's death – that he had been diagnosed with cancer, that he had hidden this from his wife and son for months, that he had taken an overdose of sleeping pills that last night and lay down in bed to die – by the time the story had been pieced together, it had an apocryphal ring to it, a tale invented from hearsay and rumour, something hypothetical, or unproven. Nothing seemed real. By the time Paul got home, the house had been taken over by strangers. Mrs MacMillan and his aunt Janet had assumed responsibility for his mother, and for the funeral arrangements; someone else had taken possession of the body, and removed the incriminating glassware from his father's room. Had it not been for his aunt Janet, Paul would never have known what had happened: the official story was that, having been ill for some time, his father had died mercifully in his sleep.

The moment he arrived, Paul was aware of a change in the house. He had always associated home with his father; or rather, the image of his father was bound up with an idea of home, with an essence that was both commonplace and mysterious. It had to do with specifics – with the smell of coal or wax, with the winter morning's taste of frost and marmalade, with his father's opera records and the dusty, almost threadbare red and blue kite he kept hanging in his bedroom – but it was always more than the sum of these parts. It was something discovered, then reinvented, moment by moment: a map he had drawn up in his mind which, even if some of the landmarks shifted, was always of the same terrain. Now, all of a sudden, the house was different: nothing had changed as such, every familiar thing was still there, but something was wrong, as if the map had faded, or someone had altered the co-ordinates. His father was not only dead, he was absent. It was as if the lie they were constructing about his last night had given his sister and neighbours and friends sufficient cause to eradicate him completely, to replace him with a version of himself that Paul did not recognise. In the process, the house had also been somehow denatured.

As a child, Paul had never understood why his father had loved that house so much. He was always working on it, standing in his workshop in all weathers, stripping down and repolishing the old chairs and cabinets he bought at auctions, or moving quietly about the place, a ghost in overalls, repairing, or decorating, or subtly enhancing a window frame or a doorway. To Paul, the house represented his mother's sullen power. Even in the attic, which his father had fitted with wide studio windows, he felt her influence, like some magnetic force shifting beneath him in the kitchen, or the well of the stairs. It was only at night that he felt liberated from her dominion, or on those days when he was out and away, walking on the shore or hanging around the harbour, watching the men work on their boats.

It had been a long time – right up until he was just about to leave – before he saw that his father had managed, by some gradual alchemical process, to create a house of his own, a place that only he inhabited. Though Paul's parents occupied the same building, they had come to dwell in different worlds: his mother had her own willed space, where nothing could happen unless it was woven into her system of ritual and control, but over the years his father had contrived something else, a kind of parallel house, not so much an escape as a sanctuary. During the week, he would be away at work. Often he would be gone before Paul woke for school, and sometimes he did not return until after bedtime. At the weekend, he worked in his shed, or he took Paul out on fishing trips. Certain key rituals had been established: meal times, family visits, the annual holiday; these areas of their life together belonged to Paul's mother, and his father rendered them up to her, the way Jesus had said that coin should be rendered to Caesar, in order that the more important things might be rendered unto God. Everything – every moment Paul's father spent alone, in his own world – had to be paid for.

One evening Paul had come in and found his dad in the dining room, fitting new wooden shutters to the windows that faced the street. He had made the shutters himself, out in his workshop behind the house. At one time there had been shutters in all the windows; they were common in these seafront houses and, where they were still fitted, could be closed and barred against draughts and noise. His father had found evidence of the original fittings and had taken it from there; now, as he stood in the window, checking the alignment, intent on his task, Paul was aware of a happiness he had never quite understood, and had even at times resented, for the distance it created between them. It was late in the summer and the evenings were just starting to draw in; outside, at the far end of their narrow garden, the street lamp had just come on, a soft wet crimson that seemed almost physically present, like some new, improvised life-form, some vague marine creature, forming, then burning away, in those first few minutes of dusk. The shrubs by the window were filling with shadows, softening into the twilight like the foliage in a watercolour, and his father stood, surrounded by his tools, totally absorbed, like the celebrant of his own quotidian rite, hovering at the edge of some region of unlikeness, some vanishing point which – Paul had suddenly realised – he would not resist, if it took him up and absolved him of his human presence. For the first time Paul had understood what his father's life was about: he had always thought of his dad as lonely, he had always considered his endless work a distrac-tion, an acceptable way of filling the hours and keeping himself busy. Now, he saw that it was quite the opposite: his father was far from lonely, he was just a man who could only be truly happy when he was alone, and work, any work, was a refuge for him, just as solitude was not an escape, not a hiding place, but a dwelling, a refuge, a place of safe keeping for what Paul could only think of as the spirit. This happiness – not so much self-absorption as self-forgetting – was wholly imperso-nal. It had nothing to do with anyone else. Yet, at the same time as it was admirable, and perhaps a little enviable, it had seemed, just for that moment, something too exclusive, too detached. In a way, it was even cruel. It asked nothing, and it gave nothing, other than the results of its wholly disinterested work. Later, when they sat down to dinner, Paul knew that his mother might not even notice the shutters, though his father had been working on them for days; at the same time, he knew his dad didn't care. What people said or thought didn't matter to him, one way or another, as long as the work was good.

At some point during the funeral – Paul wasn't altogether sure when, for he had spent the whole day in a kind of walking trance – at some point during the buffet and drinks session after the body was safely stowed in the ground, his aunt Janet took him very quietly to one side. Janet was his father's younger sister, a thin, mischievous-looking woman with astonishing copper-coloured hair and very large, very bright blue eyes. As a boy, Paul had entertained something of a crush on his aunt, though he had not seen her often; even now, he was struck by how beautiful she seemed, how radiant, in spite of the occasion. Her voice was as light and musical as it had always been – just like wind-chimes, he remembered thinking, years before, when he had never heard wind-chimes, but had read about them in a book, and thought they must sound like that. When she took him by the arm and led him away across the main function room of the town hall, which had been booked specially for the occasion, and into the little kitchen beyond, Paul had felt awkward and at the same time privileged, as if a gift, or a promise, was being bestowed upon him. To begin with, however, Janet had merely gone through the usual stuff – condolences, concern about Paul's college work, concern about Paul. It was only towards the end that

212

she came out with what she had evidently been planning to say all along.

'You know, your dad was a good man,' she said. 'You mustn't ever doubt that.'

Paul nodded. 'I don't,' he said.

'He was my big brother,' she continued, ignoring him, 'and I looked up to him. But I have to say, he did some things I couldn't agree with.'

She waited a moment, watching Paul as if she expected him to speak – maybe even to argue – but he couldn't think of anything to say. He assumed Janet was going to criticise his father for the way he had chosen to die, without telling anyone what he was planning. It was something he had no wish to argue about.

'The trouble was,' Janet continued, 'he gave up on us all too easily.' She paused to give him a thin, testing smile. 'Far too soon,' she added, her voice dropping. She turned to the open doorway and looked out across the function room towards her sister-in-law. 'It's very hard to take. Especially for your mother,' she added, with a little tilt of the head. 'Your mother certainly didn't deserve *that*.'

Paul listened. It was strange to him, hearing people talk about his father; stranger still to be here, where his father had always been, and to feel his absence, like something real, something tangible, in the air about him. The atmosphere had been strange from the moment he had stepped through the front door into that alien house two days before – stepped, so it seemed, into a haunting, the house around him, the people who had come and gone, the whole world haunted by an apparent uncertainty, an obvious lack that he couldn't quite isolate. It wasn't just that his father was no longer there; it was deeper than that, it was more fundamental. It was like a puzzle or an exercise in logic for which the instructions are missing: he could see the pieces, he knew that they must fit together in some way, but none of it made any sense. He wondered if it surprised the others as much as it did him that, having been so quiet, so self-effacing, so nearly invisible in life, his father could be so glaringly and painfully absent in death. At the same time, in spite of the fact that she was there, in a black dress at the centre of the room, it was his mother's absence from her own life that surprised him most. In all the time he had lived with them, he had never once witnessed any exchange of affection or warmth between his parents; for as long as he could remember, they had slept in separate rooms; yet now, with the husband gone, the wife seemed suddenly empty and purposeless. He knew it was too easy a conclusion to reach, that she had loved him after all, but he couldn't help thinking that she had loved him more than he, and certainly she, had understood. At the same time, in spite of everything, she had been determined to have a Catholic funeral, with a public reception in the town hall – a place his father had particularly disliked, with its bingo club and its small-town socials – for all and sundry, from the village and beyond. Even in grief, she had had her will.

Earlier, the funeral Mass had been conducted at St Mary's, a place his father had attended only on rare occasions, at Easter, or on Christmas Eve, or for the odd wedding or family christening. It had never occurred to Paul before how alien this ritual must have seemed to his dad, how offensive, even, to his sensibilities. Paul had always seen his father not as an atheist or even an unbeliever so much as a pagan soul, committed to the unsayable truth of the earth, and water, and the sky. If he had believed in anything, it had been in something more elusive and less symbolic than a wafer and

214

some wine. His father had not been interested in the anthropomorphic, or the personal. He had more or less consciously honoured that old Pictish sense of continuum, that sense of something ancient and, at the same time, constantly new-born in the world, which was represented by nothing, but was present in the subtler magic of the earth, in the glimmer and drift of reeds and salt-grass at the tide line, in the waves of meadowsweet that marked a ditch, or the rings of dark grass where a fairy ring began. It was ironic, thinking that his father lay in that box by the altar rail, knowing this was not what he would have wanted. Yet all these people here present, from his family to the handful of loyal friends who had taken the day off work to be there, all these people thought of him as an unbeliever, a lapsed soul, because he had turned away from their church. Some of them were probably praying for him at that very moment – praying that their middle-eastern God, clouded with wrath and judgement, would accept a sinner into His heaven. It mystified Paul. These people, who were so proud of their Scots heritage – of the language, the place names, the history, the land – these people, who had wondered why he, Paul, had chosen to go so far from home to study, lived by the rules and commandments of an alien, imported religion, when they would have been so much better served by his father's hidden, unspoken reverence for the local.

He remembered a time when he had begun to tune in, without words, without instruction, to that pagan sensibility. It was on one of the country walks they used to take, when he was ten or so. His father loved more than anything to be out in the open, and he would hurry them through an early breakfast, every other Sunday morning, if the sun was shining, or even if, by some calculation whose method and data were

215

known only to him, he thought it would be a nice day later, and they would go out, taking the old coast path as far as the caves, then turning inland and following the line of a hedge as far as Kilrenny, before heading back around, past the old standing stone, and home. Paul's mother treated these walks as she would any other chore and, while his dad dictated the pace, stopping on the high ridge to gaze out over the firth, or lingering by the caves or the standing stone, it was understood, as his one concession to her desire to be home, that they never varied their route, and always made it back with an hour to spare, before Sunday lunch. When they reached home, each of them retired to his or her accustomed domain: his father to the workshop, while lunch was prepared, his mother to the kitchen, and Paul to his room, where he would sit by the radio his father had bought him, listening to the Third Programme, or reading a book. He hated the ritual of Sunday lunch, but it had to be undergone – another concession to his mother – and he would consciously prepare himself, with this moment of quiet, building up a distance in his mind that would remain for hours, impassable and silent, while they ate their stuffed chicken and greens, and his parents ran through their accumulated small talk – who in the village was ill, who was getting engaged or married, who had left for Canada, or England, who had moved jobs, or died. During these conversations, Paul's father was studiously polite and interested, but it was his mother who knew the gossip, and she seemed inordinately interested in the lives of other people, as if they were close to her in some way that Paul and his father had failed to understand.

It had been on one of those Sunday walks, as they had followed the low stone wall between the kale field and the beach, that Paul had realised, not for the first time, but fully, with a sense of immediacy, that he was fated to die; or rather, not so much that he would die, but that life would go on without him afterwards, as it had done before he had been born. It was as if, for no obvious reason, he had slipped out from the half-dormant person he had been till that sunlit morning, and become someone else, someone more alert, but also more anxious, more tuned-in to the world around him. Things that had seemed abstract to him before were suddenly real, suddenly vivid and, for a moment, it was as if he was listening for something – that he had been listening for some time, waiting for a sound to emerge from the fields or the shoreline, a new voice rising through a litter of lichened stones or a fallen birch to assume a recognisable shape – an animal, say, or a hunting bird. Of course, he had known for a long time, since before school even, that everyone he had ever known was going to die – his parents, his school friends, his teachers – and he had known that he would also die, but the idea had never quite occurred to him that life would continue without him: that these stones, this water, this stretch of shoreline, this kale field, would go on, after he was dead and buried. It had been a breathtaking moment, a moment of bewilderment, even a kind of grief. Yet, strangely enough, that had passed almost immediately and been replaced, without his quite understanding the logic of the adjustment, by a sense of calm, a kind of benign detachment. His first impulse had been to wonder how people stood it – how his father, his mother, he himself, could live so easily with this thought when, on a morning like this, the world was so wonderful, so vivid and immediate and real, so difficult to think of losing. Why were they not stricken with grief? Why were they not inconsolable? A moment later, however, he was telling himself, somewhere at the back of his mind, that there

217

was something, some part of each person's being, something that could be equated to presence, perhaps, that *knew*, beyond a doubt, that it was not the mortal person which mattered, but time itself, time and place and the life in it, which was always changing, yet, in some real way, always remained the same. After he was dead, someone else would walk here, and think these same thoughts; after he was dead, someone would tune his radio into the Third and listen; the story would go on being repeated, and it didn't matter how often, or by whom, because it was always the same story, and the same souls moving through the story. Only the characters were different. It had been an astonishing moment, as if some angel had passed and brushed him with its wing – yet he hadn't even broken pace and, a moment later, he was tuning back in to what his father was saying, something about a boat on the firth, on its way to the island, packed full of people who wanted to see the puffin colony.

Now, looking back, he wasn't sure if this memory was real, or if it was something he had constructed from images of those childhood walks and some thought that had come later, something he had read in a book, or seen in a film. The memory seemed at once intense and unverifiable: no doubt he had experienced this moment, at some time in his life, but it had not been so clear, or so articulate. It had occurred to him before now that everything – thoughts, memories, the way we created the world for ourselves and one another – the whole thing was too verbal, it had too much to do with the sayable. His memory was suspect, for being capable of articulation; the truth, the event itself, what he *knew*, had more to do with the stone wall and the warmth of the sun, the green of the kale field and the wind off the sea, than it had to do with thoughts that could be put into words. He might have said that people were not stricken with grief by the idea of dying, and the world continuing without them, because they knew that they were intrinsic to the world itself, that the spirit that lay behind the persons they were belonged to the very process of change that informed that world, and would never be lost from it, but that wasn't really what he knew. What he knew was stone, water, air, sky, kale field, earth, sunlight. You could take a picture of it, but you couldn't speak about it. And you could experience it, but you couldn't recall the experience, even though it lay in you, part of who you were becoming, part of an indelible spirit that was neither personal nor contingent. The mistake they had made, in school, and at his mother's church, was to think that the soul was a given, a part of the person which was born, and died, with him; if Paul understood anything, it was that the soul came from the world, that it was always changing, that it was no more a part of the person he or his father was, than the weather.

After the funeral came the moment that Paul had been dreading, that moment when the last guest had gone and he and his mother were left alone together in the house. His aunt's words were still there at the back of his mind, yet he couldn't help thinking that she had been mistaken. No doubt she wanted to see things in the best possible light, but that desire had blinded her to the reality of her brother's home life. Paul had lived with his parents too long not to know that something had gone wrong in their life together. They had tried; they had managed a quiet, more or less civilised life, but theirs had been a marriage in name only. Long ago, it had soured for them and Paul saw no particular virtue in their having kept their problems hidden for decades.

Now, as he changed out of his funeral clothes, he was

wondering how long he needed to stay, wondering what would be a decent interval before he could go back to Cambridge. It was late. He would have to go down, of course, but he hoped his mother would be tired and go to bed soon. It seemed heartless, but the truth was he didn't know what to say to her. He lingered in his room for as long as he could, listening, as she moved about downstairs. It was such a familiar sound – yet there was something almost obscene about it, about this very familiarity, on this of all days.

'Paul?' His mother was at the foot of the stairs. 'Would you like something to drink?'

He did not answer. Instead, he stopped where he was, and listened to her listening. 'Paul?'

'Hello?' His voice sounded odd and distant to him. It was the first time he had been aware of himself speaking all day. He crossed the landing to the top of the stairs. His mother was wearing her apron.

'Would you like a cup of tea?'

She seemed to have made a full recovery. Two days before, she had been under the doctor's supervision. Even at the funeral, she had been a ghost of a woman, accepting the condolences of her guests in stricken silence. Now, she was up and about making tea and tidying up, as if nothing had happened. Paul was tempted to refuse, but he couldn't do it. He nodded.

'That would be nice,' he said, lamely.

The kitchen hadn't changed over the years: it was, as it had always been, the dead centre of his mother's world. From here, she had exercised control over the entire house, making the ordinary everyday decisions that had filled their lives with meaningless, unseemly clutter. His father had never seemed to mind it but, for as long as he could remember, Paul had thought about getting away. Though it had meant leaving his dad, he wanted nothing more than to step out into light and air, into sunshine or drifting snow, closing the back door on his mother's world of tortoiseshell cats and fake fur, the doilies and handmade crafts, the endless pots of tea and the old wives' remedies she had for everything, poultices and tisanes and milk warmed in a saucepan with a clove of garlic whenever anyone had a cold.

His mother had made tea in the best pot, and laid out a plate of cakes and biscuits – miniature Battenburgs and slices of Swiss roll, a couple of Digestives, some petticoat tails of shortbread. By the time Paul got to the kitchen she was already sitting at the table, pouring the tea. She looked tired. Here and there, on the counter his dad had built across the middle of the room and on the various work surfaces, the cups and saucers and cake plates of the handful of guests who had been invited back to the house were waiting to be washed up and put away.

'You ought to get some rest,' he said. 'I'll stay and clear up, if you like.'

'That's all right,' his mother replied. She had never relinquished the sovereignty of her kitchen to anyone. 'It won't take me long.'

Paul nodded his assent and took a sip of tea, trying hopelessly to think of something to talk about.

'It was a good turnout,' he said, finally.

His mother gave a tight, unhappy smile. 'Yes, it was,' she said. 'Your dad would have liked it.'

Paul couldn't help thinking that she was wrong there – and he wondered if she knew, if she had even the remotest idea of how much his father would have hated the ceremony she had contrived for his corpse.

221

'You had a little talk with Janet, I saw,' his mother continued. She was probing. In spite of Janet's obvious goodwill, Paul's mother had never entirely trusted her sister-in-law.

'She was just telling me a story,' Paul lied. 'About when they were kids.'

His mother looked interested. 'Really? What story was that?'

Paul scoured his memory for something to tell her. Janet had told him quite a few stories over the years – it was one of the reasons he'd had such a crush on her, because she had talked to him as a person, not as a child – but it was a moment before he came up with anything.

'She was telling me about the time when they were kids, and Dad built a kite,' he said. 'About how he won some kind of competition with it.'

His mother nodded. 'That's right,' she said. 'Your dad was always good at things like that. In fact, if it wasn't for the kite, we might never have met.'

Paul was surprised, suddenly, by her tone, and by the sense he had that she was about to confide in him. 'How do you mean?' he said, trying not to sound too interested.

'Well,' his mother's face brightened a little. 'It was when he was trying out one of his kites – not that first one, but one of the bigger ones – that we met. Over at Burntisland, out on the sands.'

Paul smiled. He was interested now. 'Why – what happened?' he asked.

'Nothing, really,' his mother said. 'I just saw this young man in a white shirt, out on the sands flying this big red and blue kite. And he looked so handsome, and so – I don't know

222

– graceful, I suppose, out there on the beach. He had lovely golden hair in those days. It got darker later.'

She stopped to remember, and her eyes suddenly brightened with tears. Paul felt sorry for her now.

'It's okay,' he said. 'It's all right.' Even as he said it, he knew it was wrong – it wasn't okay, it wasn't all right, but he couldn't think of anything to say. Immediately, his mother pulled herself together.

'Well,' she said. 'I'd better get this stuff put away. It'll be a long day tomorrow.' She stood up and carried her teacup over to the sink. 'You go up now and get some rest,' she said. 'I'll finish up here.'

Paul sat a moment, feeling helpless and absurdly lonely. Then he finished his tea, and stood up. 'Good night, Mum,' he said. He hadn't called her mum in a long time.

She didn't turn round. 'Good night, son,' she said.

The next day, around noon, he went for a walk around the harbour. It was a bright, warm day: people were out and about, shopping, or sitting on the benches opposite the little pier, eating ice creams or fish and chips. Some of the faces were familiar; occasionally someone would stop him to offer condolences or ask if his mum was all right, but most of the people here were strangers. Even when he recognised the faces of those who greeted him, he couldn't recall their names, or where they knew him from. At the same time, it struck him that, although he barely remembered any of the people in this small town, he knew every timber and bolt in the pier, every stone in the wall of the library, every door along the seafront, just as surely as he knew his own skin. It didn't matter how long he had been away: all of it, every least detail, was familiar to him. It was as if his mind contained a map of this place, as if everything here had been recorded forever in the folds of his brain. It was something he had done all through childhood, through windstorms and gusts of rain and that half-hour before the dark when the year's first snow began to settle; it was the one skill he had been given, the one innate gift, to draw up this inner map of the world, to draw it up and then, more carefully, in greater and finer detail, redraw it with an almost perfect attention, so that he knew every fence-post, every dock leaf, every smear of bird lime, every nebula of moss and lichen on the churchyard wall. And, insofar as he missed anything when he was away from home, he missed this.

He remembered something Richard had said to him once, over one of their afternoon teas early in the previous winter. It had been raining all day; as usual Richard had provided a lemon cake, and a plate of fruit thingummies from the little bakery on Trumpington Street. Maybe it was the weather – Richard always suffered from a vague, pleasing melancholy on wet days – but the conversation had taken a distinctly dark, rainy-day turn.

'If you had to lose everything,' Richard said, 'what would you miss most?'

Paul didn't answer. He knew a rhetorical question when he heard one.

Richard gazed out across the garden. He seemed sad. 'It wouldn't be anything gross, like the big house, or the fancy car, assuming you had such things. It wouldn't be your impeccable reputation, or fame, or the regard of others. No; if you had to lose everything – I mean *everything* – it would be the things you most take for granted now that you would miss. It would be different for each person, and it would probably surprise you to know what it was: a lilac tree in flower, the sound of a train in the distance, the smell of marmalade or hot buttered toast. Rain on a windowpane. A fruit thingummy.'

He regarded the plate of pastries with absurd fondness.

'Everything that is commonplace, everything ordinary, everything we take for granted – these are the things it would be unbearable to lose.' He cut himself another piece of lemon cake. 'You hear about prisoners in torture cells, how they keep themselves sane thinking about an old school book, or the smell of new bread, or some banal poem they had to learn by heart in school. When they are finally released, they have been purged of ideology, they inhabit a new politics, a new order that nobody else understands, a politics of the ordinary, of the commonplace, the irreplaceable. A glass of milk. The sound of laughter in the next room. Early morning trams.' He fell silent, then he shook his head and laughed. 'I don't half talk sometimes,' he said.

'I'll say.' Paul felt an overwhelming surge of affection for his friend.

'Sorry,' Richard mumbled through a mouthful of lemon cake.

'Don't mention it,' replied Paul.

The days passed slowly. Paul had nothing much to do other than read and walk around the town. Sometimes, he would meet someone he had known in school, and he would listen patiently, with feigned interest, to their stories of marriage and babies, or job promotions, or impending moves. One day he met Caroline Henderson outside the Post Office: she had a child with her, and her face had gone soft and a little slack, but there was still a glimmer of the beauty she had once possessed in her schooldays. Paul felt mildly embarrassed, remembering the fantasy about her that he and Nancy had concocted over the vodka, and it wasn't till later, when he was walking away, that he remembered how young she was. She had been two years behind him in school – which made her nineteen, or at most twenty now, but she had a baby, and a husband, and debts. To Paul, this seemed a wholly unacceptable loss.

Walking about the town like this – town transformed by the sudden fact of his father's absence – brought back memories he hadn't known he had, phantom memories he wasn't altogether sure of, suspecting himself of filling in the blanks, inventing small elaborations and flourishes, inserting odd details for the sake of exposition or continuity. Yet, no matter what he recalled, there was always something else, some original memory, which eluded him – and that was the worst of it, he thought, *that* was what lay at the root of the grief he felt, that inability to properly remember, to *see*, in his mind's eye, the father he had lost. Worse still, the memories that did come to him vivid and entire were trivial, or banal, or even humiliating, like the recollection he had of an afternoon at the fair long ago, when he was maybe nine or ten. He didn't know why this memory had returned so forcefully, yet it seemed important, and he kept thinking about it, mulling it over, trying to decipher it.

Every year, the fair came to town and set itself down on a piece of open ground beyond the sorting office, a beautiful, tawdry village of lights and rockabilly music that drew Paul like a magnet. It was a small fair, with no more than six or seven rides, but it wasn't the rides that interested him. It wasn't even the noise, or the patchwork of new scents – candyfloss, fresh nougat, dry grass, spilt diesel; it wasn't anything he could see or hear or touch. Naturally, it was nothing he could explain to his mother.

'I don't want you going down there by yourself,' she would say. 'Not amongst *those people*.'

Paul was never entirely sure who *those people* were: the freaks and roustabouts his mother had seen in old movies, the local bad kids who seemed to have free run of the fair, or some other, darker but more nebulous group of spirits who waited behind the painted façade of the ghost train or the dodgems, to taint the hearts and minds of impressionable boys.

His mother didn't want him going there by himself; on the other hand, she had no intention of going with him. That job was left to his father. His dad seemed oblivious to the charms of the fair but he would walk down to the patch of waste ground and watch as Paul tried his hand at shooting a pop gun, or attempted and failed to pull plastic ducks out of a pool with a hooked stick. To make it more of an occasion, they would go on the dodgems together, or Paul would be despatched, alone, on the ghost train while his father waited, mock-anxious, for his return three minutes later. The main attraction, though, was the promise of something – something Paul couldn't have defined or even hinted at – a promise that had to do with the night, and the cheap fairy lights, and the way the sound of the music, or the screams and laughter of the other fairgoers, could shift away into the distance, even at such close quarters, as if it were happening elsewhere, somewhere out to sea, or somewhere above them, in the very night itself. As they walked around, eating candyfloss or ice cream, their faces blurring into the warmth of the lights and the generators that stood between the stalls, the sky would gradually darken, turning a deep, cool blue above their heads. At times like that, Paul could see it all as if from above, and the promise was almost made manifest, a coolness, a sense of distance, a

227

remoteness that he felt he might enter, if he could just grasp it, if he could only see it for long enough.

Most of the time his father would take him to the fair on a weekday evening, so they would still have the weekend free for other things. Once, however, they had been obliged to go on a Saturday, on one of those perfect, still, weekend afternoons in midsummer when it was a blessing to be out of doors and away from home. As they had expected, the fair was crowded, mostly with the kind of feckless boys Paul's mother so mistrusted, but there were also families, and bands of girls in their best clothes went walking amongst the stalls, aware of the boys, but feigning disdain for their catcalls and show-off antics. That year, the fair had seemed disappointing, perhaps because of the crowds, but more likely because it was so different in the day, so colourless and cramped, lacking the imagined distance of the night. His father had sensed Paul's disappointment and, to make up for it, he had been particularly generous in doling out money for rides and games – which was the main reason that Paul finally succeeded in winning something. What he won, however, wasn't what he had expected. He'd had it in mind to take his mother a little glass vase he had seen on one of the stands, but after he pulled the winning straw from the tin that a tall, curly-headed man offered him in exchange for a warm clutch of pennies, he found himself in possession of a single, bright-red goldfish in a plastic bag full of very clear and unbearably vulnerable water.

His dad had already started back and was waiting about twenty yards away, while Paul had lingered for one last go. After a brief and utterly pointless argument with the curly-headed man, he had decided there was no option but to make the best of it, and he was carrying his prize back across the piece of open ground between the rides and the sorting office when a boy in a white T-shirt flashed by, pursued by a gang of friends. Paul managed to avoid the first kid, but one of the gang careered into him, knocking the plastic bag out of his hand, and sending them both sprawling. Immediately, Paul looked up to see if his dad had seen – he had a horror of having his father share in this childish moment of pain and humiliation – then he picked himself up, while the other boy scrambled to his feet and ran away.

The fish was gone. He found the plastic bag, empty now, in a pool of water on the dried-out summer grass, but it was a good minute or more before he located the tiny, thrashing goldfish, a sliver of red life already fading on the brownish earth, a single eye gazing up at him, the mouth gaping. He plucked it up but, having found it, there was nowhere to put it. The bag of water was gone – and, as soon as he had it between his fingers, the fish slipped loose, squirting out and landing a few feet away, while a new gang of boys stood around him, laughing, and his father, who had finally noticed that something was wrong, made his way back from the edge of the field. By the time he arrived, scattering the boys like a flock of gulls, there was nothing to be done.

'I'm sorry, son,' he said. 'I'm afraid it's dead.'

Paul nodded. The fish had stopped thrashing and lay still now, its mouth open, the brightness and colour fading from its body, the way stones fade when you pick them from a rock pool, till they are lifeless and dull, and you forget what they looked like before, when they had caught your eye in the bright salt water.

'It doesn't matter,' he said. At that moment, he was afraid his father would offer to buy him another, which was the last thing he wanted. He had stood there and watched the fish die, and he didn't want a replacement, he just wanted to wait a

229

moment, to stand there, to isolate the strand of a thought that shimmered in his mind, as bright and elusive as the fish, as bright and as impossible to hold. It had something to do with uniqueness, with the fact that everything is single and unrepeatable in time and space, and that sense he had of the sky above his head, of the moment's warmth and light and stillness.

He needn't have worried, however. His father stood with him a moment and said nothing more till they were away from the fair, walking home the long way round, by way of the harbour and the little gift shop on Shore Street. There, he stopped and bought a small blue ceramic vase, with a wreath of yellow flowers painted around the rim.

'Why don't you give this to your mum,' he said. 'She'd like that.'

Paul took the vase, still in its cardboard box. 'We can tell her it came from the fair,' he said.

'If you like. Wait a minute.' His father bent and peeled a label from the lid of the box.

'There,' he said. 'That'll do it.'

Now, looking back, Paul couldn't see why this memory of his father meant so much to him. What he recalled was nothing but a typical act of kindness, a typical moment of discretion. It wasn't till long after the funeral, when he went upstairs and, pausing a moment to be sure he could hear his mother moving around below him, stepped into his dad's room, that something else occurred to him – nothing big, nothing important, nothing *meaningful*. The room was as his father had kept it: simply furnished, almost bare, the bed in the centre, facing the window, the old kite pinned to the wall above. There was nothing here that revealed his father's personality, or interests; his shed out in the garden, crammed full of tools and instruments, or his bookshelf in the hall, with its Italian atlas and old books about flight, would reveal more of the man than this, his private, sacred space, where nobody else had ever been permitted to go. But then – and the thought came to him suddenly, like a revelation, though it was something he ought to have seen long ago – surely it was this very stripped-down quality, this *absence* of something, that mattered most. This was his father's real world, not the books, not the tools, not the work with which he kept himself occupied. This was his father's essential reality: a separateness, a solitude and, with that separation, a hard-won discretion which was open to be shared, but which was never imposed, never even offered to the larger world. It was the solitude of a craftsman, the isolation of someone who had traded the social, traded the human, for something else, something he couldn't explain or share.

A week after the funeral, Paul's mother was already working on the brave face that said she didn't need him at home any more. She wanted him to feel free to leave when he was ready. Nevertheless, they didn't talk about his going back to Cambridge for another several days. Paul had been making calls – to Mrs Yazz, who was keeping his room open for him, to Richard, who didn't answer the phone, to Nancy, who hung up on him as soon as he started speaking, and on one occasion to the number Hannah had given him. The phone had been answered by a brusque, foreign-sounding woman, who told Paul that Hannah had gone to Switzerland. This had come as something of a surprise, until he reminded himself that he really didn't know anything about Hannah. When he asked when she would be coming back, the woman gave a harsh, impatient grunt and hung up the phone. After that, he

231

kept trying Richard, to see if he knew anything about what was going on. It was after just such a failed attempt to reach his friend that his mother suggested he go.

'I'm fine,' she said. 'You get back to your friends.'

Paul knew enough to hear this suggestion with at least feigned reluctance. 'I'm all right here,' he said. 'Term doesn't start for a couple of weeks.'

'I know,' his mother replied. 'But you have your friends. And your things. You should go back.'

He protested for what he thought was a decent length of time, before giving in. He was struck by how magnanimous she had been: in the past, she would complain at how short his visits home had been, as if she suspected the real reason for his long absences. It was only later, as he was packing, that it occurred to him that she wanted him to go, that she either needed or wanted to be alone.

KITE

It was the sky he wanted. He had been building kites for a long time, and with each one he made he had a different idea of the sky. He had flown them from the cliffs, and on the hills and ridges inland, but it was only here, at the edge of the water, where he could see the horizon and feel the earth moving in infinite space, it was only on the shore that he knew how much he had always longed for the blue of distance. Out here, in the wind, he had a sense of the world he had inhabited as a child, when he had lived closer to matter, and to the elements. Alone on the beach – for with the kite he was always alone, even when the beach was crowded – he remembered how real it all was, and how the very existence of the material world was a miracle in itself: earth, sky, water, zenith, sun, space, stars. If being alive had any purpose at all, it had something to do with this, with being aware, and learning to take nothing for granted.

He flew the kite on his days off and sometimes in the evenings, if he got back early enough. In his hands, the line was like a live nerve, a living fibre connecting him to the wind and so to the sky. He never tired of that sensation: it was where the life of the thing was, this tensed line of his perfected longing. He'd read, as a child, how the sky wasn't flat, the way it looked to a casual observer; he had come to see that it had depth and variation, that it had layers, that it was a subtle, responsive thing, like skin. He knew, of course, that it wasn't blue, any more than the sea was blue, but that people spoke about the blue of the sky as an idea, as an essence, because there was always blue somewhere amongst those folds and layers. Still, it was the blue he wanted when he sailed the kite high into the air, feeling it shift and slide in the wind, guiding it, letting it guide him, action and reaction, question and answer, in an endless and subtle series of movements and responses. Everything he did, every smallest movement, had its equivalent in the sky. It was a correspondence, of sorts, a kind of dialogue. Sometimes, he would think that the sky was the only thing to which he was certain he belonged.

At first, he didn't notice the girl. He knew someone was there – on these cool, late evenings in September the beach would empty soon after four – but he had no sense of who it was. All he knew for sure was that it was a woman. She had been watching for some time, not saying anything, her eyes fixed on the kite, but it was only when he became aware of a shift in her attention, when he knew that she had turned her eyes to him, that he realised who it was. He'd noticed her before; she was the pretty one he had seen on the promenade from time to time, the pretty, dark-haired girl with the smaller, hard-faced friend; he'd seen them on the promenade eating toffee-apples, or walking around the little fair at the end of the pier. Today, she was alone, though, pretty and neat in a yellow dress and a white cardigan, her thick, dark hair pulled back and away from her face in a tight ponytail. After a moment, he began reeling the kite in, bringing it down carefully, elegantly, so it looked as if it had decided to come down of its own accord. Then he turned to see her better.

'Hello,' he said.

234

The girl smiled and looked at her feet.

'Would you like a go?'

She shook her head then, her eyes still fixed on the sand. 'No thanks,' she said, quietly.

'It's all right,' he persisted. 'It's easy enough.'

She looked at him. From the expression on her face, he could tell that she wanted to try it, but she wasn't sure about him. How old was she? Eighteen? Nineteen? Her eyes were very blue, he noticed. Blue, like the blue of the zenith on a summer's afternoon.

'Come on,' he said. 'I'll show you.'

The girl took a few steps forwards, hesitated, then seemed to screw up her resolve. She took the line from him, but he kept just enough of a hold to control it, as he moved alongside her, guiding her hands. He'd done this before a couple of times, with other girls; with them he had circled his arms around their bodies, moving in close, flirting and watching to see how they responded. It was a game, mostly. Now, however, he felt an odd restraint. A respectful distance had to be observed between them, and he stood alongside her, the way he might with a child, or another man, showing her what to do. It wasn't as easy as it looked, of course. That was the first thing anybody learned – but it got easier, much sooner than that first impression suggested, so they could begin to feel how it all worked and tune into the thing. That it had almost nothing to do with the eye was how they would begin to understand it; it all had to do with feeling, with tension and movement flowing back through the nerves and into the spine and the belly. Maybe, if they were lucky, they would at least guess that it was also about longing, about wanting, not so much to fly, as to become the sky.

The girl was smiling. He guided her carefully, speaking

softly, his hands touching hers, then retreating, creating a tiny theatre of the delicate between them, of words suggested and left unspoken, of the infinite possibilities of touch. This wasn't flirting for him, the way it had been with the others. He kept looking at her face, at the blue of her eyes, at the set of her mouth as she concentrated on what he was telling her. After a while, though, he didn't talk any more. He let the line speak, the line and the occasional shock of contact between their hands. Her skin was amazing: so cool, so smooth. He had always been so warm-blooded — it was a joke in his family that he never felt the cold, that he could go out in the snow in his shirtsleeves and still not feel it — but she was so cool that, even at the surface of the skin, she suggested a distance; a still, blue remoteness. Once, she laughed, and he was entranced by the brightness of the sound. It was familiar to him, this laugh; at the same time, it was infinitely strange and new, and he understood in a moment how easily one person could become lost in another.

When they stopped, she turned to him. 'Thank you,' she said. She was smiling softly, but her voice was serious. 'I liked that.'

He smiled, but he kept his voice serious too. 'So did I,' he said, adding quickly, before she had time to get away, 'we could try it again, if you like.'

She looked away along the beach. 'I have to go some-where,' she said, and he sensed regret.

'I meant another time,' he said. 'Tomorrow, say.'

She shook her head. 'I'm not sure,' she said. 'I might have something on—'

'Or Saturday,' he put in, quickly. 'Would you be free on Saturday?'

She looked up at him and smiled. 'I don't know. I'd have to

see.' She was already thinking about where she had to be now, and she wasn't sure about Saturday, but he knew she wanted to come.

'That's fine.' He didn't want to push too hard. 'If you can come on Saturday, I'll be here. All right?'

'All right,' she said. Then she turned and walked quickly back up the beach, towards the little flight of steps to the promenade. It had already started to darken a little and, over her head, all along the front, the lights were coming on in the shops and houses, though it was still too early, and the sky was still almost, but not quite, blue.

SIERRA

Richard stood a long time gazing out across the slow-moving, yellow water. He had been in Cordoba three days now, and every afternoon he had drifted back to the river, vaguely dissatisfied with the place, and with himself, for expecting anything other than the hot, noisy, unappealing city he had chosen for his first stop. As a traveller, in Italy, in the Far East, in Australia, he had prided himself on seeing through the tourist stuff – the neat temples and museums; the streets full of quaint shops selling local crafts and produce; the historic or culturally significant locations marked in the guide books, where tour parties lingered for the allotted time, then moved on – but this was his first visit to a town he had always thought of as magical and remote, and he had been hoping for a connection, for a way in that would offer itself only to him: a drift of music or scent on the evening air; a cool wind off the river; a perfect, deserted courtyard packed to the highest balcony with geraniums and marguerites. He had even imagined an encounter of some kind, some fleeting romance with one of the extraordinary women he saw everywhere he went: dark, slender, almost impossibly beautiful creatures, whose language he did not speak, and whose gestures and expressions, when he encountered them in shops or cafés, seemed to him deliberately alien and enigmatic: solemn, but far from serious; courteous, but not altogether friendly; interested, but never quite engaged.

He had hoped for a romance; instead, in high summer, he was stuck in a bad hotel with a bunch of rowdy American high-school students who were advancing through Europe behind a fat, commanding woman named Georgia Platt. Georgia had taken something of a shine to Richard on that first day, when they had fortuitously checked in together, and found they occupied adjoining rooms – Richard tired after the journey from Madrid, and embarrassed by his poor Spanish; swaggering, portly Georgia blissfully indifferent to her ignorance of this or – as far as Richard could tell – any other European tongue. Now, for three days, he had been wandering the city trying to avoid, not only his unappealing neighbour, but all of the Georgias who had invaded this crowded, hot city with their umbrellas and maps and half-digested facts, escorting parties of the rudest people the world could offer, from Texas to Tokyo, shuffling from one spot to the next, tired and hot and irritable, but still avid for Culture and History, even if slightly uncertain as to where they actually were.

Richard had quickly come to realise that, under the present circumstances, Cordoba was pretty well unnavigable. He had seen the famous Mezquita, its Moorish beauty sunk under an ugly Christian superstructure; he had walked the narrow side-streets in the afternoon heat, in a vain attempt to escape the crowds; he had sat in dark, crowded little bars and bought a couple of records in a dingy, ill-stocked music shop. Now, he had given up. Every day, he made his way to the old Roman bridge, to enjoy the faint breeze that followed the course of the river, and thought about where to go next. He had reserved the room at his hotel for five days, but he was thinking of moving on, of catching a bus or a train to Granada, then making his way up into the mountains, into the cool of the Sierra, where there was nothing for the tourists to see, and no Georgia in the next room, waiting for that discreet knock at her door.

Meanwhile, he studied the river. This was the Guadalquivir of which he had heard so much, but all he saw was a watercourse choked with mud and reeds, and a few islands of willow and scrub where egrets fluttered like white handker-chiefs caught in the branches of the trees, and the odd funereal-looking heron drifted slowly across the muddy stream. It was odd: up here, halfway across the bridge, he couldn't quite convince himself that the city was real, yet he kept going back to gaze across the clouded water and listen, through the chatter of the egrets and the swish of traffic, for a low, sweet sound that, for moments at a time, he could almost detect, the faint, musical hum that was the truth of the place he had come looking for. Maybe it was nothing more than the wind in the reed beds, or the sound of water from somewhere dark and hidden under the paved bridge, but he kept thinking, for no good reason, that he was on the point of finding something – and it struck him as ironic that he felt closest to the thing he had intended to discover in Cordoba when he reached the undistinguished, rather ugly statue of Saint Michael at the midpoint of the bridge, its pedestal covered with wax and grime, the saint's pale feet surrounded by rotting flowers and by the red votive candles that were lit each day, in the blazing heat of the afternoon, by an elderly woman in a long grey dress and dusty, broken-down shoes.

Now, with the idea of escape forming in his mind, Richard felt more at ease. A quick calculation on the journey out had reassured him that he had enough money for a couple of

240

months before he had to decide what he would do next or –
an idea that he kept inviting in, then putting quickly from his
mind – before he had to *go back*. Going back was permanently
there as a probability – as a necessity, even; but as long as it
could be deferred, it didn't really bother him. He knew from
experience that, as long as a sufficient time-lapse intervened,
going back was never a return to the same as before, that things
changed much more quickly when he was away than when he
was there, living through it all. By the time he got home, Gina
would have moved on; he might even see her at a party, or on
the street somewhere, and feel a slight but delicious pang of
regret or longing, and he would take pleasure in wondering
about what might have been.

For the moment, though, he was glad to be out of
Cambridge. All of a sudden, it had seemed a less temperate
place: in the months before his departure, it had become ugly
and self-conscious, a city that was watching itself, thinking too
much, trying too hard to justify a way of dealing with the
world at large that, for all its faults, worked better than most. It
wasn't just the rapist that was the problem – though that was
bad enough; there was something else, something more
diffuse; an unease, an unsettled feeling. Over the last few years,
there had been new developments, tawdry new buildings had
gone up throughout the city, and there was more to come, he
felt sure. Places he had loved, places to which he had become
accustomed, were being lost. The old Lion Yard of memory
and fable had been destroyed to make way for a soulless
shopping centre, and there had been rumours for a long time
now that the Kite – that tight, higgledy-piggledy region
between Parker's Piece and Newmarket Road – would be the
next to go. Some buildings had already been demolished,
other properties were being allowed to run down. Richard

241

had always loved that part of the town, with its little restaurants and cafés, its shops, its place names – Eden Street, Paradise Street, Adam and Eve Street, Orchard Street. He could hardly stand to think that it would all go under, for no good reason.

But then, it wasn't just buildings that were being destroyed. He knew well enough that the rapist could have cropped up at any time, but there was something about the public reaction – the nonsense written in the press, the ways in which the case had been used by politicos on all sides, the defensiveness, or defiance, of the men he knew – something about the way it was all being used as a diversion from the *real* that appalled him. Whenever he'd got into a discussion about what was going on – the rapist, the so-called developments, the apparent rise in incidences of grad-bashing – he felt something close to despair. Nobody was being radical enough. It was all political, it was all contingent. The revolution – the non-political, non-dogmatic revolution of the spirit which he felt, somehow, he had been promised by a decade or more of experiment and risk – was melting away, before it had even begun to be fully imagined. It was like music heard in the distance as you approached, the music from a fairground, or a dance, heard across a field. It had been there for so long, getting louder and louder as he came closer, but now, all of a sudden, it was gone. Now, there was no music, only noise.

In the face of that noise, Richard had been drained, almost entirely, by a sense of loss. Yet now, gazing out at the muddy river, he allowed himself a wry smile. It had been a mistake, of course, to believe in that revolution. There were too many people with their own ideas of what was right, too many people willing to sacrifice the basic decencies to win the arguments they were having with the world. He remembered

242

the time, at one of Alex's parties, when – hidden behind a Japanese screen in the corner of the room – he'd overheard his friend arguing with a woman who had, a moment before, passed loud and destructive judgement on Gina – or rather, on the fact that Richard had brought Gina to the party looking 'like a tart' in her electric-blue dress and high-heeled shoes. Alex had barely known Gina at the time, but his loyalty to his friends was inclusive and unforgiving.

'I don't think it's up to you,' he said, 'to dictate how another person should or shouldn't dress.'

'Really?' Richard could hear the contempt in the woman's voice.

'Really,' Alex said. 'It's – discourteous.' Alex had chosen his word carefully. He didn't mean rude or impolite; what he wanted to indicate had to do with a whole set of ideas – ideas about which this woman knew nothing – that Alex had developed over a period of time.

The woman laughed. 'Discourteous?' she said, with exaggerated surprise. 'How quaint.' Some others around her joined in. People often found Alex quaint.

'Discourteous,' Alex said. 'Ungracious. Lacking in courtesy. You know what courtesy is, I take it?'

The woman snorted. 'I'm a single woman in a man's world,' she said, playing to the gallery now. 'I don't do courtesy.'

'Then maybe you ought to learn.'

The woman had laughed again, but her laugh had sounded forced. Perhaps she had thought herself safely amongst like-minded souls.

To most people, Alex seemed weak. He was easy to dismiss as a poor little rich boy: all his life his parents had given him money in exchange for attention but, contrary to the usual expectations, Alex had thrived on it. He loved *things*. He had the house, which he filled with beautiful objects: ukiyo-e prints, tea bowls, woodcuts – this very Japanese screen, painted with cranes and bamboo, behind which Richard was hiding, had been acquired a few days before, in an antiques shop in Oxford. He loved giving parties and dressing up. He loved playing games. But more than any of these, he loved ideas. When he was on the track of something – some thought, some notion – he was like a terrier. Lately, he had been reading Romance literature, in English and French, because he was intrigued by the model of courtesy they constructed, and he had come up with a set of charming, though wholly impractical, theories about social behaviour. According to Alex – who was as much unlike a medieval warrior as it was possible to be – the knights of the romances were ideal beings, from whom much could be learned in our own time. Their concept of manliness, he said, had nothing to do with toughness, or power. What they valued, what the Grail represented, and what the knightly ideal expressed, was grace – and, in pursuit of that elusive spirit of grace, they had created a complex, beautiful system, the courtly ideal. As Alex saw it, this ideal was one of the great art works of the Western world.

'The true and cortais knight,' he would say, 'dedicates himself to remaining sensitive and aware and open in every situation. This is what the Grail Quest is about, about being wholly alive, in a mysterious and dangerous world. An alarming world. They wanted to be aware of others, alive to subtlety, open to possibility.'

Richard would laugh. 'Fine,' he would say. 'But it isn't real. It's just a literary convention.'

'I know that.' Alex could easily become exasperated at his

friend's inability to see the point of his researches. 'I know it isn't a historical reality – but it *is* the truth. It's a literary convention – yes – but it's also *true*. This literary convention – this writer's dream – allows us to see that courtesy is not for others, it's a perfect strategy for maintaining and protecting your own sensitivity.'

Richard had only nodded then, and let Alex carry on expounding his theory. At times he had been charmed by his friend's trust in the courtly ideal. At times he had even imagined how fine it would be, if people could live according to some impossible order. But, in the end, he had always dismissed Alex's notions.

Nevertheless, here in the south, it had occurred to him more than once that he might be wrong. There was something about Andalucia, some remnant of an older world, of another culture, that seemed imbued with that courteous ideal, with that notion of grace to which Alex had become so attached. You could see it in the way people dealt with one another: a distance, a formality, a sense of respect, which was at once social and otherworldly. People here were, in their dealings with strangers at least, both formal and gracious. Richard had a sense that courtesy – as opposed to politeness – *mattered* to these people. When he compared the way the Cordovans carried themselves with the behaviour of the tourists who had invaded their city, there was an obvious dignity, an obvious self-respect, that set them apart from their uninvited guests. In spite of everything – the superstition, the corruption of a Fascist government, the impossible heat – the Andalucians had something, some indefinable quality, that the British, in particular, seemed to lack. Richard couldn't help wondering if cities like Cordoba had their equivalent of the Cambridge Rapist. But no, he thought – amused at how naïve he was being, how desperate he was for something fine – even if they didn't, they probably had something just as bad, or worse.

And yet it was always there, that . . . something. It was always present: a mythical life behind the ordinary lived existence of the people you saw on the streets and in the bars. Every city had its own version of that life, every village, every region, every state. What Richard had come to detest wasn't the superficial, factual reality of the rapist, or the property developers, or the jackboot politicos who seemed to find their way to Alex's innocent parties, it was the mythic life, the essential truth, behind the city he had been accustomed to loving. Just as Cordoba struck him as a process of conceal-ment, where the rich, dark earth-colours of some Moorish past were buried under the gaudiness of the Catholic present, so the green dream of Cambridge and its environs had become obscured by the monochrome of politics and commerce. Neither place, he saw, was sufficient for his present needs. But tomorrow, or the next day, he would leave the city and go out, first to Granada, and then onward, up into the mountains, to some village that still remembered snow and spring flowers, and he would stay there for as long as he could: alone, silent and untouchable. He couldn't stay there forever, he knew that. Before long, he would want to go back, if not to one city, then to another, back to people, back to the noise and movement, back to the possibility of love that only a city could offer. He regretted it, but this was how he was. Standing on this crowded bridge, over a slow-moving, mud-coloured river, he knew he belonged more to the world than he would have liked. Yet tomorrow, or the next day, he would leave it – for a while, at least. He would spend an afternoon walking in the gardens of the Alhambra, then he would travel up, into the mountains.

He could already taste the cool air of the Sierra.

SWALLOWTAILS

Back in Cambridge, Paul found the house utterly transformed. All the downstairs rooms were freshly painted, making them seem brighter and more spacious than before; the staircase and the landing had also been spruced up, and Mrs Yazz had replaced the hall carpet. His own room was untouched but the bathroom and the room at the back, the one Steve had occupied, were similarly bright and airy. Best of all, the kitchen was completely new. The old units had been ripped out and replaced, the floor had been covered with new linoleum, something had been done to the sink, so that it sparkled. It was as if Clive had never existed. In addition, Mrs Yazz had another deal for him: he could stay in the house till Christmas at the same rent as he had paid over the summer, if he would agree to take pictures of all her houses, for what she mysteriously called her 'records'. Paul was only too happy to agree.

The new term brought a few surprises. Two days into the first week, he met Penny who, seeming at once more distant and more friendly than she had ever been when they were going out, treated him to a coffee at Belinda's, so she could tell him all about her engagement. With a breathtaking lack of irony and a wholly deliberate disregard for any lingering feelings Paul might have for her, she described in some detail how she had met a fascinating man named Michael, and fallen in love over the vacation. Michael was training to be a chartered accountant, it seemed, and had very good prospects; he had taken Penny to the most wonderful restaurants; on the last night, he had proposed, 'in the old-fashioned manner'. Paul made a supreme effort not to let his amusement show.

'And how is Marjorie?' he asked.

'Oh, she's fine,' Penny answered. 'She's going up and down to London, researching this paper she's been working on.'

'Really? What's it about?'

'She's doing some interviews with prostitutes,' Penny said. 'She asks them about their lives, about their ambitions, about their relationships. Stuff like that.'

Paul didn't know why, but he was surprised and a little impressed by this news. He couldn't imagine Marjorie out in the real world, amongst real people, talking about their lives. She had always struck him as the theoretical type. Still, he didn't say anything. He let Penny talk, listening to her, watching her with something close to amazement. Finally, when it was obvious there was nothing more to be said between them, she gathered up her bag and her coat and made ready to leave.

'How's Richard?' she asked.

The question struck Paul as odd, and he wondered if perhaps she had heard something about his friend's sudden disappearance.

'I don't know.' He stood up and very pointedly helped her on with her coat.

'What do you mean, you don't know?' Penny didn't actually want to be helped, but she allowed him the gesture.

'I haven't seen him,' Paul answered simply. He didn't want

this to go anywhere. 'I imagine he's gone away. He was thinking of leaving—'

'Oh, well.' Penny shrugged on the coat, and turned to him. 'If you don't mind my saying, that's Richard all over.'

Paul did not reply. He did mind her saying. Whatever the facts of Richard's sudden disappearance, it was a more complex matter than Penny would ever allow.

'I never much liked him,' she continued. 'You know that. You always thought of him as a friend, but I don't think he was ever a friend to you.'

Paul smiled and shook his head. 'It's not that simple,' he said.

'But it is,' Penny answered, knowing he wanted to let it go but unable to move on without one last word. 'People like Richard get away with far too much.'

He thought she was about to go on, to say more, but abruptly she stopped. They left together, but parted at the corner of the market square.

'Well,' Penny said, outside the bookshop. Paul thought for a moment she wanted to shake hands. 'Goodbye, then.'

Paul nodded. 'Goodbye,' he said. They managed a smile before they moved off, but Paul knew he wouldn't see her again – or, if he did, it would be as apparent strangers. It was hard to believe that she had meant so much to him for so long – or rather, that he had imagined she had. Everything that had ever happened between them seemed like so much ancient history.

But then, everything had shifted now. It was as if the solitude Paul had begun to learn out at the field station had quietly taken over his life. For some weeks, he was even alone in Mrs Yazz's house. Apparently, Clive was gone for good. Not only had he not returned to his lodgings, but he had failed to show up for lectures and was officially considered a dropout. Steve had got his sister to send a note to the house to say that he would be moving back to Huntingdon when he got out of Fulbourn and wouldn't be requiring his room any more. Meanwhile, Richard really did seem to have vanished. Paul had cycled round to the house a couple of times, but nobody answered the door. He left a note, but he knew it was a waste of time. The only friend he'd made in Cambridge had moved on, and he hadn't even bothered to leave a forwarding address or a note.

Paul's solitude deepened. With Richard gone, he didn't go to parties any more; with Clive out of the picture, the house was still and quiet. Paul took to going out at night, or in the early mornings, rediscovering the city he loved, a city of darkness, of stillness, of endless subtleties of light and shadow. It was the same city he had always known, the city he had shared for two years and more with all those others, but the map of it that he held in his mind was different now. It was the map of a place without people, like one of those empty cities in old films. The places he chose to go now, places like Kettle's Yard, or the graveyard behind it, places out on the fen, where he would cycle at weekends, small villages up the river – they were all places to be alone, where nobody knew him, and where he seemed almost invisible. And – except for his work, except for the camera in his hand and the pictures he took – he *was* invisible. At the same time – and he knew what Penny would have made of this – Paul didn't really mind. He was alone. He had always been alone. Everything else – friends, lovers, even family – was transitory and, in an odd way, almost inconsequential compared to the basic truth, the utter finality, of that aloneness. Though he didn't expect anybody else to see it, there was a satisfaction to be gained from the mere recognition of the fact.

A few days later he cycled up to the field station to see if Tony was still there. He'd not heard anything from the man since that day he'd found the rabbits and, though he wasn't surprised, he was a little disappointed. Tony knew where he lived, after all. He could have sent a note, at least.

It was late on a clear, cold afternoon with a hint of evening frost on the air, when he reached the insect station and, with a pang of nostalgia, of regret even, propped his bike against the tool-house wall. Tony was in the locust room, huddled over one of the larger cases. Paul tapped at the open door.

'Can I come in?'

Tony looked up. He had the preoccupied but happy look of someone who has been alone for hours, and there was something else to him, Paul noticed – a clean, exact quality, a gravitas and, at the same time, a new brightness that hadn't been there before.

'Paul.' Tony was surprised. 'You're back.' He straightened up and closed the locust case. 'Come in.'

As he stepped into the room, Paul was struck by several things at once. There was nothing very different about the place, yet it was, nevertheless, utterly transformed: cleaner, more orderly, the locust room seemed brighter, and fuller now, than it had done. It was a moment before Paul realised that the room contained more than just locusts.

'As you can see,' Tony said, 'I've changed things around a bit.' He glanced off into the far corner. 'And I've made some additions.'

Paul followed his gaze to the large, dim case by the office

door. He couldn't make them out at first, but he knew, anyway, what Tony was talking about.

'Swallowtails,' he said.

Tony smiled. 'Touch wood,' he said. 'Can I interest you in some tea.'

Paul nodded. He had been nervous about coming, but he felt suddenly at home here. He followed Tony through to the office where, he noticed, the other man had installed a new kettle, a tea caddy, a small, round plastic container for sugar and a similar, but jug-shaped, one for milk.

'I've tidied up in here a bit, too,' Tony said. 'Made it more homely. Take a seat.'

Paul sat down and watched in silence as his former boss made him tea, and produced a packet of Digestives; it was then he noticed the real difference, the change in Tony's appearance that he should have seen at first glance.

The white coat was gone. That ugly, grey, foul-smelling lab coat that Tony had always worn, its pockets and lapels streaked and blotted with suspicious green and brownish stains, had finally been replaced by a bright, red-and-green-check shirt and faded blue jeans – and this minor detail had made all the difference. Tony, it seemed, was a different man.

The transformation wasn't just a matter of appearances, however. Over the next hour or so, Tony explained how he had spent the last couple of months – ever since he had found Paul, camera in hand, at the door of the rabbit room – thinking about what he was doing, and what he wanted from his job. He explained that, at first, he had imagined some kind of conspiracy: the rabbit experiment had always made him uncomfortable, and he had suspected Paul of trying to photograph it for some ulterior motive – prurience, say, or some vague desire to make trouble for the Zoology Department. That was what had made him react so angrily, that discomfort with what he was doing, but it had taken him a while to see it. When Paul hadn't returned, Tony had assumed his assistant, whose work, he said, he had come to value, had left the field station in disgust.

'You still have some back pay owing, I think,' Tony added. 'Or you ought to have.' He shook his head. 'A lot has happened over these last few months,' he said. 'I finally started with the swallowtails. I got rid of the rabbits. I just told them at the Department that I couldn't maintain that experiment any more.'

'You got rid of the white coat, too,' Paul said. 'I always hated that coat.'

'Did you?' Tony looked surprised. He glanced back to the other room, where the swallowtails flickered a danced in the half-light. 'Did you really?' He laughed softly to himself and shook his head.

Outside the sky was darkening. The promise of frost Paul had noted on the cycle ride up the Huntingdon Road had turned to a hint, and there was a faint, sweet scent − windfall apples, old smoke, the faintest trace of burnt sugar − that reminded him of home and his father's shed.

'I'd better get back,' he said. 'I just wanted to come up and see how things were going.'

Tony nodded. 'I'm glad you did,' he said.

Paul stood up. He had a sudden, unaccountable impulse to shake hands with this shy, remote man, who was so obviously happier when he was alone with his insects, cleaning out the locust cages, admiring the swallowtails, or standing after hours in the powdered-gold light of the manducca room, like an old-time alchemist, assisting in the rituals of decomposition and transformation. The moment passed, however, as quickly as it came, and a moment later he found himself outside, in the cool, dark garden, picking up his bike. Tony followed him to the door, and stood watching, as if to make sure he would find his way out in the dark.

'Don't be a stranger,' he called, from the lit doorway of the locust room.

'I won't,' Paul answered, hovering for a moment over the handlebars before he cycled away into the deepening night. And even as he did, he knew it wasn't true – knew, without the faintest shadow of a doubt, that he would not come here again, that he would leave Tony to the enviable and hard-won solitude that he so obviously enjoyed.

Finally, on a wet afternoon well into the autumn, Paul met Hannah again. She was walking along King's Parade, with a huge, multicoloured umbrella, and she seemed far away, lost in thought. Paul wondered if she had seen him and was trying to pretend she hadn't – she probably thought he'd stood her up, or maybe she figured he'd taken a hint, and given up, when he didn't telephone her after the funeral – but he called out to her anyway and she waited while he caught her up.

'Hi, Paul.' She looked more beautiful, even, than he remembered her; she had cut her hair in a tight, almost severe bob, and her face looked clearer, more translucent. To his surprise, she seemed happy to see him.

'Hi,' he said. 'Where are you off to?'

'Oh, just shopping.' She smiled. 'You'd better get under my umbrella. You're getting very wet.'

'It's all right,' he said. 'I was on my way to Belinda's.'

'For tea and shelter?' Hannah laughed.

'You could say that.'

255

'In that case, I'll join you,' she said.

Belinda's was almost empty. They took a seat at the front of the upstairs café, so they could look out at the people going by in the rain. It was one of the real pleasures of the place: the sense of warmth and shelter was heightened by sitting at the rickety little table, wrapped in the scent of lemons and toasted tea-cakes, and looking out at the passing umbrellas and hurried people in raincoats, heading for lectures or meetings – not just the sense of shelter, but also, somehow, the sense of transience. Sitting there, in the rain-darkened world, Paul always had a more poignant sense of how fleeting life was. It was like the moment in a poem he had read, where the poet is sitting in his garden, listening to the birds singing, looking at the tree in blossom over his head, and thinking of how it would all continue without him after he died – the same light, the same birdsong, the same apple tree. For Paul, that moment came in places like Belinda's, on rainy days, when the place was almost empty. He had tried to describe it once to Penny, but she hadn't really understood – she had imagined he was talking about something else, some form of sadness.

They had been talking for a while before the subject of Alex came up, more by chance than anything else. Though he was curious, Paul had no intention of enquiring after Hannah's supposed fiancé, and Hannah had seemed happy to keep him out of the conversation. Besides, at this stage in the game, there was really nothing to discuss. Whatever her feelings for Alex now, it had nothing to do with a man she had met twice previously, a man who had failed even to call her when he'd said he would. They hardly knew one another, after all, and once they had talked about the summer vacation – Hannah had indeed been away in Switzerland, while, for reasons he could not have explained, and in spite of the fact that it would

256

have explained his failure to call her, Paul omitted all mention of his father's death — they were cast back on their narrow circle of common acquaintances.

'Have you heard from Richard?' Hannah asked.

'No. Have you?'

'No.' She smiled sadly. 'Something of a mystery there.' She looked out at the rainy street. 'It's Gina I feel sorry for.'

'Oh, I don't know. She's probably better off—'

'No doubt about it,' Hannah said. 'But he didn't have to break it off like that, without even talking to her. Just . . . disappearing.' She seemed troubled, momentarily unhappy, even.

Paul nodded. 'And how are things with you?' he asked. 'You and Alex, I mean.'

Hannah looked up at him. She seemed surprised by the question. 'Things are fine,' she said. 'Why wouldn't they be?'

'No reason.' His question had been nothing more than a conversational gambit, a simple change of subject. Or, at least, he had intended it to seem so. 'You're still engaged, then?'

Hannah laughed — that same dark laugh he'd fallen in love with, the first time he'd met her. 'We're not *still* engaged. Though we are engaged. We weren't engaged before. But then, I went to Switzerland—'

She broke off. 'It's a long story,' she said.

Paul clasped his hands together and rested them on the edge of the table, like a mathematics teacher waiting for the answer to a geometry question. 'I've got all day,' he said.

'It's boring,' Hannah said. 'Other people's love affairs always are. But Richard was right on that, at least. We did get engaged.' She shook her head. 'He was wrong, too — he was wrong on most things, I suppose — but he was right about

257

that.' She smiled sadly. 'Poor Richard,' she said. She refilled her teacup.

'Why do you say that?' Paul asked, surprised.

Hannah shook her head. She took a spoonful of sugar and let it trickle, a few grains at a time, into her tea; then she took a slice of lemon and let it slither into the cup.

'He was always so careful,' she said. 'He wasn't going to get caught out. He wasn't going to become trapped. He made all these rules for himself, and then he got caught up in them.' She looked at Paul curiously. 'You were good friends,' she said. 'Weren't you?'

Paul shook his head. 'I don't know,' he said, 'now that you ask. I used to think so. But I don't think I ever really knew him.'

'There wasn't that much to know, I think. He was just a man who knew what he didn't want. He didn't want commitment. He didn't want responsibilities. He didn't want to get bogged down.'

'Fair enough, I suppose,' Paul ventured.

'Yeah, sure,' she said. 'Fair enough.' She brightened. 'I thought the same way myself, for a long time.' Paul could see that she was growing restless, already thinking about leaving. But she continued to make conversation. 'And how about you?' she asked.

'How about me?'

She smiled, unfazed. 'Are you "still engaged"? I mean – are you still seeing—'

Paul shook his head. 'No,' he said; then, because he had sounded abrupt, added, 'I suppose I like my own company too much.'

Hannah considered this for a moment. 'Alex always says that about me,' she said. 'I could imagine it being true about someone like you. Though I don't know you at all. But it's not me.' She smiled, almost apologetically it seemed. 'I need people.'

'Well,' Paul said, 'we're all alone, when it comes down to it.'

'Maybe.' Hannah looked unconvinced. 'We're alone, and we're not alone. Who was it said that the first rule of the human condition is that we are always and everywhere alone, and the second rule is that we cannot fully exist without others? Or something like that—'

'D. H. Lawrence.'

Hannah looked at him in surprise. 'Sorry?'

'It was D. H. Lawrence,' Paul said, 'who said that.'

'Ah.' Hannah couldn't resist a smile. 'I should have known you'd know.'

'Oh.' Paul wondered if he ought to be offended, at least mildly. 'Why's that?'

Hannah shook her head. 'It's just — how I imagine you, I suppose.'

After that they sat quietly for a while, watching the rain. It was beginning to slow up; somewhere, at the far end of Trinity Street, the sky had begun to lighten. Hannah stood. 'I have to get on,' she said. 'It was nice seeing you, Paul.'

'It was nice seeing you.' Paul smiled. He felt a momentary sense of loss, as if something was still unfinished between them.

'No doubt I'll see you again,' she said. 'It's a small town,'

'Yes.' Paul nodded. 'I'd like that.' He didn't know whether he should go out with her, or wait. It seemed better to let her go. She had her coat on again, and she had taken her umbrella from the corner where it had been propped up to dry, but still she hovered, as if she also thought there was something still to be said – though whether it had to do with Alex, or Richard, or something else, he couldn't have said.

'Well,' she said finally, 'goodbye.'

Paul smiled. 'Goodbye,' he said. He felt an odd sinking, a shiver of something that came close to grief, as she turned and headed for the door, and the impulse to jump up, to ask her to stay a while and talk some more, was almost irresistible. He stayed where he was, though, till she was outside. She gave him a short, happy wave as she passed the window, pulling her umbrella open; then she was gone, heading back towards King's Parade and into the crowd.

Later, as he headed back, he saw Aqualung for the first time in months. The man was standing under the street lamp at the centre of Parker's Piece, his face turned to the sky. It was still raining, though it wasn't so heavy now; fine misty droplets hung in the air, clinging to every surface like a second skin – what his father would have called a wetting rain. Aqualung was soaked through; he had to have been standing there for some time, in his heavy greatcoat and thin baseball shoes – but he didn't seem to mind that. In fact, if anything, he seemed happy, his face lit up from within with what seemed to Paul, as he paused a moment in his walk home, a kind of mystic joy, as if this strange, unkempt creature had been afforded a glimpse of the secret at the heart of things, a secret that could never be told to anybody else.

FOX

When term ended, Paul surprised himself by refusing his usual
job on the Christmas post and going home to spend the
holidays with his mother. Part of him had always wanted to be
at home for Christmas – or rather, for midwinter, which was
what he really loved. It had nothing to do with the festive
season, so called, nothing to do with presents and a tree and
carols, especially not now that his father was gone. What
mattered was the sense he had, at midwinter, of something
just, something *right* about the world, a turning point, a pivot
in time, a sense of some underlying shift through completion
to a new beginning. This moment happened best at home, or
perhaps it simply came more easily, because he had always
experienced it there: the harbour quiet for the winter, its few
vessels up on stocks alongside the walls; the boatyard
icebound, its vagrant colours sealed between fissures and gaps
in the wooden hulls, the craquelure of paintwork and frosted
mortar catching the light; local thaws breaking out along a
sunlit wall, seepages from wood and brickwork in every
possible colour – amber, cobalt, leaf-green, watery ochres and
cooled golds, the new water fish-scented, rusty, viscid or shot
with light, like the water from some source, some vital origin.
It was a world of stillness and of separation, yet two streets
away from the front, everything would be different – and this

was what struck him most about the little town in winter, this gift it had for dividing itself into distinct regions of light and dark, or stillness and motion. Away from the front, the little gardens along each street, stalled under snow and deep shadows, would suddenly become places to be lost in, joined one to another, in spite of fences and walls, or emerging slowly from the grip of the cold, a litter of scaled holly leaves here, or the shed snakeskin of acanthus there, everything desiccated and, at the same time, muddled and self-concealed.

His arrival was no less of a surprise to his mother. To begin with, she even treated him with something close to suspicion, not altogether sure what to make of this sudden access of filial duty. Or, at least, that was what Paul first imagined, when he saw how awkward she seemed in his presence, over those first couple of days. It wasn't till Christmas Eve, when they were sitting together in the front room after dinner, that he fully understood what had been going on in his absence. Dispensing with the usual tea, his mother had produced a bottle from the sideboard.

'Would you like some sherry?' she asked. She seemed studied, overly casual.

Paul nodded. 'That would be nice.' He was surprised at the sherry; his mother had never been a drinker to his knowledge. Still, it seemed appropriate to the occasion, and he didn't really start to worry about it until about an hour later, when they were on to their third glass, and his mother's voice began to blur slightly. They had got round to talking about his dad, all of a sudden, talking about him as one long dead now, a creature locked into the past, into the world of simple memory. Yet Paul could feel his mother working up to something, moving towards a fixed point in her mind.

It had started with talk of his dad's car, the old, but perfectly maintained Citroën. Paul's mother didn't drive, and she was telling him that she had no use for it, that he should take it back to Cambridge in the New Year. Paul had remarked, then, how that car had been his father's pride and joy, that he felt a little nervous about driving it. His dad had always been so careful, such a perfectionist. He had remembered the time his father had told him, on one of their driving lessons out at the airfield, that the essence of real intelligence was courtesy, and that a driver without courtesy was an accident waiting to happen. He hadn't really understood the remark at the time – he wasn't sure he understood it now, but, whether it was the sherry, or because it was Christmas, he repeated his father's words with something close to reverence. He wasn't sure he had the courteous intelligence his father had considered so important in a driver.

His mother smiled grimly and shook her head. 'Not long after we got married, three or four years before you were born, your father was involved in an accident,' she said. 'You didn't know that, did you?'

She uncorked the sherry bottle and waved it vaguely in his direction. He shook his head. She topped up her own glass. 'It was about this time of year,' she continued. 'Just coming up for Christmas. He'd been out for a drink at lunchtime with some of the other men from work.'

She shot Paul a quick, shy look. He knew that what she was about to say was, in her eyes, the betrayal of something, but it was also something she wanted, or perhaps needed, him to know.

'He liked a drink in those days. Though he only had a couple, because he was in the van. The police said he wasn't over the limit.'

Paul watched as she raised her glass and drank again – and it occurred to him that she had been waiting to tell him this story for months, maybe even years, that the sherry wasn't just for Christmas, but a necessary part of the process.

'He was driving back,' she continued, after a moment. 'About four in the afternoon it would have been, and he passed a woman on a bike. He saw her clear enough, though it was already getting dark, and he swung out to avoid her, but something happened, the door at the back of the van wasn't shut properly, or it came loose – something like that. And it hit her.'

She leaned back, cradling the sherry glass in her hand, and sat silent for a moment, as if she was trying to recall some detail she had forgotten.

'It wasn't his fault, though. It was an accident, that's all. He wasn't over the limit, nothing like that. And the woman didn't have a light on her bike. But he blamed himself anyway, because he'd taken a drink. I mean, everybody took a drink in those days, there wasn't all this don't-drink-and-drive campaign. You were just careful. But your father didn't take it like that. It was his fault that the door came loose, it was his fault that he'd stopped off at the pub in the van.'

Paul listened in silence. To begin with, he had suspected her of a lie, or an exaggeration at least, but now, as he watched her talk, her eyes averted, her hands cradling the drink, he knew that what she was saying was more or less true.

'After that,' she said, 'he was a different person. His whole life changed. Even though he wouldn't talk about it, not to me, not to anyone, he never stopped thinking about what happened.'

'What about the woman?'

She looked up. 'What about her?'

'Was she all right?'

264

His mother turned away. He wondered if she was upset now, or whether she was just trying to remember something.

'No,' she said, turning back to him. Her eyes were clear again, unrelenting. 'She was badly hurt.'

She waited a moment, as if to find the precise words that would convey her meaning and, at the same time, be as fair as possible to both the living and the dead. 'He went to see her in the hospital. He told her everything that happened. She said it wasn't his fault.'

Paul nodded. 'Well,' he said, 'it sounds like it wasn't.'

His mother sipped her sherry. She was on her fourth now. 'Maybe so,' she said. 'But that wasn't the end of it. It was only the beginning.'

'How do you mean?'

'I mean that he didn't really care about that woman. It was himself he was worried about. It was all about him. He changed his whole life, so he would never make a mistake like that again. And in the process, he made himself into somebody else. Somebody I didn't know at all any more.'

She laughed. Paul realised she was a little drunk now. 'You're always reading in magazines, how it takes two to make a marriage work. How you have to work at it. How it gets better and grows all the time, if you work at it. But he wouldn't do that, would he? For him, it was just—'

Her voiced tailed away, and she peered down at the glass cupped in her hands. It was empty again.

'Anyway,' she said. She set the empty glass on the table. She looked old and tired. Paul waited for her to speak again, but she sat quietly, lost in her own mind and for a moment he experienced an almost unbearable sense of a last chance being lost, of a moment passing, and their lives moving on, leaving something unsaid forever.

At the same time, he had a sudden, very strong sense of *déjà-vu*. Something like this had happened before, long ago, in childhood; he had only to find it and it would be a question answered, a doubt resolved. As he sat, watching his mother – who had sat back in her chair slowly, and seemed on the point of falling asleep – he tried desperately to recall that childhood memory. For a moment it hung at the edge of his awareness and he thought it was about to dissolve before he could fix it in his mind, to break up and fade, before he knew what it was, and he made an effort to be still, to stop his mind and let it come. It had something to do with the kitchen; it was something that had happened when he was a child, maybe five or six, maybe a little older; it had happened in winter, on a day like this, with snow in the air, the kitchen windows fogging, the radio playing – the radio, yes, and he remembered it, though it was nothing, nothing at all, just a memory of his mother in the kitchen on a Sunday evening, listening to the radio. It was what she always did on a Sunday: she would switch the radio on and stand at the sink washing dishes, or sit at the table, making pastry, and she would sing along to the music quietly, almost under her breath, as long as she thought nobody was listening. And that one evening, he had stood at the door, arrested by the sound of her voice, which had risen, little by little, joining in with a song she knew – 'Little Brown Jug', 'Don't Sit Under the Apple Tree', one of those pop songs from the Forties. That was when they still had that show on the Light Programme – and for all he knew, maybe they still did – an easy, light-hearted, homely show called *Sing Something Simple* – and the song was the one that didn't make any sense till you saw it written down – *Mares eat oats and does eat oats* – and even then it didn't make any sense, but it was one of his mother's favourites, and she was singing it in this

266

light, quite musical voice that he didn't know she had. From where he was standing, he could only see the side of her face, but she looked wistful and suddenly old and locked up inside a lost version of herself – *and little lambs eat ivy* – somebody she remembered and was surprised she still was, in some hidden angle of herself – *a kid'll eat ivy too* – a girl who had once been in love, or happy, or just filled with the ordinary trust, the unquestioning expectancy of something good, something simple. It had been a surprise to him, finding this woman in the kitchen, and he had stopped to listen, clinging to the sweet, thin voice, not wanting to lose it, half-believing it was the beginning of something he had suspected was there all along. Then she had turned around – it had lasted a minute, maybe a little longer, but not much, and when she saw him, she stopped short and stood up. She had a colander in her hand, full of curly kale, which she proceeded to carry over to the sink. The radio had gone on singing – a new song now, something about a smoothing iron – but she had stopped and he knew it was because he was there. Finally she spoke.

'Get me some butter out of the fridge,' she said, in a voice that seemed incapable, now, of music.

That was all. Behind it all, behind this sliver of memory, lay a whole hinterland of snow and night and crimson lamplight along the street – the blizzard of '63, say, when the buses stalled in the road, and the children had been obliged to walk to school, going out earlier than usual, in thick winter coats and hats, to a morning darkness that still tasted of night and ice. Some of the grown-ups had stayed home from work for days, holed up indoors with magazines and old books; others had made the effort, men like his dad, who had never missed a day, even when he had to drive fifty miles north, up through the Sidlaws, or over to Grangemouth, where the snow was even thicker and some of the roads were closed. Just before Christmas, the pipes had burst in all the classrooms, and they had been sent home from school; with nothing to do, he had hung around moping all day, till his mother had brought out the Christmas decorations for him to look at, fragile glass ornaments wrapped in old fruit wrappers, tiny bells dusted with glitter and smelling of citrus. She had done it to amuse him, to keep him busy – he'd even known it at the time, but now, remembering, that didn't matter, because there had been a moment when she had come in, with a plate of scones and some hot barley water in a cup, and she had smiled at him as she set them down on the table, as if this were the usual life they lived, as if being happy was normal. Out in the kitchen, the radio was playing, and the snow was falling, so thick and dark at the window that he could almost feel it brushing the glass and settling against the walls, burying the house in whiteness and sealing them in.

Now he looked at her closely, as if for the first time. This woman was the same woman he had seen, in those fleeting moments, and she had dedicated her whole life to hiding that fact. Now, having come to the brink of something, having almost given herself away, she had slumped in her chair and, her breathing heavy and laboured, was suddenly far away in sleep, forgetting him, forgetting everything. And quietly, showing a consideration for her that was half fear on his part that she might wake and resume the conversation, he stood up and crept out of the room, leaving her there alone, lost in what he hoped were pleasant dreams.

It was only as he prepared for bed that he saw, for the first time, the irony of his mother's situation. Though she had been estranged from her husband for years, this woman to whom an empty house might have seemed a blessing was, in fact, painfully lonely. The luxury of solitude, a luxury which she might have been expected to appreciate, was nothing less than a daily hardship to her. He imagined her, over the long months since the funeral, moving from room to room, cleaning the house, tending the garden, trying to keep herself occupied; he imagined her sitting in the kitchen with the radio on for company, drinking sherry, whiling away the dark autumn evenings. She had seemed so keen for Paul to leave, after the funeral, that he had imagined her coping well with the situation; now he saw that she was as lost and alone as it was possible to be. And because this loss had taken her by surprise – because she had probably been entirely unprepared to mourn her husband's death – she had no way out of it that Paul could see. Without an acknowledged wound, how could she be healed? Without a recognition of grief, how could she emerge from her period of mourning?

Paul remembered something Richard had said, one afternoon, over tea in his garden: something to the effect that the principal philosophical discovery of the twentieth century had been that we are alone and homeless in the world. It was the kind of nonsense Paul had come to expect from Richard: a half-truth, so exaggerated as to seem grotesque, yet half of a truth, nonetheless.

'Everybody seems to come to the same conclusion.' Richard was trying to appear serious. 'Freud, Sartre, Heidegger—'

'W. C. Fields—'

'W. C. Fields. Yes. In his later work, anyhow.'

'So,' Paul played along, 'redemption comes of accepting our lot, and making the best of it all.'

Richard shook his head. 'There's no redemption,' he said.

269

'There's just this. Homelessness. Solitude. The sooner we get used to that, the better.' For a moment, he had sounded almost serious.

A moment later the mood had passed and they had moved on to something else. Yet Paul had not been able to forget the question Richard had raised. For some reason, it had struck him with some force. Hannah had said something similar, at their last meeting, over tea in Belinda's. We are alone, and we cannot be alone. We need other people, even if we cannot stand being with them. That – and it struck him now, far too late, that she had been talking about herself and Alex – *that* was what she had meant.

Well, maybe it had been true for her. But it didn't need to be true. It hadn't been true for his father, after all. Now, when he considered his mother, alone in what was, for her, an empty house, it struck him that whatever redemption there was came as a result of accepting solitude, of taking homelessness as a starting point, and then of seeing this starting point as the very condition of grace. There was no home other than the home you invented anew each day from the empty house you were obliged to inhabit, once all the distractions were stripped away – and, for a moment, he was seized with an almost unbearable grief that, no matter what happened, he could never tell his mother this. It was all he had learned so far, all that he knew, and he wanted to go to her and say it, in so many words. At the same time, he saw that it was nothing she needed or understood. Now that his father was gone, she lived alone, in an empty house. It was as much of a surprise to her as it was to him, but she was a woman stricken by grief for a man she had long ago ceased to recognise, a man she had convinced herself she no longer loved – and, for that, Paul knew, she would never forgive herself, just as she would never forgive her dead husband for becoming so much a part of her existence.

The next morning, he rose early and went out for a walk. He had planned to go over to the graveyard to see his father's headstone; instead, he found himself drifting in the direction of the old railway line. Earlier, as he'd lain awake, he'd become aware of something – a presence, a spirit, suspended in the half-light. It was nothing supernatural, it wasn't even very strong, but he could feel something there, something imminent at the back of his mind, like a voice which was just about to speak, or had perhaps just finished speaking. It wasn't in any way the spirit of the man they had buried five months before, however. It was the father hidden in every man's mind, a father Paul had carried with him all his life: a good phantom composed in part from the man he had known and, in equal part, from a figure he himself had invented. He'd had the impression of someone about to speak, but this presence was not a voice in the physical sense. It resembled more the sense of words that arose out of text, when you read it to yourself, hearing the music of it in a quiet place at the back of your mind. At the same time, Paul couldn't help thinking that the essence of this spirit, its reality, had more to do with silence than with speech, with the kept secret rather than any possible disclosure.

Now, as he followed the old familiar path along the railway line out into the woods, it began to snow. It had been cold in the night, the grass was streaked with hoar-frost, the puddles along the line were fretted and starred with ice, but this was the first real snow he had seen all year. It started slowly at first, large white flakes drifting down between the trees through the still air; after a while, though, it began to thicken, quickly

271

settling on the grass, and on the sleepers between the tracks. It was utterly silent.

He had expected no sign of life on a day like this: people would be at home, opening their gifts, or in their various churches, or getting the lunch started in their kitchens all over the town. There were no birds, no dogs barked; there wasn't even traffic on the road below. He had expected no sign of life. Yet as he walked, he caught a glimpse of something through the thickening snowfall and, after a moment, he made out a lean, dark-muzzled fox, loping towards him along the tracks. He was surprised to see it on such a day; surely, he thought, it was too cold for it to be out hunting. He wasn't even sure how long the fox had known he was there; before he'd made out what it was, the animal had stopped in its tracks, and it was waiting now, watching him suspiciously from about ten yards' distance, with a cast look in its eyes that was so different from a dog's look. It didn't move: it seemed confident, ready for anything that might come.

Suddenly, for no obvious reason, Paul remembered Patrick, that boy from the woods all those years ago – and he saw all at once that the boy was a fraud, that he had been a fraud all along. Tough as he had seemed, Patrick had been just another scared kid, whistling in the dark to seem brave. As he crouched to his fire, the smoke wreathing around his face, his fag smouldering, he'd been putting up a front. Maybe he didn't know what Paul had made of him, and possibly he didn't care. He had gone out to the woods to be alone, because being alone was less demeaning, less inauthentic, than being with other people. Paul understood that choice; he could even respect it. But it wasn't necessary – out of fear, or pride – to become the imaginary werewolf hiding in the undergrowth, growling softly under his breath, feeling the hair

272

grow on the back of his hands, dropping into a crouch, suddenly in possession of bright, sharp teeth and claws. Paul had never really believed that the creature in those old horror films was real, but he had been afraid of that boy, alone out there in the woods, stooping in under a tree out of the rain, oddly beautiful, but also undeniably pitiful. At the same time – and this was something far worse than anything you could see in a movie – he had come to see that the monster was true. He and that boy had dreamed it up together, they had made it up as the expression of a distant, silent kinship. The monster was true and he was standing in a room somewhere, with a double-edged blade in his hand, and a grotesque leather mask to hide his too-ordinary, unremarkable face. The monster was this, and nothing more – and Paul realised suddenly that, every time he had read a newspaper report, every time he had talked about the rapes with Clive, or Nancy, every time he had imagined the events that had taken place in that room, he had only seen the monster, never the woman. That was the rapist's triumph: the assailant, the perpetrator, the ordinary man wanted to render his victim invisible and nameless, so that everything in the picture, even her pain, even her fear, belonged to him. He acted, she was acted upon; he existed, she did not; the camera followed him as he crossed the darkened room, it lingered on his hands and mouth and the knife he laid to the victim's throat till it made him out as the phantom, the werewolf, the monster that he was not, and could never have been. Like the boy in the woods, his motive for being there, in that room, had been fear all along and only the meaningless pain of another could assuage the dread which sat at the core of his being like a tumour. It wasn't sex he wanted; it wasn't power. It wasn't even surrender – that would have involved something given on the other's part, and he didn't want to be given anything, he only wanted to take. Somewhere in his fantasy, he had always known that people would see him, they would witness his moment of possession, his self-assertion. It was disgusting, it was pathetic, but that little man felt it as a victory, and he wanted his victory to be seen, if only in the mind's eye: he wanted to be seen, the hidden camera watching him, recording his every act in loving detail, while the woman vanished, trickling through his hands, insubstantial beside him. And what was there to oppose that sad little man with his desire for visibility, and so, victory? What was there to set against this invented monster? Not the hero, surely.

At last Paul understood. He saw his father working in his shed; he saw him out in the rain, digging or pruning, or standing at the edge of a loch, casting his line. He saw all the men who had ever seemed to him weak and indecisive, and he understood that the one perfect and impeccable gesture any man could make was to refuse victory in any form, to see it for what it was, and to refuse it, as fact and as illusion, in order to be free. It was a surrender, it was a relinquishing of power – to become, for one's own sake, a helpless, tender, unvictorious human being. That was why they had taken themselves away: men like his father, the boy in the woods, all those quiet, shifting figures that had hovered around the edges of the social. They had understood that the only way to become themselves as they could be was to be alone. Each of them, in his own way, had come to understand the need for surrender – which was not only different from, but even the opposite of submission. Surrender was an act of will, a relinquishing of visibility and power, in exchange for the tenuous moment of grace. The boy in the woods had been afraid, but that was where the possibility of grace began, in that first inkling of fear. All this time, he had been missing the point. It made Paul want to laugh out loud, knowing that what really mattered was this fear, and the grace that came with it, when he surrendered himself to the world.

On the surface, his father had still engaged with the world, that is, with other people and the expectations they had foisted upon him, in order to earn a living, and to keep up appearances, but at a deeper level, at every level that mattered, to him at least, he had surrendered something. At the last, his father's world had become nothing other than the land, the weather, the elements. It had nothing to do with thoughts, or ideas, only with work. For the process of becoming, the process by which grace was achieved, was something entirely physical, of that Paul was certain. His father had decided to stop wanting the things he had thought he wanted, to allow a space to form in his mind, a space where the unexpected might happen. And like his father, Paul had also begun – without even knowing – to surrender something, to allow that same space to form. As he stood quite still, gazing along the tracks to where the fox stood watching him, there was nothing to which he could truthfully say he belonged, other than to this world of silence and light, and this dangerous nostalgia for the other animals. It was this nostalgia, this longing for the unnamed world of other creatures, that made him homeless in the world. At the same time, it struck him that this homelessness, this longing, was the one thing worth pursuing, the one thing he needed to understand. If he was homeless, he was, for this very reason, capable of anything. A necessary recognition lay at the core of this state of being: a recognition that, while he could never say at any particular moment that he was free, he was always at the point of freedom. And even in that, he was not alone. Generations of

275

unfathered men had picked up their unseen burden and moved on into the same darkness, the same accommodation with homelessness that he had begun to imagine for himself.

For months, he had been trying for something: that had been his first mistake. He had wanted a beginning, a marker; but now he knew that the only possible beginning was a long process of relinquishment, a giving up of everything external to the work, everything inessential. A logical abandonment of desire, to be open to anything that might come, any image, any word, any texture or sound or movement. All of a sudden, it struck him how mistaken he had been: the photographer he had wanted to become had been predicated upon a disappearance, whereas what he needed was to remain where he was; not to disappear, but to become invisible. The only way to inhabit this fox's world was to become invisible in his own. It was not a question of an inner life, of drawing a barrier between one state and another, between mind and world, between soul and person, it was simply a necessary choice between estrangements. Yet, oddly enough, he was beginning to see that this quality – of estrangement, rather than alienation – was the best asset he had. It was the starting point for a process that led inevitably to invisibility. To care nothing at all for being seen. The grace of the forgotten: the tree that falls in the woods.

He looked up along the tracks. It was possible that he had made some sudden movement, but it was just as likely that the fox had weighed him up and decided he did not constitute a threat; whatever the reason, it was moving away, loping off into the thickening snow, not looking back now, but going about its business. It seemed to be interested in something it had seen, or scented, somewhere in the hedge. Even when Paul walked on, it did not run, or even break pace for a moment. Obviously, it had forgotten him. Quietly, Paul turned and started making his way back home, to where his mother would already be preparing their Christmas lunch.